Crossing the Line

WHITECAP

A SINGLE MOTHER SMALL-TOWN ROMANCE

JESSICA PRINCE

Welcome to Whitecap! I'm so excited for you to start this new series with me.

When I originally started writing Crossing the Line, my intention was to make this book 11 in my Hope Valley series, but as I started writing, I realized it just wouldn't work there. You'll understand as you read.

Now, while the series name and location might have changed, it's still the same characters and same storyline I originally planned. And it's still got that same small-town feel you've come to love from my stories.

You'll see some Hope Valley characters that you've come to love, plus a few other fun Easter eggs thrown in.

I hope you love Trent and Cheyanne's story as much as I do.

Happy Reading!
   -Jess.

Discover Other Books by Jessica

<u>WHITECAP SERIES</u>

Crossing the Line

My Perfect Enemy

<u>WHISKEY DOLLS SERIES</u>

Bombshell

Knockout

Stunner

Seductress

Temptress

<u>HOPE VALLEY SERIES:</u>

Out of My League

Come Back Home Again

The Best of Me

Wrong Side of the Tracks

Stay With Me
Out of the Darkness
The Second Time Around
Waiting for Forever
Love to Hate You
Playing for Keeps
When You Least Expect It
Never for Him

<u>REDEMPTION SERIES</u>
Bad Alibi
Crazy Beautiful
Bittersweet
Guilty Pleasure
Wallflower
Blurred Line
Slow Burn
Favorite Mistake

<u>THE PICKING UP THE PIECES SERIES:</u>
Picking up the Pieces
Rising from the Ashes
Pushing the Boundaries
Worth the Wait

<u>THE COLORS NOVELS:</u>
Scattered Colors
Shrinking Violet

Love Hate Relationship

Wildflower

THE LOCKLAINE BOYS (a LOVE HATE RELATIONSHIP spinoff):

Fire & Ice

Opposites Attract

Almost Perfect

THE PEMBROOKE SERIES (a WILDFLOWER spinoff):

Sweet Sunshine

Coming Full Circle

A Broken Soul

CIVIL CORRUPTION SERIES

Corrupt

Defile

Consume

Ravage

GIRL TALK SERIES:

Seducing Lola

Tempting Sophia

Enticing Daphne

Charming Fiona

STANDALONE TITLES:

One Knight Stand
Chance Encounters
Nightmares from Within

<u>DEADLY LOVE SERIES:</u>
Destructive
Addictive

Whitecap Playlist

"Carry on Wayward Son" by Kansas
"Simple Man" by Lynyrd Skynyrd
"Bad Moon Rising" Creedence Clearwater Revival
"Can't You See" by The Marshall Tucker Band
"Free Bird" by Lynyrd Skynyrd
"House of the Rising Sun" by The Animals
"Burnin' for You" by Blue Öyster Cult
"Paint It, Black" by The Rolling Stones
"All Along the Watchtower" by Jimi Hendrix
"Gimme Shelter" by The Rolling Stones
"Slow Ride" by Foghat
"(Don't Fear) The Reaper" by Blue Öyster Cult
"In-A-Gadda-Da-Vida" by Iron Butterfly
"Whole Lotta Love" by Led Zeppelin
"Black Dog" by Led Zeppelin
"One Thing Right" by Marshmello and Kane Brown

Prologue

CHEYANNE

THREE AND A HALF years ago

I'd managed to rack up more regrets in my twenty-two years on this earth than most people could accumulate in an entire lifetime.

It seemed like, no matter how many mistakes I made, the lessons I was supposed to have learned never really stuck. I wasn't sure if my problem came from poor decision making or if maybe I was just cursed, but I guess, in the end, it didn't really matter.

The downward spiral that was my life started when I was just a little girl. My parents had died when I was only seven years old, and after that, everything went downhill pretty damn quickly. My twin sister and I were shipped off to live with our next of kin, a cousin of my mother's we didn't even know, and to say the woman and her husband were lacking in affection was a laughable understatement. They seemed to forget we were even around half the time, and when they did remember . . . let's just say it wasn't pleasant. They didn't beat us or anything like that, but their complete disregard was so bad, it was almost negligible.

It wasn't long after we moved in that, out of nowhere, my sister was taken away, and I never saw her again. Losing my parents had been a crushing blow. But losing Charlotte was like having an arm and a leg ripped off my body. She was my twin, my other half, and without her, I never could manage to feel whole.

As I got older, I clung to the relationships I'd formed with an iron grip. I'd hold on too tight, eventually stifling friends or boyfriends to the point they'd take off. I couldn't really blame them. It was way too much responsibility to put on anyone: taking care of the broken little girl who was desperately looking for someone to love her. But still, it never failed to break my heart, time and time again, whenever one of them let me go.

That all built up to me making the first of my most profound mistakes when I was only nineteen.

I let myself be pulled in by a wolf in sheep's clothing.

Graham Knightly had a talent for saying and doing all the right things. He promised me everything I'd ever wanted: love and affection, money and security . . . *family*. He'd distracted me with shiny bobbles and velvet words, and the view from behind my rose-colored glasses was so beautiful I didn't see him for what he really was until it was too late—pure evil.

We'd gotten curious stares at the start of our relationship. After all, I was only nineteen and he was already thirty-one, but I convinced myself they were just jealous that I had him and they didn't. In the beginning I'd liked the age difference. It meant he was already established. He had a successful career in politics, a beautiful house, a bank account—which was a whole hell of a lot more than I could say for the boys my own age.

We'd only been dating a few months when he proposed, just weeks shy of my twentieth birthday. I'd said yes with stars in my eyes, thinking that day was the first day of a new life—a better life.

That was the second worst mistake I'd ever made, because the honeymoon wasn't even over before he pulled the veil back and revealed the truth that had been lurking behind it the whole time.

He didn't want to love me or give me a better life. He'd wanted a pretty, young thing on his arm during fundraisers and galas and public events as he ran for office, someone who'd make him look like a family man in the eyes of the voters, a trophy to hang off his arm and look good in photos. He'd wanted a woman that other men would covet and other women would be jealous of. Someone naïve and easy to manipulate. He'd wanted a girl with no family to her name so there'd be nobody to ask questions, someone he could control completely.

When I wasn't doing my part in all of that, I was his own personal punching bag, the doormat he liked to wipe his shoes on at the end of every night.

The beautiful life I thought I'd have turned into the very worst nightmare I'd been trapped inside of for two years. During an event last year, someone made a joke that all sociopaths were either serial killers or politicians. At the time, everyone had laughed, thinking it was hysterical and totally unfounded, but I was the only one who knew the truth. I was the only one standing in that circle of people beside the man I'd married while he played the role of doting husband and *knew* the joke that had just been told was based on unquestionable fact.

I was the only one who knew the much-adored senator liked to beat the hell out of his wife night after night, that he smiled as he punched and kicked her, that he laughed hysterically as she writhed around on the floor of their bedroom in agony. I was the only one who knew the word "no" could set Graham Knightly into a rage, leading him to take whatever the hell he wanted anyway.

Sure, there were people who suspected, members of his security team, friends he kept close who were just as sick and twisted as he was, but I was the only one who knew as a definitive fact that he was a monster down to his very soul.

And now, sitting on the bed behind the locked door of our extravagant bedroom—my very own gilded cage—staring down at the little plastic stick in my hands, I was also the only one who knew about the tiny life currently growing inside of me.

And that changed *everything*.

Before this, I'd been resigned to my life. Well, that wasn't really true, it was more that I'd been beaten down to the point I just didn't give a damn anymore. However, that was back when it was just me, when I wasn't responsible for the wellbeing and safety of another human being. But now I had someone else to live for, someone to protect and keep safe from all the evils in the world, even if that evil was its own flesh and blood.

Staying was no longer an option.

For the life growing inside of me, there was only one choice.

I had to run.

One

SAWYER

Now

"Hey, Sawyer."

"Morning, Sawyer."

"Hi, Ms. Darcy."

The early morning hustle and bustle of Whitecap, Oregon was in full swing, and it was so different than what I'd been used to back in Ohio. There were more people on the sidewalks, heading to work on foot, than there were cars on the streets. It was the quintessential small town, where everyone knew everyone and neighbors brought baked goods to all the newcomers to welcome them to the block.

It was that warmth and acceptance that made me pick this place over all the others I'd stopped in when I was on the run. The fact that you could hear the waves crashing along the shore and smell the salty sea air also played a big part in my decision. It gave the whole town a peacefulness that I wanted to give my child once she finally came into the world.

So once I landed in Whitecap, I'd shed the skin of the past, of Cheyanne Knightly, and became Sawyer Darcy, a soon-to-be single mother who was just looking for a place to settle down and build a life.

The people had accepted me graciously, and the picturesque seaside town had become my home, as well as my hiding place from the evils lurking in the world—one in particular who I knew would probably never stop looking for me.

I waved and smiled, returning greetings from the people I passed by.

"Hey there!" I looked across the street to Monica Killborne who was in the process right that moment of opening Drip, the local coffee shop, for the day. "How's it going, Sawyer?"

"It's good, Mon."

"How's that precious little girl of yours?"

I smiled, thinking of my daughter, Renee. "She's great," I answered back, totally at ease with shouting a conversation across the street. It was just what people did in Whitecap. Being in a rush was no excuse for not being neighborly with these people. "An endless bundle of energy and destruction, as usual."

The woman smiled so big I was able to see her teeth from across the street. "Ah, the life of a toddler."

"Tell me about it. I'm hoping she wears herself out at daycare today, but I'm not holding my breath."

"True enough. Well, I'll let you get going. Stop in for a coffee later."

"You got it."

I finished my stroll down the block to Warren's General Store, where I'd been working since shortly after arriving in town a few years back. It wasn't some fancy corporate job where I had to wear heels every day and sit behind a desk in fancy designer skirts and blouses, and I freaking loved it. The work was honest, the husband and wife who ran the place were amazing, and the customers who came in were great. I loved the idea of this town being so small it had this quaint, family-owned, one-stop-shop kind of place where you could grab pretty much anything you needed instead of being littered with chain big box stores every couple blocks that blemished the homeyness of the place.

Here, I got to see friends and neighbors on a regular basis and keep up with most of the local gossip—which also meant I was among the first to know if any new faces popped up in town. That made this whole hiding in plain sight gig a hell of a lot easier. I'd learned over the years to make sure I knew everything about my surroundings, that included all the faces —even those who were just passing through.

I kept my eyes and ears open, always prepared, and if I got even the slightest hint that something was off, as much as it would hurt, Renee and I would be gone before anyone had the chance to notice we were missing.

The bell over the door tinkled serenely as I pushed it open and stepped into the store.

A head full of frizzy slate-colored curls popped up over the top of the shelves of cereal boxes. "Morning, Sawyer!" my boss called in her usual cheerful voice.

"Hey, Georgia." I flicked my wrist out in a wave as I headed for the cash register. Georgia Warren and her husband, Desmond, owned Warren's General Store. It had been handed down to them from Desmond's father, who got it from his father before him. When they finally decided to retire they had every hope that their only son would come back to carry on the family legacy, in spite of the fact that he'd been gone a really long time. I didn't have the heart to tell them I wasn't sure that was going to happen.

Apparently, he'd left their small town with dreams of bigger and better things than what Whitecap had to offer. In the years I'd been living here, he'd come back less than a handful of times for holidays and birthdays and such, and those trips never went past the three-day mark.

Georgia was incredibly proud of the family history behind the little store, and never failed to talk the ear off any new face that came through the doors, spouting on and on about the generations of Warrens that had been in Whitecap since the town was founded.

"How's life?" I asked as I stowed my purse beneath the counter and pulled my nametag out of the little bin, pinning it to my chest.

"Well, I'm still here and kicking, so that's a plus."

I shot a wink her way. "You'll outlive us all."

She let out a harrumph. "Damn straight I will. My big behind will outlast all those new-age hippy-dippy dieters with all their no sugar, vegan, gluten-free crap." She waggled her thumb toward her chest. "A pack of bacon every morning does a body good."

I wasn't so sure about that. I was pretty certain her doctor had already lectured her on her cholesterol quite a few times, but who was I to burst the woman's bubble?

I headed down the aisle, shooing her away from the boxes of inventory she'd been in the process of shelving. "Go ahead and get that aforementioned behind to the register. I'll finish this up for you."

She stood from her crouch, her knees and hips cracking frighteningly loud, making me wonder how it was possible she hadn't broken, or at the very least, dislocated something on her way back up. "Thanks, honey," she said with a groan, reaching around to massage the small of her back with a wince. "On the inside I feel like I'm nineteen. Then my body has to go and mock me."

"Yeah, well. That's what you have me for. To do the heavy lifting—literally. Now go on."

She scuttled down the aisle toward the counter at the front of the store. I watched as she hoisted herself up on the cushioned stool and pulled out one of the many romance novels she kept hidden at the back of the shelf beneath the register, thinking we didn't all know her little secret. We all knew. Hell, when things were slow, I tended to raid her stash as a way to pass the time. She had a penchant for historical romances that had rubbed off on me. I'd take a sexy plundering pirate or a rakish duke over real-life men every day of the week.

I shook my head on a grin as she started reading, and got down to re-stocking, moving my way through the shelves. Just as I was finishing up with the cereal, the bell tinkled as the door whooshed open in a rush, bringing the sea breeze in with it.

"What's the rush, Luna?" Georgia asked from her place at the counter.

I lifted my head, and my eyes landed on my friend just as hers found me. "Oh good, you're here!"

I lifted my arms out at my sides. "Where else would I be, Lu? I'm here five days a week. It's my job."

Luna Copeland was the closest thing I had to a best friend, considering the only things she knew about me were the lies I'd told her and everyone else in Whitecap. She only knew me as Sawyer Darcy. She knew absolutely nothing about Cheyanne Knightly. There had been a few close calls over the years—mainly after we'd had a bit too much to drink during our monthly Margarita Mondays—when I came *this* close to telling her all my secrets, but I'd always managed to pull myself back before my mouth could get away from me.

It wasn't that I didn't trust her. If there was anyone I knew I could count on, it was her, but the risks were just too great. I had to put Renee's safety first. I'd run before Graham could discover I was pregnant. If he found out about the daughter we shared, he'd hunt us down and take her away from me, and that wasn't going to happen. I kept her safe. I loved her. I did everything in my power to protect her. If her father had the first clue she existed, she'd be in danger and I'd die before I let that happen.

Luna skip-walked down the aisle, a huge, shit-eating grin on her face. "Have you seen him yet?" she asked excitedly.

"Seen who?"

She let out a whistle and danced a little jig. "If you're asking that, you definitely *haven't*."

I smacked her in the stomach with an unopened box of marshmallow puff cereal. She snatched it out of my hand and peeled the flap open, tearing the interior bag and stuffing a handful of cereal into her mouth. "Will you stop speaking in code and just spit it out already?" I pointed at the cereal box. "And you're paying for that."

She rolled her eyes like I was being ridiculous before explaining through puffy, cereal-packed cheeks what had her in such a state. "So I heard from Dina who heard from Carley who heard from Addy that she had a new renter at the beach house on Sandstone Lane right down the street from your house."

The skin between my brows puckered as I frowned in confusion. "That usually happens with rental properties, right? People *rent* them. It's kind of the whole purpose."

Luna's cheeks flushed a pale, excited pink as she leaned in and lowered her voice like she was about to reveal she knew who shot JFK or that she'd stumbled on Coca Cola's secret recipe or something. "Yeah, but according to *all of them,* she's never had a renter that was this gorgeous."

I snorted as I turned away and began breaking the empty box down with a box cutter. "I seriously doubt that. Tourist season brings people from all over the country. There are hot men all over the place during the summer."

Luna let out a wistful sigh and fanned her face. "Don't I know it," she replied dreamily. "Damn, I miss the summer."

"It's still technically summertime, babe."

"Yeah, but it's the *end* of summer, which means all the talent has headed back home or been sampled already."

My friend was what I liked to refer to as a seasonal dater. She was basically the female version of the world's most notorious bachelor, keeping her dalliances strictly to men she knew wouldn't be sticking around for more than a couple weeks. Three months out of the year she went nuts with the hot, single men passing through, and as soon as fall hit, it was like she went into hibernation until the following summer.

Her thought was she was still young enough that the tick of her biological clock was just a distant noise at this point, and she intended to soak up as much fun as possible before she even considered such things as settling down and monogamy.

She refused to get involved with any locals, claiming things tended to get a bit messy when you took a guy home from the bar and the dude you'd wham-bam thank-you-ma'am-ed a few weeks before lived just up the block.

"Anyway," I said, shifting the focus back to the matter at hand, "I'm sure Addy was exaggerating. You know she tends to do that."

"I thought the same thing. But then Sherry at Gas and Go said she spotted him when he swung through to gas up his ride, and she confirmed it. So I'm going to need you to be on the lookout for me, 'mkay?"

"What? Why me?" She let out a huff that scattered cereal crumbs all over the front of my shirt. "Oh, come on. You're so gross," I said on a laugh as I dusted myself off.

She finished chewing quickly and swallowed. "Sorry about that. And you know why. You have that crazy weird juju where you can get a read on a person just by looking at them."

She wasn't wrong about that, but it wasn't exactly juju. It was a skill that came from years of hiding and lying about my identity. I'd basically grown to be suspicious of everyone around me. It wasn't the easiest or healthiest way to live, but it kept Renee and me safe.

"Why do you think I never hook up with a guy until I've gotten the okay from you?"

Oh yeah. And it had also turned me into a walking creep detector for my best friend.

"What if this guy's not just passing through? What if he's planning to move here?"

She gave me a look that screamed, *oh, you precious, silly girl.* "If he's as hot as people are claiming, I'm willing to make this one exception. You know, for the greater good."

I gave her a snide look. "Oh of course. For the greater good."

She started skip-walking backward. "So you'll be on the lookout for me?" She lifted her hand to her ear, pinky and thumb out to mimic a phone. "And call me if he stops in here."

"Yes, because all I have to do with my day is watch out for your next hookup," I said dryly.

"See? I knew we were besties for a reason." She shot me a wink as she got closer to the door. "See you soon. Loveyoubye!"

"Wait! You didn't pay for the"—she fluttered out of the store, the door closing behind her—"cereal," I finished on a sigh.

"That girl," Georgia stated with a fond shake of her head. "One of these days she's going to meet a man who knocks her on her ass, and I can't wait to see it."

That made two of us.

Two

SAWYER

I PUSHED into the coffee shop later that day, in desperate need of caffeine to beat back the afternoon lull that usually hit me around 3:00, making it nearly impossible to stay on my feet or keep my eyes open.

"Hey, Mon," I greeted, brushing my wind-blown hair out of my face. She stood behind the counter, her elbow resting on the wooden top, her chin in her palm as she stared off. "How's it—?"

"Shhh!" She waved her free hand in my face to silence me.

I clamped my lips shut and rolled them between my teeth. It was then that I noticed the coffee shop was eerily quiet. "What's going on?" I whispered as I looked around. It seemed every woman in the building was staring in the same direction as Monica.

"New guy came in a few minutes ago," she whispered

back. "And holy walking orgasms, Batman. Pretty sure my panties went up in smoke the minute he pulled the door open."

"You're as bad as Luna." I shook my head good-naturedly. "He's just a man," I continued as I turned to look to the person everyone was gawking at. "You'd think no one here ever saw one before—holy God. *Is that him?*" I hissed when I finally caught sight of the man sitting at the small, round table in the corner.

His rich, chocolate-brown hair was a little long, flipping at the ends around his neck and ears. As I stared, totally transfixed, he raked his fingers through the dark strands, pushing them back from his face and giving me an unob-structed view of his profile. And what a profile it was. From that angle I could see he had thick, arched brows, a straight nose, a strong, square jawline that hadn't been shaved in a few days, and distinct, chiseled cheekbones.

Golden tanned skin stretched around a thick, veiny forearm and a bicep that bulged as he lifted the coffee cup to his mouth and took a sip. There was no missing the fact that his hand was so big, the mug looked dwarfed beneath his long fingers and a wide palm. But what had to be the hottest thing about the guy just then was that he wasn't just sitting there messing around on his phone, oblivious to anything other than what was happening on the screen. No, on the table before him was a hardcover book that held his complete attention.

There was just something about an attractive guy reading

a book that made him off-the-charts hot. At least to me. And from the collective sigh that filled the air from every ovary-carrying adult in the room as the stranger turned the page, it was easy to tell I wasn't the only one who felt that way.

Monica gave me a snide look, arching a brow. "You were saying?" she teased.

"Whatever," I grumbled, forcing my gaze from the stranger. I'd been staring so hard I was beginning to feel like a voyeur. "I'll admit he's attractive—"

"Oh no, honey. 'Attractive' doesn't begin to cover it. Get close enough to a man like that and I'm pretty sure your eyebrows will melt right off your face."

"Colorful," I said on a chuckle.

With a sigh, she returned her chin to her hand and resumed her gawking. "What is it about a man reading a book in public that sets my lady parts all aflutter?" Monica asked, voicing my earlier thought. Well, all except for the lady parts bit.

"I'm sure your husband would just love to hear that."

She waved me off without a care. "Meh. It's like when I read a particularly steamy book. I get all hot and bothered, and he gets to reap *all* the benefits . . . if you know what I mean," she added with a wink.

I pushed down the cringe that came with that overload of info, as well as the unsettling feeling that came from being drawn to a man I'd never seen before, and tried to pretend that everything was normal. It was just another day. There was no dude who looked like he belonged on the cover of a romance novel, his shirt hanging open and fluttering in a breeze as he ripped the bodice of some duchess's dress in half with his bare hands, sitting in the corner of my local coffee shop.

It had been a *long* time since I'd been with a man, and the last one had turned out to be a nightmare in the very truest definition of the word. It was a road I had no intention of going down again. My reasons were totally different, but just like Luna, I refused to do relationships. However, unlike her I stayed away from intimacy altogether.

"So, can I get a coffee or what?"

She blew out a raspberry in mock frustration. "Fine, Debbie Downer. You want the usual?"

"Yes, please." I focused harder than necessary on Monica as she went about making my drink, tracking her movements like I was going to be tested on them later. It was either that or leer at the stranger, which was a big fat *no*. My eyes tried several times to drift in his direction, and I had to actively keep myself from glancing back over. It was a whole hell of a lot harder than it should have been.

The hiss of the milk steamer cut through the hushed whispers I heard coming from the women behind me. No doubt, they were tittering on about the newcomer. The smell of roasted coffee beans filled the air, going a long way in perking me up. I wrapped my hands around the warm paper cup as soon as Monica slid it my way and lifted it up for that first sip. The hit was instant, and I closed my eyes to savor the taste, letting out a grateful moan.

"Thanks so much. You're a lifesaver."

"It's what I do." Monica blew on her nails and buffed them against her shirt smugly. "Don't look now, babe, but I think you might have an admirer."

A shiver ran across my spine as I peeled my eyelids open wider. "What?"

"Mr. Sexy Reader over there is scoping you out." A tingling sensation spread across my back between my shoulder blades, that itchy, crawly feeling that came from the sense of being watched.

My body acted of its own accord, and before I could stop myself, my head swiveled and my eyes landed on the stranger. Sure enough, he was looking right at me—or more specifically, at my ass.

My movement must have caught his attention, because his gaze traveled up to my face, a sheepish grin stretching across his lips at having been caught ogling. If I thought the man was something to behold in profile, it was absolutely *nothing* compared to what he looked like facing me full-on.

"My God, it should be criminal for a man to be that good-looking." Monica breathed, and from the corner of my eye, I saw her fanning her face. "Damn, if I didn't love you, I'd hate you so bad right now. As it is, I'm all kinds of jealous."

Ripping my attention from the insanely gorgeous man, I looked to Monica, trying to ignore the fact that my heart rate had suddenly kicked up into the red zone. "You do remember that you're married, right?"

She blew out a raspberry. "I'm married, not dead. I'm allowed to appreciate a fine work of art when I see one. And Sam better watch out or this dude might just unseat him as hottest in town."

Monica's husband, Sam Killborne had been the most popular bachelor in town when he moved here several years back. To hear Monica tell it, the women had all but dueled over him. Eventually, he saw the treasure who was Monica—again, her words—and quickly put a ring on her finger, snubbing all the other ladies. I'd seen for myself how that hadn't stopped the single women in Whitecap from drooling just a bit any time he entered a room. And for good reason. The man wasn't just good-looking, he was built like a brick house.

Having had a successful career in the NFL before retiring—something that had kept the man *in shape*—he was now the head coach of the high school's varsity football team. But that wasn't the only reason he garnered so much attention and adoration. Not only was he handsome as hell, but he was also an all-around incredible guy.

Instead of taking his summers off once the school year ended, he spent that time acting as the town handyman, using his natural skill with tools to help out friends, family, and neighbors with any home repairs or projects they might need done. When a nasty storm had blown through last year, a tree in my yard had fallen and put a hole in my roof. Without me even having to ask, he'd shown up the very next day to patch the roof and remove the tree.

He was the polar opposite of Graham in every single way,

and I knew better than most how lucky Monica had been to land such a solid guy.

"I don't think Sam really cares about being the *hottest in town*," I said, using finger quotes on the last three words.

She snorted and shook her head. "Please. He'd have you all believing that, but trust me, he secretly gets off on it. His male pride is a very delicate, like a precious baby bird. If he didn't have me to stroke his ego once in a while, he'd probably spend all his time huddled in a corner, rocking back and forth."

I snorted sarcastically. "Well thank God, for you then."

"Exactly." She suddenly narrowed her eyes and stuck her finger in my face. "I see what you're doing. I'm on to you. I know you're trying to change the subject from the fact you've got a perfect ten currently checking out your ass like he wants to eat his next meal off of it."

I made the mistake of taking sip as she spoke and proceeded to choke on my coffee. "Jesus, Mon," I wheeze-laughed once my airway was clear.

She smiled, looking way too damn happy with herself for garnering such a reaction. "You should go over and say hi."

"That's not going to happen." I fought against my body's reaction to turn and look back at the man as I thumbed through my wallet for some cash to pay for my drink.

"Oh come on," she insisted. "You've been single way too damn long. Would it really kill you to take that dude out for a test drive?" She waggled her brows as she passed me my change, adding, "I'm sure your lady bits could use a little dusting off."

"My lady bits are just fine, thank you very much. No dusting required."

I heard the sound of a throat clearing as soon as that last word passed my lips, and Monica's eyes suddenly grew comically wide, making her look like a cartoon character.

"Hello," a deep, raspy voice laced with humor rumbled from right behind me.

I swiveled on my heels slowly, knowing before I made a full rotation who I was going to see standing there. Sure enough, the stranger was only a few feet away, and the intensity of his attractiveness from a distance had nothing on the magnetic pull of all that was him up close and personal.

His velvety stare beat against my ribs like a xylophone. From so close, I could see his eyes weren't just brown, they were also speckled with flecks of gold, and the edge of his irises were rimmed with a dark green ring. They were show-stopper eyes, and at that very moment, they had rendered me completely speechless.

"For the love of God," Monica whisper-yelled, "say something already."

All I could come up with was, "Uh . . ."

The man grinned, revealing two rows of straight, pearly white teeth and, Holy Weeping Angel Babies, a set of devastating dimples. "I'm Trent," the handsome stranger stated.

I blinked slowly. "Chey—" I started before my brain

finally reengaged and I caught myself. My eyes bugged out as I clamped my mouth shut so fast my back teeth clacked together painfully. His eyes might have made me mute, but those damn dimples apparently made me flat-out stupid. That grin stretched into a full-blown smile, deepening those divots in his cheeks, and dear Lord, he just kept getting better.

"Ouch!" I cried when Monica reached across the counter to pinch the skin on the back of my bicep. Whipping around, I shot her my deadliest killing look as I rubbed at the stinging flesh.

"Excuse my friend," Monica butted in. "Sometimes her brain disconnects."

"Not a problem," the guy said with a chuckle. "At least you're willing to admit you're shy, right?"

"This is Sawyer," Monica continued on my behalf.

"Sawyer," he said, like he was testing my name on his tongue. "Nice to meet you. So, are you a local?"

"Um . . . I-I need to go," I blurted, grabbing my coffee and taking two quick steps back. "Nice to meet you too," I muttered as I turned on my heel and speed-walked toward the exit. "Enjoy Whitecap. See you."

One last glance over my shoulder showed Monica staring after me like I'd just lost my damn mind. She wouldn't have been too far off the mark. I'd already made one infinitely idiotic error in nearly spouting out my real name. I couldn't risk another brain fart.

Humor danced in the stranger—Trent's—eyes as his gaze

tracked me. "Yeah. See you around," was the last thing I heard from him before the door shut behind me.

"God, I really hope not," I whispered to myself as I scurried around the corner of the building and out of sight of the large windows.

Luna had been right that I was pretty damn good at reading people, and something about that man set my radar pinging in all directions. My gut was telling me he was all kinds of dangerous. Just maybe not in the way I'd expect.

Three

TRENT

I PUT my rental truck in park and let it idle, waiting about a block down from the building where the GPS said "Sawyer Darcy" was.

Letting out a sigh, I grabbed my phone from the cupholder in the center console and scrolled through my contacts until I got to my boss's name.

He answered after the first ring. "Sheppard."

Lincoln Sheppard, or Linc as all his men knew him, was the owner of Alpha Omega, a private investigation and securities firm based out of Hope Valley, Virginia. He'd started the place when he got out of the Corps years back, and when business started to grow and he needed to bring on more people, he hired ex-military guys like me who were struggling with the return to civilian life and needed a job that let us use the skills we'd developed and honed from years of serving our country.

It wasn't a very big operation, and the town we were based out of was small as hell—though not quite as small as this place—but the reputation we had as being the best in the business had us taking jobs all over the country, so desired we got to pick and choose the kind of jobs we worked, referring the rest to other outfits in the business because we didn't have the time.

Even still, despite the fact we were all swimming in work, when Dalton, another member of our team, came to us, asking for help, none of us had hesitated to throw our hat into the ring. Dalton was a brother in a way that was stronger than blood for me, making his fiancée, Charlotte, family, so when we got word she wanted to find her long lost sister, worried that she might be in trouble, that became our highest priority. Everything else was placed on the back burner. It wasn't about money or making a name for ourselves. It was about family helping family.

Linc let his guys loose, providing us with anything we needed to help aid in our search. However, even with all our skills combined, tracking down Cheyanne Knightly had proven to be harder than expected. It was as if the woman had disappeared off the face of the earth.

Days turned into weeks that inevitably turned into months. Each lead took us to a dead end. I'd followed one trail after another, the most recent sending me all the way across the country to some tiny dot on the map in the middle of nowhere Oregon called Whitecap.

"It's me," I said into the phone, my eyes pinned to the building some ways down from where I was parked.

"Hey. Any news?"

"Made contact yesterday," I informed my boss before giving him the information we'd all been hoping for. "She's going by the name Sawyer Darcy, but it's her."

Silence echoed through the line for several seconds before he asked, "How sure are you about this?"

"Not a doubt in my mind, man." I'd set myself up at the coffee shop in the hopes my target would do like most people and swing in for an afternoon pick-me-up. I didn't have to wait long, and as soon as I caught my first glimpse of her from across the room, the shock had been instant. "I know Dalton said they were fraternal twins, but swear to Christ, I thought it was Charlotte at first."

Not to mention the fact that she slipped when I introduced myself, nearly giving me her real name instead of the alias she'd been living under for years. The fear that flooded her expression as soon as she caught herself was palpable, causing the air around us to grow thick and swampy with tension. She nearly ran out of there like her ass was on fire. It was only because of her friend temporarily distracting her that I was able to sneak the tracking device into her purse without her noticing before she took off.

"Jesus Christ," he grunted. "I can't believe we finally found her. You call Dalt with the news yet?"

I felt a tingling sensation crawl across my skin as I read the words on the sign that stretched across the top of the small cottage that, along with most of the other houses on this street, had clearly been converted into a business. "Not yet. Wanted to check in with you first because we may have a problem."

Sure enough, as soon as the words came out of my mouth, the door to a converted house pushed open and the woman now known as Sawyer stepped out, an adorable little girl with dirty blonde pigtails resting on her hip.

"What's wrong?" Linc asked, pulling my focus off of them.

"She's got a kid, brother. Two or three years old from the looks of it, so it's not a long shot to think that Knightly prick is the father."

"Fucking hell."

After a local case involving crooked police and murder had garnered national attention, splashing Charlotte's face all over the news outlets, Graham Knightly officially put himself on our radar when he sent one of his men after her to find out what she knew of her sister's whereabouts, a sister she hadn't seen in nearly two decades. Things had escalated to ugly, and it didn't take much digging for us to discover Ohio's Lieutenant Governor was all kinds of dangerous, and that his wife's disappearance and reports of her death reeked of some sort of cover-up.

"If I had to guess, that kid's the reason she went on the run and has been living as a different person this whole time."

I could hear the weariness in Linc's sigh, clear as day.

"Which means she probably won't be too thrilled with us tracking her down for a long-awaited family reunion."

"That would be my guess." I watched through the windshield as she and her daughter moved along the sidewalk. Cheyanne—no, that wasn't right. *Sawyer* looked like a completely different woman just then as she beamed at the toddler in her arms. Her whole face was lit up like the Fourth of July, happiness practically radiating from her pores. The anxious woman I'd encountered at the coffee shop the day before was completely gone as she smiled and laughed at her little girl, saying something I couldn't hear through the glass and distance between us. "Not so sure letting Dalton know I found her is the best idea just yet," I admitted, feeling shitty for having to say it. Unfortunately, it was the truth. "He's all about making his woman happy, not that I can blame him there, and Charlotte finally connecting with her sister after all these years would definitely make her happy. But he'll want to move in fast and if I do that now, she might get spooked and take off again."

"I agree." He hesitated for a second, then clipped, "*Fuck.* Wish I didn't, but I see your point, and I think you're right. If we told them now, I don't think we could keep them reined in. Know for a fact Charlotte would jump her ass on a plane before any of us could stop her. Hell, she'd probably stab anyone who tried to stand in her way."

He wasn't wrong about that. Charlotte Belmont wasn't the kind of woman to take orders—or hell, even a polite request if she wasn't in the mood. She might have looked like a tiny little pixie, but she had a fire in her that screamed *do not fuck with me*. She wouldn't hesitate to cut you if she felt you deserved it, and her wrath would make most men's balls shrink back up inside them. Dalton had his hands full with that one, and he fucking loved every second of it. As much as that woman could terrify me, I had to admit, I could see the appeal.

"So how do you want me to play this?" I asked as I continued to watch mom and daughter. Sawyer had lowered the kid to her feet, and now they were literally skipping down the sidewalk. As they got closer, I could hear the muffled sounds of the little girl giggling like crazy, and it made a smile tug at my lips.

"For the time being, just keep her and the kid in your sights, yeah? You're just another tourist enjoying some time off by the beach. If you can, feel her out. We'll give it some time and reassess later on."

"All right, boss. Sounds good to me."

"This'll stay between us for the time being. Keep me posted if anything comes up."

"You got it."

I hung up a second later, my eyes on the reflection of Sawyer and her little girl in the side-view mirror as they passed by my truck and continued down the sidewalk. I'd do what Lincoln suggested and keep an eye out. I just hoped like hell that now that we finally managed to find her, it wouldn't turn the world she'd created for herself and her daughter upside down.

Four

SAWYER

WITH BATH TIME done and teeth brushed, I helped Renee into her jammies, pulling the nightgown with a sleeping cartoon teddy bear over her little belly.

"Boo!" she shouted the moment her head popped through the neck hole. I let out a little squeak and held my hand to my chest, feigning fright. "Gotcha, Mommy!"

"Sure did, sweetheart. Now hop up here and spin around to I can brush your hair."

She did as instructed, grabbing hold of the comforter in her tiny fists and tugging herself up onto the bed. She crawled across the mattress until her knees bumped mine and plopped down with her back to me.

I picked the brush up off the bedside table and started carefully pulling the bristles through her damp hair. My little girl was almost three years old, and I'd never once taken her for a haircut, so the silky dark blonde locks hung past her shoulder blades. It was a few shades lighter than my own hair, and much darker than Graham's natural blonde.

I still had a few pictures from my childhood stashed in a box tucked in the very back of my closet, high up on a shelf, and as Renee got older and her features went from those of a baby to a little girl, I pulled that box down to make a comparison. Sure enough, my precious girl got her hair from my sister. My twin. I hadn't seen her in what felt like a lifetime, in fact, we were only a few years older than Renee when we were ripped apart, but I could still remember clear as day that Charlotte's hair had always been a little lighter than mine.

My baby also had her aunt's eyes. Our mother's eyes. It was a wonder I could still remember what they'd looked like all these years later. I'd been so damn young, after all, but I did, and the pictures I'd carried everywhere with me, keeping secreted away from prying eyes all my life, helped fuel those memories.

Where I'd taken after my father, getting his brown eyes, my girl had taken after my mom and sister, having the most gorgeous hazel gaze that turned different shades of green, blue, or brown depending on what she was wearing.

"All done." I put the brush back on her nightstand beside her adorable little daisy lamp. "Up you go. Under the covers." She scrambled up the bed as I stood, pulling the comforter and sheet back so she could climb between them before tucking them under her chin. "Did you pick what book you want as a bedtime story, doodle bug?"

"Pwincess stowy, Momma" she demanded.

"The princess story again? That's five nights in a row."

"Pwincess stowy!" she exclaimed loudly.

I let out a sigh of fake exasperation and sat down beside her, my heart swelling and chest warming as she snuggled into my side. "Once upon a time, in a castle high up in the clouds, there were two little princesses."

"Sistews!" she cried out.

"That's right, sweetheart. They were sisters. Twins, actually."

"Theiw names, Momma," she whispered excitedly, already knowing the story I'd made up for her by heart. "Say theiw names."

"Their names were Cheyanne Riley and Charlotte Renee."

"Like me!"

I hugged her tighter against me and gave her side a little tickle. "That's right. You're named after the oldest princess because you're just as special as she was. Anyway, the little princesses were loved by their mommy and daddy, the king and queen, so very much. The whole magical kingdom came out to celebrate the day they were born, and as they got older, they grew closer than two sisters had ever been. They were best friends, two halves of a whole.

"But sadly, when the little princesses were still very young, a mean dragon came to their castle in the clouds and stole them away from their mommy and daddy."

I continued on with the story, detailing the king and queen's heroic effort to save their daughters and how they had slayed the dragon and finally brought the little princesses home. By the time I reached the part where the sisters had grown up into young women and met two handsome princes that they married, Renee was out like a light, her mouth opened slightly and her lips pursed into a pout in her sleep.

Carefully easing from her bed, I bent to press a kiss to her forehead. "Love you, doodle bug," I whispered before flipping off the daisy lamp and heading for the door. Like I did most every night, I stood in the open doorway and stared back at my little girl snuggled beneath her fluffy covers. I counted my lucky stars at the same time the fear for her safety threatened to consume me.

For as long as I could remember, all I'd ever wanted was a family of my own. Growing up the way I had, having the most important people in my life stripped away, I'd clung to the idea of becoming a mother with both hands, knowing that when I had children of my own, I'd finally have someone to give all the love and affection I'd been carrying around inside of me. I remembered how wonderful my own parents had been before they died, and all I wanted was to give that to my own babies.

There wasn't a day that passed that I didn't thank the powers that be for giving me Renee. But with that feeling came an overwhelming sense of guilt. This wasn't the life I'd wanted to give her: constantly hiding, the threat of having to run again around every corner. I knew the life I'd built for us was as unstable as a house of cards in the middle of a hurricane. What I'd wanted to give my child, the dreams I used to have, had gone up in smoke all because I'd been so desperate for love I'd picked the first man to spout pretty words.

"Yo, helicopter mom," Luna called from the kitchen, pulling me from my melancholy. "Move your ass. These margaritas aren't going to drink themselves."

With a low chuckle, I pulled Renee's door partially closed and headed down the hall where Luna was waiting to kick off our Margarita Monday.

"The little rug rat down for the count?" she asked as I rounded the corner. One of the reasons I'd fallen in love with this little cottage was because of how open and airy it was. From the living room, you could see right into the kitchen and dining area. There was a big sliding glass door to a deck that overlooked the beach and ocean that I could open up to bring the smell of the sea into my home. The whole place was great for entertaining, something I did pretty regularly here.

It was funny, really. In my old life I'd hated having people over. It was always such a performance. Fake smiles, fake laughter, small-talk that felt like pulling teeth with people I didn't like all that much. And there was always an objective. None of them were friends, they were players in the game to help Graham get to where he wanted to be. I couldn't stand any of them. But here, I loved when my friends would gather in my house, around my kitchen, on the deck, or kick back on the couch. The only reason for their visits was to catch up and enjoy each other's company. No one expected anything from the other person.

"Yep. She's out cold."

Luna smiled big. The ice in the silver cocktail shaker rattled around as she shook it with a flourish before dumping the concoction between two glasses with salted rims. "First round is up. Time to get this party started."

I grabbed the glass she slid across the bar and lifted it to my lips, taking the first sip. The tartness exploded on my tongue first, followed a second later by heat.

I gave her a wide-eyed look. "What is that? Why does it taste spicy?"

"Jalapeño," she answered before taking a big gulp. "Wanted to try something new. What do you think?"

I took another sip. "I actually like it. The sweet and spicy works really well together."

She gave her shoulders a little shimmy as she rounded the bar and headed for the sliding door. "Just like me."

"Exactly."

I left the door open so I could listen for Renee in case she woke up and flipped on the white twinkle lights I had strung around the deck before curling up on the small patio love seat facing the inky black ocean and star-speckled sky. Sliding off my flip-flops, I pulled my feet up and tucked them beneath me. I loved sitting out here during the summers, before the weather started to turn and the temperature dropped. No matter how hot it got during the day, there was a continuous breeze blowing off the water that kept things pleasantly comfortable.

She took the chair catty-corner from me and kicked her bare feet up on the glass coffee table. "So," she dragged out dramatically, "I talked to Monica this morning, and she had some pretty interesting gossip."

I rolled my eyes and took another drink. "For the love of God," I lamented. "This town and its gossip."

"Hey, don't knock small-town gossip. It's one of the reasons I love this place so damn much."

"Of course, because you're one of the worst gossips here. You and Monica both."

She didn't look the least bit offended as she decreed, "Amen to that, sister. And I think it's funny you haven't asked what it is I heard."

"I haven't asked because I already know, which means I also know for a fact that whatever you heard wasn't interesting at all and definitely exaggerated."

"So the new hottie *wasn't* scoping you out at Drip a few days ago?"

"He just looked at me, that's all." Although, I did catch him looking at my ass, and it sure as hell felt like he'd been checking me out. But I wasn't about to add fuel to Luna's fire.

"Well, Monica said it was more than that, that the dude was ogling you like you were a three-course meal and he hadn't eaten in a month."

"Like I said, she exaggerated."

Right?

Nope, I silently screamed to myself. I wasn't going to start questioning it because it didn't matter. Not at all.

She looked at me, her expression pinched with skepticism. "Was she also exaggerating when she said she thought you'd stroked out for a minute and lost the power of speech when he came up and introduced himself to you?"

I snorted and took a gulp of my margarita, smiling as I admitted, "No, she might have been spot-on with that one."

Luna's head fell back on a laugh. "At least you're willing to own it."

"It's not my fault! There isn't a woman on the planet who could help it," I defended. "I mean, the dude had dimples, for Christ's sake. *Dimples.*"

"No way," she breathed, her attention rapt.

"Have you seen him yet?"

She let out a beleaguered sigh and poked her bottom lip out in a dramatic pout. "No," she said grumpily. "And I'm starting to feel really bitter about it. It's like I'm the only one in town who hasn't spotted him yet. It's not fair."

"Yeah. Well, I'll tell you, the rumors don't do the guy justice. I thought I was going to swallow my tongue. I can't even remember the entire interaction. I think I blacked out for a few seconds."

She choked on the drink she'd just taken, and we both burst into laughter.

"I'm serious," I giggled when the hilarity finally tapered off. "I thought you all were being ridiculous when you talked about him, but I get it now. For real."

She dropped her head back on a groan. "Oh my God. And he totally hit on you. I hate you so much right now."

"Trent didn't hit on me," I insisted.

I realized my mistake as soon as her eyes bugged out. "*Trent*?" A wicked grin pulled at her lips.

"You're ridiculous," I groaned into my margarita.

"And you're on a first name basis now," she teased in a sing-song voice.

"What? It's his name," I cried on a bewildered laugh, throwing my free hand out. "What else am I supposed to call him?"

"Oh no, *Trent* is fine. I bet *Trent* would love you using his name."

"I hate you," I grumbled into my glass. "I really do."

"So *Trent* is hot, huh?"

"Yes. Unnaturally hot."

"Damn." She collapsed back into her chair. "I knew it. So what are you going to do?"

My brow furrowed in confusion. "Do about what?"

"About the new guy!" she cried in exasperation. "You going to hit that or what?"

My eyes bugged out and I nearly choked on my drink. "Of course not. I don't even know the guy."

"All the more reason to get in there and bang one out," she declared. "Or maybe more than one. All the more reason to get in there and bang a dozen out."

"You and Monica are the worst," I grumbled. "I'm not banging anything out."

She looked at me like I'd just grown another arm out of the center of my forehead. "Why the hell not?" she asked in a tone that was equal parts bewildered and accusatory.

She sat up, removing her feet from the coffee table and leaning forward with her elbows braced on her knees. "Seriously, when was the last time you had sex? And don't give me that shit about not remembering. A woman remembers."

She was right, I did remember the last time I had sex. It was right before I found out I was pregnant. I wish I could forget about it, truly, but every horrible memory from that time in my life was burned into my brain.

I didn't miss a single thing about Graham. Even with all the running and hiding and constant worry, I was happier these past few years than I'd ever been with him. But I'd be lying to myself if I said I wasn't painfully aware of my lack of a sex life. My vibrator ran through batteries at an alarmingly fast rate.

"It's . . . been a while," I hedged when it became clear she wasn't going to let this line of questioning go.

She arched a brow, her silent demand for me to get more specific.

I rolled my eyes on a huff. "It was around the time I realized I was pregnant, okay?"

Her back shot straight, a look of horror etched across her face. "Oh, God. You poor thing."

I rolled my eyes skyward. "Will you stop it? It's not a big deal. And I certainly don't need to be pitied by a woman who slept with a guy whose claim to fame was being a 'latte foam artist.'"

She lifted a finger in defense. "First off, he was very

passionate about his work, so who am I to judge what some people consider art?"

"It's not art. The dude was a glorified barista at a Starbucks."

"That's beside the point." She waved me off. "And secondly, that guy rocked my freaking world. I was walking funny for a week, thank you very much."

I wrinkled my nose at her overshare before relenting. "Fine. But what about the guy with the Harry Potter hang up?"

Her mouth opened but no words came out, like she knew there was no rebuttal for that one. She pursed her lips like she was in deep thought for a second before saying, "Okay, I'll give you that one. I wasn't a big fan of him shouting, 'I solemnly swear I'm up to no good' every time he was about to come. It was a real lady boner killer. Also, I'm going to stop telling you things if you're just going to throw them back in my face."

"I *wish* you would stop. You tell me too much. I have images scraped into my head that I'm never going to be able to get out. *Never.*"

She blew out a raspberry. "*Pfft.* My ability to overshare is one of the things you love most about me."

"It really isn't."

"And we've gotten way off point. Are you honestly telling me Renee's dad was the last person you slept with?"

I threw back the last of my drink so fast the tartness and

spice burned a path down my throat, pooling in my belly like fire spreading across gasoline.

"Holy shit." She sucked in a breath, my silence all the answer she needed. "Wow. I just . . ." She gave her head a shake. "You never really say anything about Renee's dad. Don't get me wrong, that's totally cool. You'll tell me if or when you want to, I'm not going to push."

"There's nothing to tell," I said, feigning a casual attitude I certainly didn't feel. "It was just a short fling. I didn't really know the guy." The lie slipped off my tongue so easily it was almost scary. It wasn't that I didn't mind lying. Truth was, I hated it, but the lie about Graham was easy enough because it was what I *wanted* to be true. It was the very same lie I told myself day after day as a way to solidify my new life and the person I had become.

Lying was so much easier when you wanted it to be the truth.

"Then what's the deal? If you aren't still hung up on this guy, why haven't you put yourself back out there? You're a stone-cold fox, babe. You could have any man you want. Trust me, I've heard more than enough rumblings from the guys in town."

She wasn't asking simply to be nosey. She genuinely wanted to know. Since I rolled into town, my non-existent sex life had been one of the world's greatest mysteries—at least according to Luna.

"No reason." Another lie I wished was the truth. See? Easy. "I have Renee to take care of and a job and bills to pay. Being a single mom doesn't really leave time for much else."

She let out a slow, steady breath, silent for several beats and staring off like she was lost in contemplation before finally speaking again. "You deserve to have something of your own, Sawyer."

"I have something of my own. I have Renee. That's all I need."

Luna gave me a look, telling me she knew I was being intentionally obtuse. "You know what I mean," she said flatly.

I did, unfortunately.

With a sigh, I uncurled from my tight little ball on the love seat and leaned forward to place my empty glass on the coffee table. "I don't know why we're talking about this. The guy—"

"*Trent*," she interrupted with a wry grin.

I shot her a glare. "He probably isn't interested, so this whole conversation is totally pointless."

"Did you miss the part where I told you you were smokin' hot, or did you just choose to ignore it?"

"I—"

She held up her had to silence me. "That was a rhetorical question. Obviously you just ignored me. Anyway, all I'm saying is that if you just put yourself out there, there's not a man alive that wouldn't trip over his own two feet for a shot with you. Clearly, Renee's dad is the dumbest boy in school for letting you get away. So don't let that asshole be the last guy you get naked with. You're in your prime, babe. Have some fun. Live a little, for crying out loud!"

A lot of what Luna had to say went in one ear and out the other because pretty much all of my friend's advice tended to hover on the very edge of ridiculous. But I'd have been lying if I said she didn't have a point with this.

Graham was the last man I'd had sex with. Hell, he was the *only* man if I wanted to be technical. I wasn't sure I could count the couple careless teenaged tumbles in back seats I'd had back in high school. Those guys were so clueless about what they were doing I'd never even gotten off during the five seconds they'd lasted.

If I was being honest with myself, I secretly hated that Graham held the title of the only man to give me an orgasm. And those few only came *before* I realized the monster he truly was. It might be nice to be touched by another man— especially one who didn't make my skin crawl every time I looked at him.

"I can practically see the wheels turning behind your eyes. You're considering it, aren't you?"

"No! Well, maybe. I don't know." I pushed out a weary sigh and reached up to rub my eyes. "What happened to *you* wanting to take a tumble with the new guy, huh? You were practically floating around town just at the thought of it a few days ago."

She shrugged casually. "Hey, what kind of BFF would I be if I stood in the way of my sister from another mister getting her freak on? But if I graciously step aside, like the incredibly magnanimous person I am, and you don't take your shot with Mr. Dimples, I'll never speak to you again."

"I am way too sober for this conversation," I lamented.

She shot up from her chair, bending at the waist to snatch up my glass. "Don't, worry, girl. I got you."

With that, she skipped back into the house and started preparing round two.

Five

SAWYER

My bed rattled and shook, making the drum line in my head beat against my skull even harder.

Damn Luna Copeland. Damn her straight to hell.

After a few years and countless Margarita Mondays with that evil woman, I'd learned a long time ago that I had to pace myself. Two margaritas were my limit, but she'd gotten one over on me by making the second one strong enough to choke a freaking horse.

Despite my efforts at self-preservation, I'd still ended the night more than a little buzzed, which, given my embarrassingly low tolerance, meant I was going to be in hangover hell this morning.

It was my own damn fault for drinking it even though there was so much tequila in the damn thing, I'd have ignited if I went near an open flame.

"Mommy! Mommy!" Renee jumped on my bed,

bouncing as high as she possibly could while her shrill voice grated on my ears like nails against a chalkboard. "Wake up!"

After a pitiful groan into my pillow, I forced myself onto my back and pushed to sitting. "I'm up, doodle bug. I'm up."

"Lu-Lu's on da couch," she said as she belly-flopped into the comforter.

I reached out and scooped her up, pulling her into my lap and swiping her silky hair out of her face. "I know, honey. Luna stayed the night last night."

"She makes a loud noise in hew sleep. Like a dump twuck."

I smiled, my girl's constant joyfulness working wonders to soothe my pounding head. "Yeah? Why don't you go wake her up while I hop in the shower? She loves it when you flop on her belly."

Renee's eyes went round with excitement. "Okay!"

I waited for a beat as she all but threw herself off my bed and blazed down the hallway.

"Lu-Lu! Wake up!"

That was followed a second later by a pained grunt from my best friend. "Dear, God," I heard her wheeze and smiled at my evil brand of payback. "Be gone with thee, Satan!"

"I'm getting in the shower," I called through the house. "You're on kid duty."

"I hate you so much!" she returned.

I threw my legs over the side of the bed as Renee prattled on loudly to her Lu-Lu, and forced myself to climb out and pad to the bathroom.

I cranked the water as hot as I could stand it and scrubbed at my body and hair until I felt somewhat normal. The whole bathroom was full of steam by the time I got out and scoured the last of the tequila from my mouth with my toothbrush.

I could have hurried so I could relieve Luna of her babysitting duties, but I figured this was the perfect payback for her heavy-handed pours the night before. So instead of rushing, I took my time exfoliating and moisturizing my face and body.

It was only once I was all fresh and dewy and feeling a million times better that I threw on an old pair of joggers and a tank top and headed out. I didn't bother blowing my hair dry. Once I stepped out into the salty sea breeze, it would do whatever the hell it wanted anyway, and that usually meant going wild and wavy.

Luna looked up from her coffee mug as I came into view and hit me with a glower. "Took you long enough," she grumbled before taking a hearty sip of the strong brew.

"And good morning to you too, sunshine."

Renee swung around on her stool as I rounded the bar toward the coffee maker. "Mommy! Lu-Lu made me waffles!"

I looked from the plate of tiny, precisely cut squares of frozen waffles to my girl's syrup-covered smile. Even hung over and grumpy, Luna was the world's best babysitter. She loved Renee so much, there wasn't anything she wouldn't do, including making the only version of breakfast she was any good at. If it couldn't be toasted or microwaved, Luna didn't want anything to do with it. "I see that, honey. Did you say thank you?"

"Yup!"

"Did you have a nice shower?" Luna asked crankily once I poured myself a cup of coffee and joined her at the counter across from my daughter. "You were in there long enough."

I gave her a big smile I knew would only rile her up more in her hungover state. "I did, thanks. And it's what you get for turning that last margarita into a triple. Or a quad. Is that what comes after three?"

"I don't know," she groaned, closing her eyes and massaging her temple. "I don't know. My brain isn't working right now."

"I told you to stop after the third one. Not my fault you didn't listen." I leaned closer and gave her a sniff. "God, you smell flammable."

"And my mouth tastes like someone lit a dumpster on fire."

I let loose a giggle and patted her shoulder. "There's a spare toothbrush in my medicine cabinet you can use. And you can borrow some of my clothes if you want to take a shower."

"Yes. Please and thank you." She started out of the kitchen with mug still in hand, calling over her shoulder, "Just so you know, I'm using all that sugar scrub you love so much."

"We'll be out in the workshop when you're done."

The workshop was another huge selling point for the cottage. It was originally a detached single-car garage that sat a little farther back from the house, closer to the beach, and faced sideways, overlooking the backyard and beach. It was closer from my car to the front door if I just parked out front, so I never used it for its intended purpose, making it the perfect place for me to work.

Making pottery had been a hobby of mine since I took a class in high school. In a life that felt so unstable and unhappy, it became an escape for me. When I was sitting at that wheel, wet clay between my fingers, creating something beautiful, I was able to forget, even temporarily, how lonely I was, how badly I craved someone to just love me.

Over time, it became a form of therapy for me, then, after marrying Graham, an escape from the world all together.

A couple of the local shop owners were nice enough to sell some of my pieces out of their stores, and while the extra money was nice, that wasn't why I did it. I did it because I loved it.

She gave me a lazy wave before disappearing around the corner toward my bedroom and bathroom, and I turned back to my girl, grabbing the syrup-covered plate and giving it a serious scrubbing before asking, "Hey, doodle bug, you want to help me in the workshop today?"

The pieces I didn't put up for sell, the ones I kept for myself, were the ones I gave to Renee to paint. She loved to join me out there, creating random, colorful patterns with no rhyme or reason. I glazed those and kept them. Every dish we ate or drank from in my house was a one-of-a-kind Renee original. My baby girl's brilliant creations.

She sucked in a gasp dramatically, and I knew exactly what was coming next. Sure enough, an instant later she let out a shriek that was so damn loud I thought she might shatter the glass in every window in the house.

"*Yes! Yes! Yes!*"

I heard a thundering rumble coming down the hall, and a second later Luna skidded around the corner, wearing nothing but a towel wrapped around her. Her momentum was too great, and she crashed into the couch, nearly toppling over the back of it.

She popped up, brandishing my curling iron like a sword. "What's happening? I heard screaming. Is someone being murdered?"

I waved her off and took another pull of my coffee. "Nah. That was her excited squeal. You know how she is."

"Oh, thank God." She sucked in a huge breath and put her hand to her chest. "It nearly gives me a coronary every time. I don't know how I always forget about that."

"I birthed the girl and it still sneaks up on me sometimes."

"I'm gonna paints Mommy's awt today!"

Luna cinched the towel around her tighter and gave my daughter a thumbs-up. "That's good, shorty. But how about you try really hard not to give your Lu-Lu a heart attack from here on out, yeah?"

Ignoring her all together, Renee turned on her stool, lifted her arms, and made grabby hands. "Mommy, down."

"Yeah, that's about right," Luna mumbled. "All right, I'm going to wash this alcohol off, if you don't mind." At that, she turned and disappeared again.

I looked to Renee, seeing stickiness and sugar all over her. "Let's get you cleaned up first."

Grabbing a washcloth, I wet it under the faucet and scrubbed my girl down before lifting her off the stool. The sun was already shining, glistening off the water like light refracting off glass as I slid the patio door open and stepped outside. The sound of the waves crashing at the shore settled me in a way I couldn't explain as I held Renee's hand in mine and moved across the small swath of backyard—it really wasn't anything more than a thin strip of grass that ran to the small picket fence that divided my property from the beach beyond—to my work shed.

I grabbed the handle of the garage door and lifted it up all the way, letting the sunlight and sea breeze fill the space.

Two of the three walls were lined with shelves that were filled with pottery: vases, bowls, coffee mugs, flower pots, plates, you name it. Some were completed, just waiting for me to pack and take to the stores to be sold. Some were still in the process of air drying, and some had already been bisque fired and were ready for glaze or paint. I set up a little card table and chair for my girl in the back corner, complete with paints, brushes, and foam stamps in the shape of butterflies and rainbows and such. Anything a little girl could possibly need to make her creations.

"What do you feel like painting today?"

She lifted her hand and tapped her little finger against her chin in contemplation, the seriousness of her expression making me smile. "I wants to paint you a pwetty cup."

I had an entire cabinet designated solely to "pretty cups" already, but I was more than happy to add to my collection.

I grabbed a ceramic mug for her and got her all set up at her little table before moving over to my own work station.

My workshop was my church. The feel of the cold clay in my hands as I worked it around was my confession, and, as I sat down at my pottery wheel and began working the clay into something beautiful, I was awash with that lightness I felt every time I perched on that stool.

I was lost in the nothingness, my mind completely blank except for the sounds of the ocean outside and the gently hummed tune coming from my baby girl as she lost herself in her painting. She was just like me in that way. She had all the crazy chaotic energy of any toddler, but when she was in my workshop, she was oblivious to everything else, concentrating in a way most other kids her age probably never did.

I looked up when Luna's voice broke through the white noise created by the crash of the waves and call of the seagulls just outside. She stood propped against the door frame, her ankles crossed and one of Renee's coffee mugs cupped between her hands. "You know, every time I see you at that wheel I have this insane urge to come up behind you, à la Patrick Swayze in *Ghost*."

I giggled as I pinched the edges of the clay and slowly dragged my fingers upward. "Should I put on some 'Unchained Melody' to really set the mood?"

"Don't temp me," she teased.

"Feel better?"

"God, yes. There isn't much a hot shower and a steaming cup of joe can't cure. Although, this was all I could find in your wardrobe that even came close to fitting me." She plucked at the front of the large slouchy T-shirt she'd borrowed, pairing it with plain black leggings, and curled her top lip. "Not exactly stylish."

"Yeah, well, not all of us can be built like a pin-up girl." I was actually envious of Luna's curves. The woman was built to be on every single one of those car calendars you saw hanging in garages across the country when you took your car in to be serviced.

She rolled her eyes dramatically. "Don't hate. It wasn't until adulthood that these curves became a blessing. You can't imagine what a nightmare middle school is for a girl who's already a C-cup and has what her grandmother referred to as 'birthing hips.'" She gave a mock shiver before pointing at me, swirling her index finger in the air. "And don't act like you aren't rockin' a pretty little figure yourself. Or have you already forgotten what we talked about last night?"

I dipped my hand in the bucket of water beside me to

make the clay more malleable while letting out a groan. "Don't start that again. I already told you, nothing is going to happen between me and the new guy. Hell, I probably won't even see him again before his trip is over."

A wry smile stretched her lips, a wicked gleam filling her eyes. "I wouldn't be so sure about that."

The tiny hairs on my back of my neck stood on end at her tone. "Why do you say that?"

"Because there's a fine hunk of man jogging on the beach right now. And he's coming this way."

Oh shit. My hands clenched involuntarily, destroying the shape of the clay. "Luna, don't you dare—"

Before I could finish my warning, she lifted her hand in a finger wave and called out, "Yoo-hoo! Hey there, neighbor. Come say hi!"

I was going to murder her so freaking hard.

Six

SAWYER

"I'M GOING TO KILL YOU," I hissed as she continued to call out to Trent, waiving her arm manically on the off chance he didn't see or hear the crazy lady shouting at him and making a spectacle. "You're dead to me. So freaking dead I can't even see you right now."

"Well you better brace yourself buttercup, because *Trent* definitely saw me, and he's headed this way right now." She pulled in a deep breath. "Mother of God, that man is gorgeous," she whispered, her eyes widening.

I shot off the stool like my ass was on fire. There couldn't have been a worse time to run into a smoking hot, dimpled man who had the whole town atwitter and set your skin to tight and itchy.

I didn't have on a stitch of makeup, I was dressed in some of my rattiest clothes designated strictly for pottery because they were riddled with stains, and my hands were currently covered in brownish, slimy gunk. Damn it, I *knew* I should have taken the time to blow my hair out!

"Crap, crap, crap," I hissed as I grabbed a rag and frantically scrubbed at my hands before brushing my wind-blown hair back from my face, silently praying it didn't look like I'd just stuck my finger in an electrical socket.

Luna turned to me, a smirk on her face as she said, "You know, for someone who isn't interested, you sure are freaking out right now."

"Shut up. I hate you," I grumbled just as a shadow stretched across the white gravel drive. A moment later, Trent came into view, and holy *HELL*. Somehow, in the days that had passed since I saw him at Drip, I seemed to have forgotten the magnitude of his attractiveness. Or maybe I hadn't and there was just something about him in running shorts and a tight, sleeveless dry-fit shirt, his olive-toned skin glistening with sweat, that took him to a whole other level.

"Hey," he greeted, those smoky greenish eyes hitting me like a sledgehammer to the chest. "Sawyer, right?"

"Uh . . ." For the love of crap. I'd lost the power of speech again!

"Yep. That's Sawyer. My very attractive, *single* best friend."

My cheeks flared with heat. "Please stop," I hissed. But Luna didn't give a damn.

"And I'm Luna."

He turned his attention her way, and it felt like I'd just been released from some sort of snare his gaze had trapped me in. "Trent. Nice to meet you."

"Oh, I know all about you, Trent," she stated. "You're the new guy everyone in town is talking about."

He arched a single brow, the dark, prominent slash lifting higher on his forehead. I'd always been jealous of people who could do that. It just looked so cool when you could lift one brow at a time.

"They are?"

"Oh, sure. It's a small-town thing. We gossip about every new face that comes through. You caught the end of summer so the tourists have died out, making you the center of attention. Congrats."

He let out a raspy chuckle, the sound like he'd gargled rocks, and why the hell was that so attractive? There was something seriously wrong with me.

My daughter came rushing up like a tornado, her attention pulled from her painting by the new person standing in her orbit. "I'm Wanay," she announced loudly, skipping to a stop a few feet in front of Trent.

He looked to my girl and graced her with a soft smile, those dimples pressing into his cheeks, and I was pretty sure one of my ovaries exploded. "Nice to meet you, Renee. That's a really pretty name."

Apparently, there wasn't a female on the planet immune to this man's good looks, because my girl's entire face flamed pink at his attention. "I'm named aftew a twin pwincess dat lives in a castle in da clouds!"

"Is that right?"

"Ya-huh! Chawlotte Wanay. I'll be fwee on my next bifday!"

Okay, so maybe I needed to stress the importance of not talking to strangers to my daughter. Especially if she planned to give them her entire life story in the span of a minute. My baby was a social butterfly practically from the moment she came squalling into the world. She'd yet to meet a person she didn't automatically become best friends with.

Those dimples notched even deeper. "Wow. That's big. You're almost a grownup."

Renee giggled bashfully, her eyelashes nearly fluttering. *Good lord.* "You wants ta paint wiff me? I'm makin' awt."

I finally managed to form words. "I'm sure Trent's really busy, doodle bug," I spoke as I took her by the shoulders and pulled her back into me.

She deflated beneath my hands like a balloon leaking air. "Oh," she muttered on a pout. "Okay."

"Maybe I could make art with you some other time, yeah?" Trent said, apparently as helpless to resist Renee's sad face as everyone else in the world. I couldn't blame him. It was a powerful look.

"Okay!" And just like that, she bounced right back, having gotten what she wanted in a roundabout way. She spun on her heel and skipped back over to her little table to resume painting.

"Sorry about that," I said, lowering my voice so Renee couldn't hear. "She's kind of hard to say no to."

"Christ, no joke." He chuckled. "That face hits you right between the ribs, like someone just kicked a whole litter of adorable puppies right in front of you."

I let out a bark of laughter at his metaphor. "Oh God. That's exactly what it's like."

"Oh shoot," Luna chirped just then. "Would you look at that? My coffee's gone cold. Time for a refill. Come on, shorty," she called to Renee. "Let's go get your Lu-Lu a refill, and maybe I'll sneak you some sugar."

"Yay!" Renee bounded away from her table, grabbing hold of Luna's hand.

"Trent, you want a cup?"

"No thanks. I'm good."

"Oh. Does your wife or girlfriend already have a pot brewing for you when you get back?"

I tried my best to stab her with my glare. *Jesus, real smooth, Luna.*

"No wife or girlfriend," Trent answered, and I could hear the struggle to hold back his laughter in his voice.

"So you're a bachelor then. In that case, you should swing by here for dinner one night. Or several nights. You probably haven't had a homemade meal in forever, and Sawyer is an *amazing* cook."

"I wish the ground would open up and swallow you," I grumbled.

Trent lost the fight and let loose a husky laugh that made my skin pebble with goose bumps. "Yeah. I just might have to do that."

"Perfect!" she exclaimed brightly. "Okay, well we'll just be inside . . ." She hooked her thumb over her shoulder as she started walking backward, leading my daughter toward the house. "You know, out of earshot and all that stuff. See you around, Trent."

"Yeah! bye, Tent!" Renee called out, skipping through the sliding glass door.

Trent watched them disappear before looking back at me, his eyes lit with amusement. "Your friend is . . . colorful."

She was *something*, that was for sure. "She's not really my friend. She's just the town crazy lady. She doesn't have very good people skills because she spends most of her time holed up at home with her twenty cats."

"I heard that!" Luna yelled from inside. "And I have *one* cat!"

"I'm so sorry she pulled you from your run and into her orbit of crazy. If you want to take off running, I'll cover for you."

He hit me with those dimples again and my knees almost gave out. "Nah, it's all good. She's entertaining."

"She's certifiably insane."

"Like I said. Entertaining." His gaze shifted over my shoulder. "What's all this?"

"Oh." I looked behind me into my workshop. "It's nothing," I answered, nerves fluttering around in my belly like a swarm of butterflies. Having the shop owners in town sell my pieces for me was one thing, but there was just something about witnessing people's reactions to my art firsthand that left me feeling exposed. My creations were personal to me, my passion. I did much better taking my cut from the people in the stores who'd sold the items on my behalf. It was one of the reasons why I didn't sell them right out of my workshop directly. "It's just a hobby," I said, downplaying what it really meant to me.

I watched, feeling itchy and tense as his gaze scanned the entire space before coming back to me. "You mind if I take a closer look?"

"Oh, um . . . sure." I stepped to the side so he could come into my inner sanctum. Other than Renee and Luna, no one else had stepped foot in here, and seeing Trent in my space felt like an invasion. But I didn't know how to explain it. It didn't feel bad, necessarily. More like he was seeing deep inside of me.

I stayed rooted in place as he moved around, taking in all the pieces lining the shelves, spending as much time on the ones that were still raw and incomplete as he did the ones that had already been glazed. Each step he took echoed the loud bang of my heart against my ribcage. Watching him as he studied everything so closely was a form of torture, but I couldn't bring myself to look away or step out of the workshop.

"You made all of these?"

"Well, Renee painted a few of them," I said as he bent to pick up one of the mugs that she'd handled the week before that was waiting to be brought inside. She'd used every single color of paint she had, making the mug look like a rainbow had puked all over it. There was a crude facsimile of a stick figure on the side that was supposed to represent her, and she'd had me paint her name in bright neon pink in an arch above it. "As I'm sure you can tell." I smiled at the thought of my baby girl.

He glanced back at me with a grin, replacing the mug, "Looks like she's quickly on her way to becoming as talented as her mom. These are amazing, Sawyer."

He picked up one of the completed pieces. It was a bowl I'd made a few weeks back. I found a pebble on the beach shaped kind of like a cone with two rounded edges, and used it to indent the sides of the clay before it was hardened to look like different sized bubbles. Then I'd used different color glazes on the inside and outside, the effect making it look almost like waves, starting in a dark navy then blending into teal and lighter shades of blue before edging the top with white.

"You're incredibly talented."

I knew from experience that my cheeks were probably glowing pink. I couldn't stop the almost-timid smile that pulled at my lips, curving then upward. "Thank you," I said quietly.

"Do you sell your stuff?"

"Yeah. A few of the stores in town set up displays and sell

them for me. Small town hospitality, you know? Neighbors helping neighbors."

"I get it. I live in a small town myself." He looked at me over his shoulder and winked, making the voice of the teenage girl who apparently lived inside my head scream like she was backstage at a boy band concert. "I'll have to look around, find the places that carry your stuff and buy a few."

That flush in my skin grew even hotter. "You really don't have to."

"I know I don't have to. I want to," he stated plainly. "Especially this one." He picked up the bubble bowl again. Much larger than a regular bowl, it was made to be used as a centerpiece, filled with whatever the owner desired. "How much for this one?"

I shifted from foot to foot, my skin suddenly feeling too tight over my bones. "You . . . want to buy it?" I didn't know if it was because it had been *so long* since I felt any kind of attraction to a member of the opposite sex, or if it was something intrinsically *Trent*, maybe he wore a cologne laced heavily with pheromones? Whatever it was, I felt like my world had shifted off its axis.

"I really do. It's cool as hell."

"Well . . ." I fumbled for the right words. God, I hated talking money with potential customers. It was so uncomfortable. "I usually sell pieces that size for about two hundred." I had to keep myself from cringing.

"Sold," he said without pre-amble.

My eyes went wide. "Really?"

"Absolutely. I'll swing by tomorrow with the cash if that works for you."

That girl in my head screamed again. "Um, y-yeah. Sure."

"You should stick around for that home-cooked meal we mentioned."

I jumped at the sound of Luna's voice and whipped around to where she stood in the open doorway, hand in hand with Renee. I pressed my palm to my chest. "Jeez, Luna! Don't creep up on people like that."

She shrugged, looking way too damn happy with herself. "Who's creeping? I made plenty of noise on my way out here. You just didn't notice." She waggled her eyebrows. "Wonder why."

"I hate you."

She was unfazed, looking back to Trent. "So how about it? You swing by with cash for that *incredible* bowl, and she'll make you dinner."

Renee jumped up and down. "Yeah, Tent! Yeah!"

I held my hand up in her face to block her from view and said to Trent, "Just ignore her. You really don't have to."

Luna smacked my hand out of her face. "Of course he does! Two beautiful *single* people? It would be sacrilege for you not to share a meal together."

I pinched my face up like I'd just sucked on a lemon, gritting quietly, "I'm going to smother you in your sleep."

"Sounds good."

At his casual response, my head whipped around in surprise, my hair smacking me in the face. "What?"

He lifted one meaty shoulder in a shrug. "She's not wrong about the whole home-cooked meal thing. It would be nice to have something other than fast food and takeout. That is, if you're okay with it."

Honestly, I wasn't sure my heart would survive a prolonged period in his company. As it was, the damn organ was trying to prison break its way through my ribs.

"I'm not—"

"Pweese, Momma! *Pweese*!"

"Yeah, Momma," Luna cajoled. "*Pweese*."

"Uh, yeah. Okay. That sounds good."

It didn't. It *really* didn't. I was a walking, talking idiot around this man. But there was officially no way out of it. "How does six work?"

I got that dimpled grin again, and the teenager in my head swooned until she passed out, face down. "Perfect. I'll see you then."

"Yeah. Yep. Uh-huh. See you then." Now I wished a hole would open up and swallow *me*.

"Bye, Tent!" Renee called, waving like crazy as he let himself out the back gate and resumed his run, returning my girl's wave over his shoulder.

"Man," Luna sighed as all three of us watched him getting smaller and smaller the farther away he got. "I think I might be a matchmaking genius. Maybe I should start a business."

I spun on her and scowled as hard as physically possible.

"One of these days, Luna. One of these days, when you least expect it, I'm going to set your house on fire."

She giggled, unaffected by my threat. "You love me," she declared before booping me on the nose. "Now move that cute behind. We need to find something *ah-mazing* for you to wear tomorrow night."

Seven

TRENT

MOVING through the gate and up the back porch steps that would lead me into the kitchen of the beach house I'd rented, I silently berated myself. I was a fucking idiot. No two ways about it.

I'd set out on my run with the intention of scoping things out. That was all. I had no plans to make contact again, at least not this soon after our first run-in. Or at least that was what I'd told myself.

I'd been trailing Sawyer Darcy for a few days now to try and get a feel for the woman and the life she'd built here for herself, but with each passing day, I was finding myself more drawn to her in a way that had nothing to do with my job. It was bordering on unprofessional, and I'd always prided myself in taking my job seriously.

There was just something about the way everyone she came in contact with responded to her, how her smile seemed to be infectious to every person in her orbit. Anyone she passed on the street had to stop for a chance to chat with her, and she was more than happy to oblige every single time, never put out about being interrupted in her attempt to get from point A to point B. If someone was talking to her, they had her undivided attention.

She was clearly loved by everyone in Whitecap, that was plain to see, and that little girl of hers may as well have been the town treasure with how everyone doted on her.

When I left the place I was renting that morning, the plan was to just wave and keep on moving if we happened to spot each other while I was jogging by, but when that redheaded friend of hers had spotted me and waved me over, my feet moved of their own accord.

I should have stuck with the goddamn plan and kept going. When that didn't happen, I should have cut the conversation short and gotten the hell out of there, not stuck around to get sucked in by a beautiful woman and the cutest little girl on the face of the earth. I *definitely* should have bailed when her friend took off inside to give us some privacy, and no fucking way I should have agreed to a small, private dinner with her the following night.

I was walking a razor's edge, dangerously close to crossing a line I couldn't cross by getting too close to a target. But in spite of the voice inside my head telling me to stop thinking with my dick and to use my brain, I hadn't been able to make myself walk away.

She looked so fucking cute, standing there with her

cheeks pink with embarrassment from her friend's behavior and that smudge of clay on her forehead she hadn't realized was there.

Her hair was a riot of wild, silky waves and curls, blowing free in the wind coming off the ocean. And those eyes. *Christ*, those eyes. They were the color of the leaves in the fall back in Hope Valley. Not just brown, but also red and yellow and orange. Like a banked fire just waiting for a bit of air to make it grow wild.

Most gorgeous eyes I'd ever seen.

So different from her twin's.

The first time I'd seen her back at that coffee shop, the differences between Sawyer and Charlotte had been hard to see from a distance, but once I was close enough, it became obvious. Seeing her earlier today, they were even clearer.

Charlotte's features were softer, a round face with a small, button nose. Sawyer's were more defined, like razor sharp edges that had been smoothed by the wind and rain over time, making her even more striking than her twin.

After spending that time with her in her workshop earlier, I no longer made the correlation between her and Charlotte being twins. In no time at all, Sawyer had become her own person in my eyes. She was just *Sawyer*. I imagined that was how everyone in this small town saw this captivating woman.

But that little girl . . . she was a different story.

She was her aunt, through and through. When she told me she'd been named after a princess who lived in the sky, one with a twin sister, it just about gutted me, because I knew, no matter how tough Charlotte acted, how hard the life she'd been forced to live had made her, she would melt into a puddle the moment she laid eyes on her niece. The niece her sister clearly named after her, a sister who obviously missed her very much.

Which made the guilt I felt at keeping this secret from her and Dalton eat at my insides day after day.

It was on that thought, as I moved through the house to the kitchen and pulled a bottle of water out of the fridge, that my phone rang, cutting off the song that had been blasting through my earbuds.

Pulling them out, I tossed them on the island and reached into my pocket for my ringing phone. Dalton's name flash across the screen.

"Hey, brother. How're things?"

"Can't complain, man," he answered as I twisted the cap off the bottle and sucked a quarter of it down.

"Can't? Or won't because your bride-to-be is within earshot."

"You're on speakerphone, ass face!" I heard Charlotte call out in the background. "And just for that, I'm gonna make you help with wedding prep when the time comes. Hope you like learning to fold napkins into swans and making goody bags filled with candy almonds and Hershey Kiss roses."

"Love you like a sister, Charlotte, but I'd rather drag my balls across shattered glass than do any of that."

"Ugh! Why are boys so gross? I'm leaving the room now so you and Dalt can bro down. Just wanted to say hi."

"Hi, sweetheart. Talk to you later."

I heard what sounded like Dalton and Charlotte making out before he spoke again a few seconds later. "All right. You're off speaker now."

"Couldn't have done that before you shoved your tongue down her throat?"

He laughed through the line. "Where'd the fun in that be?"

"I see you called just to be a dick," I said with a grin.

"Well, you been gone a while. Figured you'd be feelin' a little homesick. You're welcome."

"So glad to know you care," I said on a chuckle before draining the rest of my water. "How're things going over there? Wedding planning under way yet?"

He let out a sigh, and I heard what sounded like him moving around and a door closing behind him for privacy. "I finally talked her around to setting a date. You know she's been holding out, hoping we'd find her sister first."

My guts twisted into a painfully tight knot, my stomach rolling like I'd eaten week-old Chinese food. "I'm sorry, man."

"Nothing for you to be sorry for. Not like you aren't pulling out all the stops to find her. It's just hard watching my woman struggle, you know? All these years, she's convinced herself being apart from her twin was the best thing for her. Now she's dealing with that little taste of hope, along with concern over that fucking prick Cheyanne was married to finding her before we do. She just needs to know she's safe, you know?"

Fuck me. Every word was a goddamn knife to my chest. I felt like the world's biggest piece of shit.

"Speaking of, how's the search going? Anything pan out with that last lead?"

"Still following it up," I grunted as I squeezed my eyes closed and pinched the bridge of my nose, feeling worse as each second ticked by.

I just couldn't bring myself to tell him the truth yet. Sawyer had built this whole life. If she thought for a second that it was being threatened, she'd pack up her girl and take off. I didn't want to put her in that position. I just needed to find a way to do this so Charlotte could get what she wanted without Sawyer's world imploding.

"Yeah, I know. I'd trust all you guys with my life, you know that, but I don't think there's anyone I'd trust more to be on this job."

Christ, I needed this conversation to end before the shame and guilt forced me to curl up into a goddamn ball on the floor so tight I couldn't get out of it.

"Well, I'm glad you guys finally set a date, brother. When's the big day?"

"We decided on next January. Charlotte wanted a winter wedding."

"Not a lot of time."

He sighed through the line. "Trust me, I know. But I'm

done waiting, man. I'm ready for that woman to have my last name for the rest of our lives. Besides, Charlotte's crew is already all over helping her get shit in order, so all I gotta do is sit back, relax, and maybe give her a few orgasms if she starts losing her mind to get her back to center."

"She's such a lucky woman," I deadpanned, fighting back a grin.

"Fuck yeah, she is. But speaking of the wedding, there's something I wanna ask you."

It felt like my chest was being squeezed in a vise, my ribs tightening around my heart and lungs until there wasn't enough room.

"Will you be my best man?"

And there it was. *Fuck*.

"You know I will, man," I squeezed out, past the rocks filling my throat. "I'd be honored." And that was the goddamn truth. I'd never had any brothers or sisters growing up. The guys I'd served with and the men at Alpha Omega had become my family. But out of all of them, Dalton Prescott was the one I was closest to. He was my brother in every way but blood, and even lacking that, I couldn't imagine being closer to anyone else. I'd step in front of a bullet for the man, lay down my life for him. By marrying Charlotte, she had that exact same loyalty from me, so keeping this secret was eating at my goddamn soul.

"Good. Can't think of anyone else I'd want up there standing next to me when I finally marry my woman."

And that vise got even tighter. "Feeling's mutual."

"All right. I'll let you go. But keep me posted if anything pops up, yeah?"

"Will do."

We rang off a second later, and I dragged my sorry ass into the bathroom. I needed a shower after my run, and hopefully—though I seriously doubted it—I could wash the shame away as well.

Eight

SAWYER

THE BELL over the door of Warren's General Store tinkled, and my head shot up, my focus once again leaving the stack of receipts I was looking through to see who'd just come through the door.

"Morning, Sawyer. Morning, Georgia," Gloria, a stay-at-home mom of three, greeted as she shuffled inside, pushing a stroller while a kid practically hung off each arm.

"Morning, Gloria," I said with a smile that felt a bit stiff. Fortunately, she was too busy wrangling kids to notice, and disappeared down the second aisle.

Georgia's voice whispered in my ear, giving me a jolt. "What's going on with you this morning?" I hadn't even realized she'd moved so close until her breath fanned across my cheek.

I placed my hand on my chest and inhaled sharply. "Jeez, Georgia. Give me a heart attack why don't you?"

"That." She shoved her finger in my face. "That right there is what I'm talking about. You've been jumpy all day, fidgeting around, constantly watching the door. It's taken you three times longer to go through those receipts than it usually does."

I pushed out a heavy sigh, my shoulders slumping. "Sorry. My brain's all over the place today. I'll pick up the pace."

She gave her wrist a flick. "Please, child. I don't care about the damn receipts. You're good at your job and you'll get them done when you get them done. I'm not worried about that. I want to know what's going on with you."

"There's nothing going on with me, swear. It's just an off day, I guess." As if the universe was in cahoots with my boss and wanted to help prove her point, the bell sounded with the opening of the door, and my attention shot straight to it.

I smiled and gave William Henry a friendly wave as I felt myself deflate.

I didn't know who I was watching for. Okay, that was a lie. I knew exactly who I was watching for; I just didn't know *why* I was watching for him. I had no reason to believe Trent would be stopping into the general store today, but for some reason I felt this annoying, nagging sense of . . . hope maybe?

It was ridiculous. I knew that. I was acting like a school girl just waiting for her crush to come walking through the door of her homeroom class. Pathetic.

My boss's snort pulled me back to reality. "Off day my

round derrière. Start talking, or I'm calling Dezzy down here to get the truth out of you."

She always threatened to get her husband involved whenever she was worried about me. Not that it ever did her any good. Desmond treated me like his own flesh and blood, a daughter who had him wrapped around his little finger.

The man was a big old marshmallow. He'd rather cut off his own arm than get stern with me, and Georgia knew that.

She didn't threaten to get him involved because he'd put his foot down, she did it because she knew I couldn't stand it when either of them worried about me.

Desmond and Georgia Warren were the closest thing I'd had to parents since my own passed away when I was a little girl, so having them worry over me weighed heavy on my conscience. And don't get me started on how terrible I felt if I got even an inkling of disappointment from either of them. God, it gutted me.

"All right," I huffed. "No need to get all Momma Bear on me. I'm fine, really it's just, I think—well, I'm not totally certain, but I think I might kinda sorta have a date tonight?"

Her eyes rounded for a beat before narrowing in confusion. "You *think* you have a date? How does that happen?"

I flapped my hands out at my sides in exasperation. "It's confusing. And it's all Luna's fault," I ended on a grumble.

"Okay, sweetheart. I think you may need to start at the beginning."

I did just that, telling her the whole story, starting with the come-to-Jesus Luna had laid on me during Margarita

Monday, all the way to what had happened the morning before and how Luna had stuck her big fat nose in the middle of it. As I spoke, Georgia's eyebrows creeped higher and higher up her forehead until they were nearly at her hairline by the time I finished.

"Well then," she said on a whispered breath once I finally finished, "that is quite the pickle, isn't it?"

"Exactly! So now do you understand how I might be a little confused about the whole thing? I mean, could dinner at my place be considered a date when my daughter is going to be there and we were basically forced into it by my meddling, well-intentioned but pain-in-the-ass friend?"

She *tsked* and gave her head a shake. "That girl. She really does know how to whip up chaos wherever she goes."

"Tell me about it," I grouched.

"So you've been watching the door like a hawk just waiting to swoop down and snatch up a big fat squirrel all day because you're hoping he might come through?"

"No!" I exclaimed way too defensively. "Well . . . maybe." With a pitiful groan, I slapped my hand over my face and plopped down on the stool behind the register. "You know, this is why I'm single. I don't know what the hell I'm doing. I should just call and cancel, but I don't even have the guy's number. And there's no way I'm canceling in person. That's humiliating."

Georgia's fingers wrapped around my wrist gently, pulling my hand from my eyes. When she spoke next, her tone was somehow both gentle and firm at the same time. It was what I called the Mother Tone. And she excelled at it. I'd tried it on Luna several times, but so far, it hadn't yielded the same results.

"First off, I'm going to need you to take a nice, deep breath. I think you might have used up all your oxygen on that rant." She waited for me to fill my lungs on a huge inhale. "You feeling better now?"

I looked to the side in contemplation. "Maybe a little."

"All right, good. Now, about this date—"

"It might not be a date."

She arched a single brow. *Damn it*, was everyone able to do that but me? "Oh, sweet child. You really have been single for far too long."

My forehead pinched in a frown. "What do you mean?"

"If a man didn't want to have dinner with a woman, he'd find a way to get out of it, trust me. Especially if a child was involved. Renee is the best thing in the entire world, but let's be honest, fastest way to get rid of a man is to introduce him to your kid."

I nodded in agreement. "Yeah, that's true."

"You're gorgeous, kind-hearted, and funny. Anyone who gets to know you loves spending time with you. Of *course* this is a date."

My skin started to tingle like my whole body was gearing up from a static shock. "And somehow, that doesn't make me feel any better."

"You've just been out of the game for a while. You'll get back in the swing of things."

The door opened right that second, the bell ringing melodically. My eyes went to it, like they had all day, and that static shock let loose, coursing through my entire body and making the tiny hairs on my arms stand on end.

"Trent," I said, my voice coming out much breathier than I'd intended. With the way I reacted to him—Every. Freaking. Time—you'd have thought I hadn't just seen him the day before.

What the hell was wrong with me?

"Holy smokes," Georgia murmured under her breath so only I could hear. "That's him?"

His gaze shot to the counter I was standing behind, and those damn brain glitch- inducing dimples dented his cheeks. "Hey, Sawyer. I didn't realize you'd be here."

"Y-yeah. I work here." I nearly smacked my forehead at my stupidity. *Way to state the obvious, Sawyer.*

"Works out well for me then. I came in to pick up a bottle of wine for tonight. Then I realized you might not like wine. Now I can just ask instead of guessing."

"I-I like wine," I said quietly, my heart stuttering, my stomach flipping, and that teenager in my head gaining consciousness just long enough to faint again. I was going to have to do something about her. She was *really* annoying.

Those dimples deepened as his smile spread. "Any kind in particular?"

"I'm not really picky. Any red is fine."

"Red. Got it. Is there anything I can get for Renee?"

Oh fresh hell. If I hadn't been sitting on the stool, I probably would have melted to the floor. "You really don't need to do that."

"I want to," he replied casually. "Can't show up for dinner without something for both the ladies in the house, right?"

"She loves gummy bears," Georgia said for me when it became obvious I was struggling to find my voice. "Well, she loves the green ones, but if you just buy her a bag, she can pick them out and she'll love you forever."

"Red wine and gummy bears. Got it. I'll just"—he hooked his thumb over his shoulder—"grab that stuff. Anything else I can get for tonight? Dessert maybe? I can't cook, but I'm a pro at buying junk food."

I finally managed to unglue my tongue from the roof of my mouth. "Oh, no. You don't need to do anything else. Really. I've got that handled. Actually, I didn't think to ask if there's anything you don't eat."

"Not picky," he replied, using my earlier words. "You make it, I'll eat it. I just appreciate the meal."

A grin that probably looked as ridiculous as it felt tugged at the corners of my mouth. "Okay then. I guess I'll see you later tonight."

"Well, I mean, I'll see you in a minute when I check out, right?"

"Right. Of course. Yes. When you check out. Because I work here. That's my job. Checking you out. Wait! Not like, *checking you out*. I didn't mean it like that. But like, ringing up your stuff."

Georgia took pity on me just then and placed her hand on my shoulder, effectively silencing me. "Wine's on aisle five, sweets on seven. Let us know if you need help with anything else."

His smoky eyes glinted with laughter as he nodded. "Right. Thanks."

As soon as he disappeared from sight, I whipped around on the stool to face Georgia. "Oh God, oh God, oh God," I whispered frantically. "That was really bad, wasn't it?"

She gave me a bemused look. "It wasn't great, that's for damn sure. What in the world was that? You acted like a flipping pod person."

"God, I know." I covered my face with my hands and groaned. "I don't know why I get like that around him. I get totally ridiculous. I think maybe his cologne or something is designed to *literally* make women lose their minds."

"Well, you better get yourself together, because he'll be back any minute, and you need to act like you know how to interact with other human beings."

As far as pep talks went, it certainly wasn't her best, but it did the job. I worked on deep breathing and shook out my hands in an attempt to rid them of their tremble. I felt somewhat normal when he returned to the counter with a bottle of wine and two bags of gummy bears, still all dimples and ridiculously good looks.

I took the items he'd placed on the counter and started typing in the prices. We weren't a big enough store for a scanner, but by now, I knew all the numbers by heart. "Anything else?" I asked as I bagged up his groceries.

"You tell me. You sure I can't bring anything more?"

I couldn't help but wonder, was he really this sweet, or was it an act? I stopped to do something I hadn't had the wherewithal to do before now, and studied his face, refusing to allow myself to get hung up on the pretty wrapping. As Luna liked to say, I had that radar when it came to reading people, and I needed to see if I got any kind of vibe off this man before I let him into my house.

Nothing pinged. No alarms sounded. No red flags shot up. I got the sense he was genuine. All I read off him was humor and maybe a hint of curiosity.

"Nope," I said with a grin. "This is more than enough."

"All right, then." I gave him his total and passed the bags over along with his change.

"I'm really looking forward to tonight," he said in an almost tender voice as he stepped back from the counter. "See you at six, Sawyer."

"Yeah. See you then."

I watched him leave and continued to stare at the door like a silly star-struck girl long after he disappeared.

"Hoo-wee," Georgia exclaimed a few seconds later. "Yep, this is most definitely a date, sweetheart."

That was the very last thing I needed in my life. I'd sworn up and down after leaving Graham that I was done with men. *Done.* So why did her saying that make my belly feel all floaty?

"If you tell Dezzy I said this, I'll deny it to the grave, but I'd give my left arm to be thirty years younger and twenty pounds lighter. That man is something *else*. No wonder the ladies of this town are all in a tizzy."

"One: I'm *definitely* telling Dezzy you said that. And two: no one says tizzy anymore."

"Well obviously they do, because I just said it, and I'm cool as hell. I may be old, but I'm still hip on all the trends young people follow."

I snorted loudly, giving my head a shake, because Georgia was anything but hip on the latest trends.

"If you say so," I muttered, going back to the receipts I'd been spending far too long on.

"I do say so, thank you very much. Now let's talk outfits. I want to make sure you pick something to wear tonight that shows just the right amount of cleavage without being too obvious."

God, she was just as bad as Luna.

Nine

SAWYER

Dinner was done, the table was set, and I was freshly showered and dressed in an outfit that Luna had approved when I had a mild freak-out earlier and texted her pictures from the front, back, and sides to make sure it looked good. My hair was once again a little wild, but I'd actually taken the time to put on a little bit of makeup. Not much, mind you, considering I was doing everything to get ready for tonight *and* trying to keep Renee from destroying the house, as well as changing her outfit and scrubbing her arms when she got hold of a magic marker and decided to draw all over herself.

It was five minutes to six, meaning Trent could show up at any moment, and as Georgia would say, I was in a tizzy. I'd lit a few candles for ambiance before deciding they made everything seem too romantic and blew them out. Then I'd second guessed myself and re-lit them only to change my mind again and blow them out.

I was a mess.

"Renee, honey, no," I called out when I spotted her sitting on the living room floor in just her underwear. "You have to keep your clothes on, doodle bug."

That was kind of her thing. Since she was old enough to do it herself, she'd strip down to her diaper or pull-up or underwear as soon as we got home. I didn't know if that was a normal thing with toddlers, but my girl had a serious aversion to clothes.

"Remember? I told you we were having company for dinner, so you couldn't be running around in your underwear."

The sour look she gave me would have cracked me up if I wasn't freaking out. Ignoring the evil glare that could have peeled the paint off the walls, I snatched the cute little dress I'd put her in earlier off the floor and forced it back over her head. The mean mug was still in place when her face poked through the neck hole.

"If you keep this on, I'll give you extra dessert," I bargained as I wrestled her arms through the tiny straps. "But it has to stay on *all* night. Deal?"

I had her at *extra dessert*. "Deal!" she agreed readily. Once fully dressed, she went back to the coloring book and crayons I set up for her on the coffee table, and I headed back into the kitchen to double check that everything was absolutely perfect.

I was in the middle of contemplating re-lighting the candles when the doorbell rang.

My belly erupted with nerves so strong it felt like a swarm of hummingbirds had taken flight as I pulled in a deep breath and started for the front door. I was bound and determined not to turn into a bumbling idiot this time. I could act normal around this man. I *would* act normal, damn it!

I pulled the front door open and nearly swallowed my tongue at the sight of Trent standing on my front stoop. He looked amazing dressed down, and mouth-watering in running gear, but how he looked just then damn near fried my brain.

He was dressed in a pair of dark-washed jeans and a deep midnight blue button-down that he wore casually untucked, with the sleeves cuffed to reveal strong, corded forearms. His hair looked to still be a little damp, like he was fresh from the shower, the ends doing that insanely attractive flippy thing. There was still a coating of scruff on his jaw, but it didn't look sloppy. It looked like it actually belonged there. It was clear the man had made an effort to look nice tonight, and *damn*, did it work.

Clearing my throat and shaking off the cobwebs trying to form in my brain, I gave him a smile that only shook the teeniest bit. "Hey. Thanks for coming."

"Thanks for having me," he returned, dimples popping. "You look beautiful."

Swoon!

I'd picked a brightly colored, lightweight maxi dress that swished around my bare feet. It flowed from my body, not really revealing a lot, but was completely strapless and held in place by a tight band that cinched around my chest, holding my girls in place and revealing just the slightest bit of décolletage. It was feminine without being revealing or making me uncomfortable.

"Thanks," I said, trying to shake off the bashfulness creeping across my skin. "You look really nice too."

"Kind of an improvement from sweat-covered running clothes, huh?"

I wasn't so sure about that. He rocked the hell out of sweat-covered running clothes.

"Yeah, well, who am I to judge? You saw me in my ratty pottery clothes."

His eyes glinted with sincerity as he said, "I thought you looked beautiful then too."

I wasn't sure how, but I somehow managed to keep my knees from buckling.

Taking a step to the side, I pushed the door open wider so he could enter. "Come on in."

He stepped into the entryway, dwarfing the already small space and making the air thick with his scent. He smelled like pine trees and clean laundry and something with just the slightest hint of spice. It was a scent that would drug any woman.

"It smells amazing in here," he said, pulling me from the fog he'd created simply by existing. "I don't know what you cooked, but if it tastes even half as good as it smells, it's going to be fantastic."

"Thanks," I murmured with a blush. "I hope you like Chicken Carbonara."

His eyes took on a heavy, slightly glazed look. "Is that the pasta dish with the bacon in it?"

I let out a little laugh. "Yep. That's the one. I'm guessing you like bacon?"

"Not sure there's a red-blooded man on the planet who *doesn't* like bacon. Most important food group as far as I'm concerned. Now I'm even happier your pushy friend set this whole thing up."

My head fell back on a deep belly laugh at his spot-on description of Luna. I opened my eyes once the hilarity had died down to find him staring at me with a look that made it hard to swallow past the cotton filling my throat. His eyes seemed to have gotten a few shades darker in just a handful of seconds. The only way I knew to describe the intensity carved into his chiseled features was *potent*. This damn man was potent as hell.

I licked my suddenly dry lips, my brain buzzing frantically for something to say. Fortunately, my little girl was here as a buffer and had the perfect timing.

"Tent!" she shouted, blazing from the living room. "Hi, Tent! Hi! You came to see me!"

The tension that held my body captive, every muscle locked tight just a moment ago, let me out of its iron grip as soon as he looked away from me and to my daughter.

"Sure did. Hey there, Little Bit. How you doing?"

"I'm colowing a pictew! Wanna see?"

She got those dimples from him as he answered, "Of course I want to see. But first, I got you a little surprise."

I'd been so overwhelmed with looking at him that I hadn't even noticed the bottle of wine he had in one hand, and the bag of gummy bears in the other. But they weren't just any gummy bears, Trent had gone through the two bags he'd bought earlier that day and picked out all the green ones.

Oh my damn. And my heart just melted into a puddle of goo.

She sucked in a breath so big I feared her lungs might explode.

"Uh oh," I whispered, knowing what was coming. "You might want to cover your ears."

He shot me a quizzical look, asking, "What?" right as Renee let out her patented excited shriek.

"*GWEEN GUMMY BEAWS*!" she screamed at the top of her lungs, doing a little dance after snatching the bag out of his hand. "Yay! Yay! Yay!"

"Good God," Trent muttered, his eyes wide with fright as he rubbed at one of his ears. "Think she might have just set off every dog in this town."

"Yeah, she's kind of famous for that scream. I'm used to it now, but the first few times she did it, I thought someone was murdering her. Scared a solid decade off my life."

His chuckle was like velvet over gravel. "I can see that. So that's her excited, huh?"

"Yep. My baby girl is all about the drama. There's no middle ground with her. When she's unhappy about something, she makes it known in a big way, and when she's happy, she'll shake the house down around you." Looking down at her as she pawed through the bag, I asked, "What do you say, doodle bug?"

"Fank you, Tent! *Fankyoufankyou!*"

"You're welcome, Little Bit," he told her before lowering his voice for just me to hear. "Christ, how do you ever say no to that little face? If she were to ask right now, I'd give her all the cash in my wallet *and* call up my lawyer to have her added to my will."

I let out another laugh. "Meh, I've gotten used to it. After enough time, I was able to numb myself to the effects of those looks. It's the only way I can get her to eat vegetables and take baths regularly."

"Well, you might have to act as my buffer tonight or I'll walk out of here after giving her the deed to my house and title to my car."

"Don't worry," I said on a giggle. "I'll protect you."

Those green-brown eyes hit me, all smoky and sweet. "Thanks, darlin'."

My daughter wasn't the only one standing before me with a face that would make a person melt.

"No problem." I cleared the cotton out of my throat. "So who's hungry?"

Ten

SAWYER

As the evening progressed, I was surprised to find myself completely at ease. The brain fog I usually experienced around Trent had finally started to let up, and I was able to act normal in his presence. Well, somewhat normal, at least.

Dinner went off without a hitch. The food was actually pretty damn good, if I did say so myself, and the company wasn't anything to sneeze at either. Any lulls in the conversation were quickly filled by Renee rattling on and on, talking about everything and anything she could think of.

There'd been a few times where I'd had to translate what she'd been saying for Trent, but for the most part, he followed her toddler ramblings perfectly.

At one point, I'd actually just sat back and drank my wine, watching the two of them talk to each other. Halfway through dinner I felt this strange warmth bloom to life inside of me at their interaction, heating me from the inside out.

If this was a date—which, I still wasn't totally sure of—it would be going down in the record books as a success. At least in my opinion. But I didn't want to get ahead of myself.

Yes, I liked this guy. There was no use in denying that. And it scared the living hell out of me.

He was the first man in years I'd been attracted to, and what he made me feel was so much stronger than anything I'd ever felt before. It was completely foreign to me. The intensity was staggering. I hadn't even felt this way with Graham during the time I'd convinced myself he was my forever.

The old me—Cheyanne—would have grabbed hold of this feeling with both hands, desperate to keep it and terrified it would slip from my grasp. But that was before. Before I'd chosen wrong. Before I'd made the worst mistake of my life. Before my need to be loved came back to bite me in the ass. But I wasn't that girl anymore, and this wasn't about me. It was about Renee.

It was because of her, my need to protect her with everything I was, that I'd made the promise to myself to be done with men. I poured all my time, energy, focus, and love into that little girl, and there wasn't a single second of a single day that I'd regretted it. She was worth all of that and so much more.

I'd actually convinced myself that she was all I'd ever need. So the impact of my feelings involving Trent not only caught me off guard, but they actually knocked me on my ass and left me reeling.

And in spite of being scared half to death, it wasn't an altogether bad feeling. Thanks to Graham, I'd forgotten all the things I used to enjoy about the back and forth between a man and a woman. The thrill of the game. I'd forgotten the rush I got as a woman when an attractive man looked at me like I was something special. Those were all the things I'd felt during my dinner with Trent and Renee.

It was weird. I barely knew this guy. He was only two steps past being a total stranger, yet I got a high from being in his company that I'd never experienced before. And insane or not, I actually found myself secretly indulging Luna's suggestion to have a little fun. Trent wasn't here for the long haul; he was a tourist. What would it really hurt to let my hair down for a little while and remember what it was like to be a woman until he inevitably went back home?

It wouldn't hurt a damn thing, a voice in my head that sounded suspiciously like my best friend chimed in. *It would be fun as hell.*

It was on that thought that Renee let out a huge yawn, effectively ending the tug of war happening in my head.

I glanced at the clock on the microwave above the stove and saw that it was a quarter to eight. "Oh, wow. I didn't realize the time. Time to get you in the bath, doodle bug. It's almost bed time." Pushing back in my chair, I grabbed my plate and leaned over to reach for Trent's.

His hand came out and stopped me before I could grab hold of it. "I'll take care of this. You go handle her."

"You don't have to do that."

"I insist," he said. "You cooked, you shouldn't have to clean as well. I'll handle the cleanup while you get that one in the bath."

I stood straight, my empty plate still extended in the air. "You sure?"

"Positive. It's the least I can do after such a fantastic meal."

That warmth inside me burned even hotter. This man really was something else. "Okay. If you don't mind."

"Don't mind at all, darlin'."

I picked up a fading Renee. Apparently, being the key entertainment during dinner had taken a lot out of her. "Can you say goodnight to Trent, baby girl?"

Her arms came out and she made grabby hands at Trent, surprising us both by making it obvious she wanted him to take her.

He hesitated for a blink, looking to me for guidance, and reached out to scoop her up once I gave him a small nod.

"Night, Tent," she mumbled sleepily.

He looked down at her like he was holding a treasure. I knew exactly how he felt, because Renee *was* a treasure. The most precious one on the face of the earth.

"Good night, Little Bit. Have sweet dreams, yeah?"

I took my daughter back and headed down the hall. I made quick work of her bath and carried her into her bedroom, getting her dressed in her jammies and brushing out her hair before tucking her into her bed.

"Pwincess stowy?" she asked sleepily. When she was like

this, all soft and sweet, it was impossible to say no to her. So I sat down beside her, curling her up against me, and started telling her the princess story. I barely made it to the part with the dragon before she was letting out little chuffing snores.

I tiptoed out of her room, closing the door before moving back through the house. The sight of Trent standing at my sink, hand-drying the pot I'd used to boil the pasta, hit me right in the gut—and maybe a bit lower. The man read and hand-washed dishes. There wasn't a woman alive who'd be immune to that.

"Can I help with anything?"

He looked back over his shoulder, giving me those dimples. Damn him and those dimples! "Nope. Just about done." He angled his chin toward the counter. "I refilled your glass. You can drink it and keep me company while I finish up."

I tried to remember a time in my life when a man had actually stepped up to take care of me, even in the smallest way, and realized it had never happened. Even before things went so terribly wrong in my marriage, Graham hadn't been the type of man to do something as menial as washing the dishes. According to him, that was woman's work. Hell, he'd never even poured me a glass of wine.

This was a first, and it made those butterflies that had taken up residence in my belly all night long flap around like they'd just chugged a can of Red Bull.

"I can do that," I said in a voice hoarse with emotion as I moved closer. Grabbing the glass, I turned to face Trent and hopped up on the counter, swinging my legs casually as I took a sip.

"She get to sleep okay?"

"Yep. Out like a light. Didn't even get through the whole bedtime story before she was sawing logs."

"She's a great kid, Sawyer."

I beamed at that. "I like to think so, but I'm kind of biased."

"As you should be." He winked, and the combination of that wink and those dimples nearly made me choke on my wine. "You've done an incredible job with her."

"Thank you," I said softly, my voice infused with warmth at his compliment. "But honestly, she makes it easy."

"If that's the case, it's because she learned it from you."

Gah! Seriously. This dude was something straight out of one of Georgia's romance novels!

"Feel free to tell me to mind my own business if I'm crossing a line, but . . . is her dad in the picture?"

The next sip—much bigger that the one before it—went down a little harder at his question. It wasn't like I didn't know it was coming. I was a single mother, it wasn't exactly out of the norm for people to wonder where her father was. Didn't mean hearing it ever got any easier.

"It's fine. And no, he's not. It's just me and Renee, and that's best for both us. He was just some guy from the past. No one important." Yet another lie I wanted desperately to be true.

"Then you really are amazing."

Well, that cut through the sudden wave of melancholy. "Why do you say that?" I asked, surprised at the vehemence in his tone.

"Because you created that back there," he pointed in the direction of Renee's bedroom, "and you did it all by yourself. That little girl is smart and funny and happy. She's full of life. All because of you."

An embarrassing wave of tears hit my eyes, making them sting. I dropped my head, hiding behind the curtain of my hair before he could see them, working frantically to blink them back.

But apparently I hadn't been fast enough, because a second later, I felt his fingers beneath my chin, applying pressure and lifting my gaze to his. Concern and worry swam through all that smoke in his eyes.

"Hey," he started, his voice so gentle it forced one of those tears I was fighting back loose. "I'm sorry. If I said something wrong, I didn't mean—"

A watery laugh slipped from my throat. "No. No, you didn't do anything wrong." I sniffled and batted at my cheek. "It's just . . . it was a really nice thing to hear. I'm not sure there's a harder job in the world than being a parent. Half the time I feel like I'm screwing up, and the other half I don't even know what I'm doing. I'm constantly worrying that I'm going to ruin her life somehow. What you said was really sweet, that's all. I just got a little emotional. Sorry about that."

"Nothing to be sorry for," he husked, his voice low and

rich like melted chocolate. He curved his hand along the side of my neck, holding it there as his thumb traced across my jaw, back and forth, back and forth, sending delicious shivers across my spine. "I can't begin to understand how hard it is to be a parent, but I have enough friends with kids to know that what you're feeling is totally normal." Each word was said in the softest, most sincere voice, and I could have sworn our faces inched closer together.

"And I don't need to have a kid of my own to see that you're doing a phenomenal job. That little girl in there is special." His chest expanded on a deep inhale, his eyes growing darker. "*You're* special," he ended on a whisper.

Just like that, something inside of me snapped, a thread that had been pulled so tight it had begun to fray. Closing the rest of the distance, I pressed my lips to his.

Trent

The kiss shouldn't have taken me by surprise. I'd felt it before it happened, we'd been leading up to something explosive in those last few seconds. But it still hit me like a punch to the gut.

Her lips were softer than I imagined, and in the past several days, since that goddamn run-in at the coffee shop, I'd imagined *a lot*. Those full, pillowy lips were a temptation I couldn't deny. Hell, the whole fucking night had been a test in self-control. One I'd clearly just lost, because I couldn't stop myself from parting her lips with my tongue and dipping inside. I had to have a taste. Just one. Even though I knew it was wrong.

I was no longer teetering on that dangerous edge. I'd just stepped right the hell over, crossing a line that should never be crossed. By kissing her I wasn't just betraying Dalton and Charlotte, I was betraying *her*.

On that thought, and on Sawyer's soft, melodic moan, my brain finally caught up with reality. Placing my hands on her shoulders, I gently pushed her back, breaking the kiss that shouldn't have been one of the best I'd ever had, but absolutely was all the same.

"Trent?" she asked, her voice breathless confusion. "Is everything okay?"

I squeezed my eyes closed because it wasn't. Not by a fucking long shot.

I opened my mouth to say four words I knew to my bones were the cold, hard truth, but still felt wrong all the same. "That shouldn't have happened. I'm sorry, Sawyer."

Her back shot straight, humiliation carved into her gorgeous face, seeping out of her pores and staining those gorgeous eyes the color of autumn leaves.

"Oh God," she breathed, slapping her hands over her mouth. "Oh my God. I'm so sorry. I thought—you were just —did I read this whole night wrong?"

She hadn't. Not at all. The truth that was being denied

all this time was that I'd fucked up long before the kiss. I'd compromised the job by developing feelings for the subject. I'd known if I came tonight something was bound to happen, simply because I wouldn't be able to help myself, and as the time ticked by, that realization only grew more obvious. The more time I spent in Sawyer's company, the more I wanted her. And now I'd formed an attachment to that little girl that felt like a physical thing pulling at my skin and burrowing down deep inside of me.

"It's my fault," I grunted, forcing myself to take a step back even as my body fought against it. "I should go. I'm sorry."

I spun on my heel and headed for the closest exit, the sliding glass door that would lead me out to the beach. As much as it killed me, I didn't let myself look back as my feet ate up the sand between her cozy little cottage and the one I'd rented.

I'd broken the number one rule in my line of work: never get personally invested.

If I were a smart man, I'd call Lincoln and have him pull me off this job, replace me with one of the other guys. But I clearly wasn't smart, because there wasn't a chance in hell of me doing that.

Sawyer and Renee's protection was my only focus, the only thing I could think about, and as good as the men I worked with were—and they were the goddamn best in the business—I couldn't trust anyone but me.

Sawyer might have been living like there wasn't a threat,

but I knew better. I knew for a fact evil lurked in the shadows, searching the entire fucking country for her. And I'd be damned if I'd let it get them.

I'd die first.

So while I knew I'd fucked up, I wasn't pulling out. I just had to make sure to keep that line drawn clearly in the sand.

And hope like hell I didn't slip again.

Eleven

SAWYER

I'd NEVER BEEN HAPPIER to have a day off in my life than I was today. It meant that, after dropping Renee off at daycare, I could go back home, keep the curtains drawn, and burrow even deeper into the dark pit I'd been stuck in since the night before.

I wasn't sure I'd ever felt such an overwhelming sense of humiliation before. I'd never read a situation so wrong. I'd been so sure he was going to kiss me, or at least that he'd wanted to. And if I looked back on the night before—something I was doing with alarming frequency—I *still* felt like that was what we'd been leading up to.

How could I have made such a huge mistake?

I knew that Georgia was probably foaming at the mouth to know how the date that absolutely was *not* a date had gone, so I at least had a slight reprieve from her. Luna was a different story. She'd been blowing my phone up all morning, and I knew it was only a matter of time before she showed up on my doorstep, demanding answers. And I couldn't even lock her out, because like a freaking idiot, I'd given her a key!

I was mid-wallow when I discovered there was no coffee in my house. If it had been anything else—like food or air—I would have convinced myself I could do without it for a while longer. But not coffee. I lived on it to the point I was pretty sure the blood running through my veins was caffeinated.

I stood in front of my coffee maker, staring at it like it owed me money for a good five minutes before finally caving and headed out into the sunshine—stupid Mother Nature. What an asshole. Going to the general store to stock up was out of the question, so I started toward the coffee shop, opting to drive to make the trip as short as humanly possible.

The only saving grace for a day as shitty as this one was the fact that Luna and Georgia were the only two people in town to know anything about my date-not-date.

Or so I thought.

I realized my epic mistake the moment I walked into Drip. Monica's gaze swung to me, and the moment it landed, her eyes began to dance with excitement.

"Oh my God, I'm so glad you're here! I want to know *everything*."

"How did you—?" I clamped my mouth shut and squeezed my eyes closed, focusing on deep breathing before my head could explode.

I was going to kill Luna. I was going to murder her and

bury her in my backyard, and if anybody asked me where she'd gone I'd tell them all they needed to know was that I'd done Whitecap a favor.

"Luna really can't keep her mouth shut, can she?" I grumbled as I stopped in front of the counter.

"Why do you act like that's a surprise? She can't keep a secret to save her life. We should all count ourselves lucky she doesn't know any of the country's nuclear codes." That worked to pull a tiny smile across my lips. "But I don't care about that. I want to know how your date went," she decreed way too damn loudly.

God, small towns were the worst!

"It wasn't a date," I replied flatly.

"But Luna said—"

"She was wrong."

"Yeah, but then Georgia told me—"

I lifted my hand to stop her. "Georgia blabbed too? Come on!"

She let out a disgruntled huff and slapped her hands down on her hips. "Will you stop changing the subject?"

"I'm not changing the subject. I already told you it wasn't a date. Now can I please get a coffee?"

"What do you mean, it wasn't a date?"

Leaning forward, I lowered my voice so no one could overhear. "Can you keep your voice down? This whole thing is embarrassing enough without everyone in town finding out."

Concern washed across her features as she braced her

hands on the counter and met me halfway across it, now whispering, fortunately. "What happened?"

"Nothing, okay? I just thought it was a date but it turned out it wasn't. That's it."

The skin between her eyebrows pinched with worry as she looked me up and down, finally noticing how I looked. I may or may not—definitely *not*—have remembered to brush my hair before twisting it up into a tangled knot on top of my head. My sweats had definitely seen better days, and when I looked down, I realized that the flip-flops I'd slid on from the pile pushed aside by the front door didn't match. Oops. Hey, at least I remembered to put on a bra, so that was a win.

"You know, I'm pretty sure there's a whole hell of a lot more to your story, but from the looks of you, it's either cleaning day or you're dangerously close to a mental breakdown. I'm leaning more toward the latter, so I'll let it slide. For now."

"Kind of you," I mumbled. "Coffee?"

I let out a sigh of relief when she moved to one of the huge industrial machines that sat behind the counter and went about making my usual. I shook off my bad mood just long enough to thank her and agree to come over to dinner with her and Sam in the near future.

I made the mistake of thinking I was home free when I turned onto my street. I'd get to resume my steady decline into the pits of embarrassment without any more interruptions. Unfortunately, when I pulled up in front of my house,

I saw a familiar figure standing on my front porch, looking all kinds of put out.

"Don't you work?" I called as I climbed from the driver's seat and shoved the door closed, beeping the locks.

"Perks of being your own boss is making your own hours," Luna declared. "And don't you take that tone with me, missy. I've been trying to reach you all freaking day. Are you wearing two different flip-flops?"

I pushed past her and slipped my key into the lock, swinging the front door open. "I am. And I know you've been blowing my phone up. Kind of hard to miss."

She followed me into the living room like a disgruntled butterfly, cranky but still flitting around, and glared when I flopped myself down on the couch with my coffee in hand.

"Well?" she demanded seconds later. "What happened on your date?"

"Wasn't a date," I said, opening the lid of my cup before taking a drink. "Oh, and by the way, thanks for going around telling people I had a date last night."

"First"—she held up her index finger—"that's on you for thinking I'd stay quiet about something this monumental. Second"—her middle finger joined the first—"what the hell do you mean it wasn't a date. Of course it was! Even Georgia confirmed."

"You two are the worst."

She threw herself down on the loveseat. "Stop deflecting."

"Okay, fine." I knew when I was beaten. Which was most

of the time with Luna. She had a gift for steamrolling her way over a conversation. Most of the time it was entertaining as hell . . . when I wasn't the topic. "It wasn't a date. I *thought* it was. I still don't know how I misread that one. But apparently I was wrong."

"How do you know?"

Here goes nothing. "Because when I kissed him, he pulled back and ran out of here like his ass was on fire."

She let out a happy yelp that had no place in this particular situation. "*Omigod*, you kissed him? That's so great!"

I lifted my brows, wishing I could pull off the whole one-brow-arch thing. "Did you just stop listening to everything I said after that?"

"No. I heard you, and the dude is obviously a turd. But I'm still really happy for you."

"Why? It was a disaster, Lu."

"Because this means you're putting yourself back out there. You felt something for this guy, and you went for it. You acted on it instead of sitting back and waiting for him to make a move."

I kind of wish I *had* waited. At least then I wouldn't have been shot down so spectacularly.

"I don't know what his deal is. I mean, I saw how he was looking at you in your workshop the other day. It was so obvious he was into you, even my great aunt Ida could have seen it, and she's got so many cataracts the doctor took her driver's license away."

"But—"

"Something had to have freaked him out. That's the only explanation."

"Yeah. Me kissing him. That freaked him out," I deadpanned.

She pursed her lips to the side in thought. "No. Something else. I saw it myself. He looked like he wanted to gobble you up." She flapped her hands in front of her. "But you know what? It doesn't matter. It's his loss, because you're shit-hot and fucking amazing. And now you've taken that first step into claiming a little piece of happiness—or at the very least, an orgasm—for yourself." She clasped her hands together and pressed them to her chest. "My little bird's grown up and ready to leave the nest. I'm such a proud momma hen."

"I think you mixed up a couple metaphors there."

"Whatever. You know what I mean, that's all that matters. Time to get you on another horse."

I set my cup on the coffee table and stretched out, propping my head on the arm of the couch and resting my feet on one of the million squishy throw pillows that covered the thing. "I love you, Luna. And I'm glad you're proud I put myself out there, but being shot down isn't very fun. You need to temper your excitement, because it'll probably be a while before I ride another horse . . . if ever."

Her bottom lip stuck out in a pout. "Don't look at last night as a failure, babe. Look at it for what it was. You were dipping your toe back into the dating waters. Okay, so a smelly little fish came up and bit you, but there are other fish who won't bite. Or they will, but only if you *want* to be bitten. And they'll do it in a way you really like." She waggled her brows.

"You are so bad at metaphors," I said with a laugh, already feeling a million times better, all thanks to her. That was why I loved Luna so damn much. She made everything better.

She shrugged. "Meh. My talents lie elsewhere." Her expression turned serious. "But seriously, are you okay?"

Yet another reason why she was the best. "Yeah, hon, I'm good. It was just embarrassing. That's all."

"Well," she started knowingly, "that, and you liked him."

There was no point in denying it. "I did. So, yeah, it's a bummer he didn't feel the same, but I'll get over it." And I absolutely would. "Trust me, I've been through way worse. I just need to lick my wounds today, then I'll be fine tomorrow."

The look on her face just then left me feeling unsettled. "You know, when you say stuff like that, it makes me want to ask questions about your past, even though I know you'll clam up on me."

She was right about that.

My chest suddenly tightened. "But you won't, because you're a good friend."

"I won't because I'm the *best* friend," she confirmed, and that vise-grip loosened. "All right. I'll let you have the day. But if we're doing this, we need to do it right." She kicked off her shoes and pulled her legs up, snuggling deeper into the furniture.

"What's the right way?"

"You're going to put on some trashy reality TV that's not actually reality at all, and we're going to sit here and judge these women on their cattiness, as well as who has the worst plastic surgery. Now grab the remote. Let's get this party started."

Twelve

TRENT

Sweat built at my temples and slid down the sides of my face, collecting and dripping off the tip of my nose onto the floor beneath me. I grunted with each pushup, the muscles burning in my arms like I'd doused them in gasoline and set them on fire.

It had been three days since I ran out of Sawyer's place, and I still felt like a world-class dick. I couldn't go on my usual morning run and risk passing by her house and seeing her outside. If I did, I knew I'd stop and try to talk to her. So instead, I'd been kicking my own ass with workouts at home that left my muscles feeling like Jell-O.

I lowered down, feeling the straining pull in my triceps before shoving my way back up. Having lost count a long time ago, I figured I'd just keep going until my arms gave out.

I managed to crank out five more pushups before my cell started ringing, pulling me out of my misery.

I rose to plank position and jumped up and shaking out my arms as I followed the sound into the kitchen.

My boss's name flashed on the screen. "Hey Linc. What's up?"

"Just checking in. You sound winded. Everything good?"

"Yeah, just finished up a workout."

"Good. Glad you're staying sharp."

"Don't I always?" I gritted. That comment made my hackles rise. Rationally, I knew I took it personally because I'd already fucked up, but knowing that didn't loosen any of the tension that was suddenly squeezing at my neck and shoulders.

"Yep. It's why I had no problem making you a part of my team." I knew he'd heard the bite in my words, but he didn't mention it. Lincoln Sheppard was the kind of man who waited for his men to come to him on their own terms if there was a problem. He was an incredible boss like that. He trusted us to know when we could work something out ourselves and when we needed a little help. "So how are things on the opposite coast? Anything to report?"

"Nope. Not—" A loud, pounding knock sounded on my front door, cutting me off mid-lie. "Hold that thought. Someone at the door."

I pulled the phone from my ear and moved through the house, grabbing my Glock and holding it behind my back as years of training kicked in. No one in this town knew me well enough to be making house calls, so I needed to be prepared for anything.

Stepping up to the door, I used the phone to push the curtain back and peek out, letting loose a sigh when I saw who was standing on my front porch. Tucking the gun in the fake plastic plant right inside the foyer, I turned the deadbolt and opened the door. "Luna," I greeted, but before I could get another word out, she jumped right in.

"Hey, dickface. I just wanted to stop by and tell you that you're the dumbest douchebag on the planet for messing with Sawyer's head like that."

Fuck. Lifting the phone to my ear, I kept my eyes pinned to Luna as I said, "Linc, I'm gonna have to call you back."

His voice was hard as he replied, "Sounds like it. And don't you fucking forget, or my ass will be on the first plane to Oregon." Then he disconnected. *Shit.* Wasn't looking forward to that conversation.

Sawyer's friend crossed her arms over her chest and stared daggers, not the slightest bit intimidated to be going head to head with a man my size. She was either the bravest chick alive, or plain stupid for having no fear. And something told me it would be a mistake to think it was the latter. This wasn't a woman to fuck with.

"I'd apologize for interrupting your call, but I really don't give a shit."

Heaving out a sigh, I reached up to rub at my temple, feeling the dull throb of an oncoming headache beating like a drum beneath my skin. "Do you want to come in?"

"Nope," she clapped back. "This will be fast, so there's

no need for me to be stuck in your space any longer than necessary."

I gave in to whatever this was, hoping she'd say her piece and move on quickly. "All right, then. Let me have it. Say what's on your mind."

I could see it on her face that my reluctant acceptance of this dressing down took her by surprise, but she quickly banked the shock and dove right in. "You probably don't know this yet, because you're a man, therefore bred to be the stupider of the sexes, but you were, hands down, the luckiest son of a bitch in existence for catching Sawyer's eye. There isn't a better woman out there than her, and she actually felt something for you. In the years I've known her, this is the *first* time that's happened. You might not get how big that is, but trust me, it's huge."

Jesus. She'd have been less effective if she'd just kicked me in the balls the moment I opened the door. Each word out of her mouth was like razors slicing through my skin. I really was a son of a bitch.

"I don't know what happened the other night—and just to dumb it down so your pea brain gets it, what I mean by that is, I don't know what you did to fuck up so epically, but I know you like her. I saw it written all over your face, so don't bother denying it." She paused in her tirade, looking at me questioningly when I remained closed-mouthed. "Wow. You're really not going to deny it."

"No point. What you said is the truth."

She let out a huff, some of her ire fading, but I could see

she was still working hard to keep a hold on her mad. "And here I was, looking forward to getting to slap some smart into you."

I fought back the grin trying to curl my lips. "Would it make you feel better if I gave you a free shot?"

I could have sworn she pouted at that. "No. It's no fun if you see it coming." She blew out a deep breath. "If you like her, why the hell did you run out of there, leaving her to think she'd made a fool of herself?"

Christ, this woman didn't pull any punches, and I could see it in her stoney expression, she wasn't going to let me get away with not answering. "It was never my intention to make her feel like that. I fucking hate that I did that to her, but I had my reasons for needing to get out of there. My leaving was best for her, trust me."

"Oh what a load of bullshit," she snapped. "I can't stand it when people claim that hurting someone was in that person's best interest. It's a cop-out. An excuse to make the person doing the hurting feel better for being a dick. Plain and simple. And if you're the kind of man to make a lame-ass excuse like that, you *definitely* don't deserve another second of my best friend's time." She whipped around on her heel and started down the walkway, pausing only long enough to shout over her shoulder, "Get your shit together or go back to where you came from." Then she was gone.

Feeling like I had weights pressing down on my shoulders, I closed the front door and threw the lock. Grabbing the Glock from where I'd stashed it, I moved through the house and returned it to where I kept it hidden—safely out of sight but within quick reach if I needed it. With no other delays, I tapped the screen and hit Lincoln's name. It barely finished its first ring before his voice came through the line.

"Before we get into what the hell is goin' on over there, I need to know right now, do I need to pull you off this case and assign it to someone else?"

A growl rumbled up my throat before I could stop it. "Not a fucking chance."

"Jesus," he hissed into the phone. "You went and developed feelings for her, didn't you?"

"It's not going to have any effect on how I do my job," I stated instead of answering in the affirmative. At this point I wasn't so much worried about him knowing the truth as I was that he'd send one of the other guys down here to take my place.

That wasn't going to happen.

"Fuckin' hell," he bit out. "What happened?"

"Look, Linc. It's not a big deal, okay? There was . . ." Christ, how to explain it. "A slip."

"There was a *slip*? What the fuck does that even mean?"

"There was a kiss," I admitted. "But I put a stop to it and made things clear." Or tried to, at least. What that woman made me feel muddied the waters in the worst way. Nothing was clear, it was a goddamn murky mess of confusion. The only thing I knew for absolute certain was that I wasn't leaving Whitecap until the threat to her and Renee was extinguished for good. "It won't happen again."

"And I'm assuming since you're still breathing, Dalton doesn't have a clue about any of this."

"You'd assume right. And it needs to stay that way. At least for now."

He blew out a heavy sigh, probably scrubbing at his face. "You sure about that? I'm not certain you're seeing things clearly anymore. You know as well as I do how bad things can go when men like us get tunnel vision on a job. You're not seein' the whole picture clearly."

"I see everything perfectly," I assured him. "If anything, this shit has tuned me in even more to the importance of why I'm here. She's created a life for herself here, Linc. This isn't just her home. She and her girl are stitched into the fabric of this place. I'm not going to let anything fuck with that, even if that means keeping Dalton and Charlotte in the dark a little longer."

"Think that might be more Charlotte's call than yours."

I gritted my teeth so hard the muscle in my jaw trembled. "Then you'd think fucking wrong," I snarled. "That sociopath already tracked Charlotte down. He knows exactly where she is. We can take every precaution known to man, but one mistake—just fucking one—and we could lead him right to her doorstep. We only had a tiny taste of what he was capable of when he sent his man after Charlotte. What do you think he'll do if he finds out the wife he's been hunting all this time, the one he's convinced half the world is *dead* just to cover his own ass, took off because she was pregnant with his kid?"

"Shit," he hissed.

"Exactly. You feel the need to send someone else down here because you don't think I've got my shit in check, that's your call, man. But I'll save you the trouble and tell you now, I'm not leaving. Not a goddamn chance. Only way you're getting me out of this town is by putting Knightly in the ground so Sawyer and Renee are safe. You get me?"

"I get you," he answered in a low, knowing tone. "But just a piece of advice, brother. I've been where you are, and I nearly lost Eden by keeping secrets."

When he'd first met his woman, her estranged brother had been a suspect in a string of burglaries and a possible homicide. Lincoln had been asked to get close to her to see what he could find out, and inevitably ended up falling for her.

To say things had gone really wrong when she found out the truth would have been the world's biggest understatement. He'd had to pull out all the stops to win her back, fortunately it worked. Now they were married, living the good life, and had a chubby little kiddo who ran them ragged.

"This isn't the same."

"You sure about that? Known you a long time, brother, and this is the first time a woman's ever gotten under your skin to the point I have to think of reassigning you, and you sound like you want to rip my head off with your bare hands for even suggesting it. You might not see it yet because this feeling is foreign to you, but I've lived it already, so I know.

Answer a question for me. Job aside, if this woman wasn't who she is and you didn't know what you know, would you be willing step in front of a bullet for her?"

I didn't say a word. I couldn't. The lump that had formed in my throat at just the thought of that happening made it impossible to breathe, let alone talk.

"Thought so," he grunted. "You're in the thick of it, man. My advice, figure out a way to tell her the truth without exploding her world. And do it fast, before it gets so far she can't bring herself to forgive you."

I finally managed to pull in a stuttered breath. "You finished?" I croaked.

"For now. Like always, keep me posted. And if you need anything, Trent, I'm just a phone call away. Whether it pertains to the job or not. Just remember that."

With that, he hung up before I could get another word in.

Thirteen

SAWYER

My hands were full of shopping bags stuffed full of what felt like every single item in the party supply store. Renee was turning three in a few days, and I was pulling out all the stops, throwing her a huge birthday party. Sure, I might have gone a little overboard, but it was my right as the mother of the most incredible toddler in existence. Seeing as I birthed her—painfully and for a *very* long time—I didn't care if my friends made fun of me.

"Thanks, Marie," I called back to the woman who'd rung up my purchase as I headed toward the exit.

"No problem. You sure you don't need any help with all that?" Her forehead crinkled as she lifted her brows. "You sure did get a lot of stuff."

"I got it. My car's right outside, but thanks. We'll see you at the party this weekend, right?"

"You kidding? Hank and I wouldn't miss it."

"Great. See you there."

She gave me a wave as I shouldered my way through the door and spilled out onto the sidewalk.

Shuffling across the cement, I struggled to rummage through my purse for my keys with my arms loaded down, finding the key fob and pushing the button to lift the back hatch just as one of the handles snapped and rolls of crepe paper streamers and paper plates tumbled to the ground. It was like a domino effect after that, handles snapping and party supplies falling. "Crap, crap, crap."

"Let me help." A husky, velvety voice came from behind me, making goose bumps prickle across my skin as a forearm came into my line of sight, stopping the tube of pink plastic cups from rolling off the sidewalk.

It had been a little over a week since that kiss, and this was the first time I'd seen him since that embarrassing night.

I'd almost completely recovered from my humiliation. The only people who knew anything about it, the biggest busybodies in town, Monica, Luna, and Georgia, somehow managed to keep their traps shut, so news of my failed date-not-date hadn't made it through the grapevine, and in time the memory of that night could die with us.

All and all, life had gone back to normal, and, with no one really gossiping about the new guy anymore, I figured he must have finally gone back home. A thought that I was trying my hardest not to acknowledge made me feel just the teensiest bit miserable.

But apparently, I'd figured wrong.

"Hi," I managed to squeak out as he gathered up a package of balloons and a banner that spelled out "Happy Birthday" in his big hands.

He looked at me, a small grin on his face, but it was still enough to make those dimples pop. Damn him. "Hey."

"You're still here." The words fell from my mouth without any thought.

"Yeah. Still here. You sound surprised."

"I just—I didn't know how long you were planning to stay in town. Thought you might have headed home by now."

"It's kind of an open-ended trip. Guess you could call it a mental health break. Just needed to get away, you know?"

"Yeah," I said in a quiet voice, grabbing the boxes of plastic utensils that had spilled from the bags. "I get that."

He looked down at his hands and at the items still littering the sidewalk. "Wow. This is a lot of pink."

I let out a snort of laughter. "Yeah. It's Renee's birthday. I might have overdone it."

His chuckle crawled across my skin. "You kidding? For something as big as a girl turning three? No way. Especially not when it's a kid as enthusiastic as Little Bit."

I grinned down at the sidewalk as I picked up the last of the items I'd dropped. "This is very true. When I asked what colors she was thinking for her party, her answer was 'all the pink in the world.'"

"That sounds like something she would say." He lifted

his head and tilted his chin toward the opened door. "That your car?"

"Yeah—Wait, you really don't have to—" He stood, taking the remaining bags from me and started in that direction. I quickly scooped up the last of my fallen purchases and scurried after him.

"It's not a big deal, really." When I reached the car, he divested me of my items, stowing them between the bags that weren't damaged and reaching up to push the button that would lower the door.

"Um, well, thank you. For helping."

"Don't mention it."

We stood there, looking up at each other in silence until it started to get awkward, the air around us getting thick and soupy. I was just about to make an excuse to get out of there when he spoke.

"Sawyer, I owe you an apology."

Oh God. "No, you really don't—"

"Yeah, I do. I'm really sorry for how I reacted the other night."

I held my hand up to stop him, the sincerity in his eyes shining in the afternoon sun. "Trent, it's okay. Really. You didn't do anything wrong, so you don't have anything to apologize for. I'm the one who's sorry. I misread the situation, and I put you in a really uncomfortable place."

"But you didn't."

"I—" My brows slashed down over my eyes in confusion. "What?"

"You didn't misread the situation, darlin'. I was attracted to you. I *am* attracted to you," he stressed.

The air whooshed from my lungs at his admission. I wasn't sure what to think or what he was getting at by telling me this. But I *did* know it went a long way in making me feel better about the whole debacle.

"It's just, the timing . . . I wish—"

"Trent, please. You don't owe me an explanation. Your private life is your own. I get it, really." I let out a small, humorless laugh at the irony of the whole situation. "I know all about bad timing. Probably better than most."

His expression softened with tenderness, slamming right into my chest like a closed fist. "I never meant to embarrass you. I do like you, very much. And if this was another time . . ."

He trailed off, and I understood perfectly what he was trying to explain. "Yeah. I get it." Letting out a sigh, I gave him a genuine grin. "Well, just because the timing sucks doesn't mean we can't be friends for the rest of your stay here, right?"

That dimpled smile was in full effect. "I'd really like that."

"Me too," I replied softly. "So how about you come to Renee's birthday party? I know she'd love it if Tent was there," I said on a giggle. "And it could never hurt to have another adult to help wrangle toddlers. They're bad enough on their own, but they'll be hopped up on sugar and excitement, so if you happen to have a tranquilizer gun, it would be welcome."

"No tranq gun," he said on a laugh. "But I'd be happy to help wrangle."

"All right then. It's Saturday at two. Just walk down the beach until you run into a massive crowd of screaming kids. Can't miss it."

"I'll be there. Looking forward to it."

"Famous last words," I called as I started around the car to the driver side door. "I'll be sure to throw them in your face later."

Those dimples pressed deep, his white smile glittering in the sun. "I'm sure you will. See you Saturday."

"See you then."

I ignored the flutters in my belly as I waved back at him and drove away. "Just friends," I told myself, determined not to make the same mistake I made the first time around. "Just friends."

"I can't believe you invited that d-i-c-k to Renee's birthday party," Luna groused. She'd swung by earlier to poach a free meal and was currently propped on one of the stools across from me with a glass of wine in her hand, watching me cook.

"There was no reason not to. And besides, it would have been really rude, considering he already knew about it because he'd helped me get the supplies in the car."

"*Pfft*! Who cares about being rude? The guy's a j-a-c-k-a-s-s."

Renee was coloring in the living room and singing along with the songs on one of her programs, so we had to spell out our cuss words. Or I should say *Luna* had to spell out her cuss words.

I looked up from the sautéing zucchini and gave her a flat look. "He is not. He's a nice guy." She mumbled something under her breath that I didn't quite catch, but I knew it couldn't be good. "What's your problem with him, anyway? You act like this was some big, star-crossed love thing and he somehow broke my heart. He's just another tourist, Lu. Sooner or later, he'll head back home, and life will go back to how it's always been."

"I'm just pissy because this was the first time you've put yourself out there since I've known you. That's a big deal. And this jerk didn't see how amazing you are. I'm not a fan of people who are too stupid to see what's right in front of their faces."

Okay, so maybe that made my heart a little squishy. Luna could be very sweet . . . in her own unique, blunt, sometimes forceful, way.

"Look, when we ran into each other earlier, he said there was a reason he couldn't go there with me, and that's fine."

She gulped down her wine and placed the glass on the bar with a *clink* before sitting back and crossing her arms over her chest. "And did he happen to say what that reason was?"

"No. And I didn't ask, because it's not my business."

She snorted indignantly. "Convenient."

Killing the flame under the pan, I placed the spoon on the cute little holder I'd made a few years back.

"I know you love me, hon, and the feeling is mutual, but there's really no need for you to be so salty about this. I'm over it so there's no reason you shouldn't be as well. Now, dinner's just about done, so be useful. Get your cute butt off that stool and set the table, would you?"

She hopped off with a huff. "Fine. But let the record show I'm only doing it because you said my butt was cute."

I gave my head a shake on a laugh. "You'll do it because if you don't, you're not eating."

"Yes, well, there's that too."

My friend could be a pain in the ass, but for the most part, she was worth it, so I figured I'd keep her around, at least for a while longer.

Fourteen

SAWYER

T HE ONLY WAY to correctly describe the level of activity at my house at that very moment was full-blown pandemonium. And I was loving every second of it.

Not only had all the toddlers from Renee's daycare class shown up to celebrate her birthday, but it seemed like at least half the town was in attendance as well.

Luna was there, of course, having shown up three hours early to help me set up. Monica and her husband, Sam, were there. Georgia and Desmond had gotten someone to cover the store so they could both attend. There was no way they were going to miss their girl's big day.

My house was going to be a disaster by the time this day was over, and I didn't care even the littlest bit. Parties like this were nothing more than dreams I'd had when I was a child. After my parents died, the people who'd taken me in couldn't be bothered to remember, let alone celebrate, my birthday. Graham had made a spectacle out of them when we'd been together, but that was only so he had an excuse to throw a lavish party and schmooze his constituents. It had never been about me. And if I hadn't run when I did, he would have defiled Renee's big day in the same way.

The people here now actually cared about me and my daughter, and they'd come out simply to celebrate my girl's latest milestone, nothing more.

People spilled from my house like a glass of water that had fallen over. The trickle started in the living room and tumbled into the kitchen, through the open slider into the backyard, and out onto the beach. You could barely hear the seagulls or waves over the sounds of children shouting and carrying on in excitement.

Until coming to Whitecap, I'd never thought something like this was possible. I'd never felt so much love in my life. Before this wonderful place, I'd never belonged anywhere. But I belonged here. My girl belonged here. If I hadn't already known that to be a fact, the turnout today would have proven it. We had more love from the people of Whitecap than I'd ever had in my entire life.

Balancing a vegetable platter—wishful thinking on my part—in one hand and a bowl of potato chips in the other, I wound my way around the counters groaning with food—thank God for potlucks, because feeding this many people would have bankrupted me—and moved from the kitchen, through the sliding door, onto the deck.

Sam and Desmond were on me before I was fully across

the threshold, shooting up from the patio furniture where they were congregated and taking the items from my hands before I had a chance to drop anything.

"Where do you want these?" Sam asked in his deep, baritone voice.

"Anywhere you can find an empty spot is great. Thanks, guys."

Desmond leaned in to press a fatherly kiss to my temple. "No problem, sweetheart."

When I started gathering up empty dishes off the long folding tables to take back inside and replace with full ones, Georgia popped up beside me, all but smacking them out of my hands. "Child, will you stop cleaning up already and come sit down? Enjoy yourself for a bit," she ordered as she took my wrist and physically dragged me to the cluster of furniture where she was sitting with Monica and Luna.

"They'll just pile up if I leave them," I argued as she shoved me unceremoniously onto the loveseat.

"Everyone here is practically family," Monica stated, putting the straw of her large insulated cup—that I was pretty sure contained sangria—to her lips, and sipping. "They'll see the empty platters and handle it. Just take a load off for a bit."

I honestly didn't mind running around like a chicken with my head cut off if it meant making sure everything ran smoothly for my girl's big day, but I also didn't mind being strong-armed by my friends into hanging with them for a bit.

I stretched my neck, looking out at the beach for my

daughter. At least a fourth of the adults had set up camp on the sandy shore to keep an eye on the kids who wanted to play down there. "Have you guys seen Renee?"

"She's fine," Luna assured me. "Someone organized a sandcastle building contest, and she was determined to kick everyone's butt." She leaned forward and flipped open one of the several coolers lining the deck. She pulled out a glass bottle, twisted off the top, and passed it to me. "Here. Drink this."

I looked at the label and arched my brows. "Piña colada wine coolers? Seriously?"

She shrugged and took a drink from her own. "It's a beach party. When in Rome, right?"

I let out a laugh and gave in, taking a sip of the overly-sweet concoction. As soon as the flavor exploded on my tongue, my face crumpled in disgust. "Ugh. This tastes like artificial sweetener and battery acid. How are you drinking these?"

She smacked her lips. "This sort of film builds up in your mouth after the first one so you can't really taste the second or third. Just push through, and you'll be good."

Monica snorted into her drink, sputtering on her sangria. "You know you're an adult now, right? You can buy the good stuff and make *real* piña coladas that won't rot your gut."

"I was feeling nostalgic. Thanks to these babies"—Luna shook the half-drunk bottle in her hand—"I had the courage to make a move on Mark Polanski during a bonfire party in the tenth grade."

It was weird to think about how different my life had been back then compared to my best friend's. While she partied and got drunk and made out with boys like pretty much every teenager alive, I'd been doing everything in my power to keep my head down and my nose clean. I didn't want to do anything that could piss off my guardians and get me sent away like they'd done with my sister.

My mother's cousin and her husband had made it abundantly clear from the very beginning that they never really wanted us, that my sister and I had been forced on them practically against their will when our parents died.

They hadn't batted an eye at getting rid of Charlotte when she proved to be more than a docile, quiet child, and I spent the rest of my years with them, terrified the same fate would befall me.

I didn't just toe the line, I stayed as far back from it as possible, something that inevitably led to the deterioration of every relationship I had. No one wanted to be friends with or date the girl who never did anything fun.

"Was Mark Polanski hot?" I asked teasingly.

"Eh. He was all right. But he was the captain of the basketball team and super popular. It was about the status, not the looks." She winked salaciously.

The four of us burst into laughter.

Leaning forward, I abandoned the still-full bottle on the patio table. "Well, I'm not nostalgic, and that one sip feels like it's burning a hole through my stomach lining, so I'm going to pass."

Monica held up her cup and gave it a little shake. "I stashed a pitcher of sangria in your fridge if you want some of that."

"I'll stick to water, thanks."

"Where's the fun in that?" a deep voice asked just as a large figure stepped up to our area, blocking out the sun and casting a shadow over us.

I looked back over my shoulder, smiling up at Trent who was backlit perfectly by the bright sunshine. "Hey, you came."

"Of course I did. Wasn't going to miss Little Bit's special day."

"He calls her Little Bit?" Monica asked on a breathy sigh, looking up at Trent with a dreamy expression on her face. "That's the cutest thing I've ever heard."

Sam, who'd been standing a few feet away, talking with Desmond and a couple of the other men in attendance, rolled his eyes skyward and broke from his group to come closer. "Honey, you mind not drooling over another man when your husband's standing ten feet away from you?"

"No worries, my love. I'm just looking. No intention of touching, I promise."

I stood, grinning at my friend's ridiculousness. "Trent, you remember Luna, Monica, and Georgia."

"Yeah, hi. Good to see you again."

They waved back. Monica and Georgia were in a state of gob-smacked awe while Luna was much more hesitant to welcome him. She was still holding a bit of a grudge, but as long as she didn't do or say anything to cause drama, I'd take it. My friend could be unpredictable on the best day.

I continued on with the introductions. "Sam, this is Trent. Trent, this is Monica's husband, Sam—"

"Killborne," Trent finished, his expression holding a mild hint of star-struck as he extended his hand. "Thought I recognized you. I'm a huge fan. Denver hasn't played the same since you and Ethan Prewitt retired."

Sam inspected Trent with a sweeping once-over before taking his hand and giving it a pump, and from the way the skin around Trent's eyes and mouth tightened, the big man was squeezing harder than necessary.

Guess Monica had been right about that fragile ego thing.

"Good to meet you, Tim."

"Trent," he corrected.

"Uh huh. That's what I said."

Okay, so Monica was *definitely* right.

I cut in before Sam could challenge Trent to a push-up competition or pissing contest. "And this is Desmond, Georgia's husband," I continued, hooking my hand through his arm and pulling him over. Desmond had a nice, calming presence about him that would help keep Sam's testosterone in check. "He and Georgia own Warren's General Store."

He gave Trent a much politer handshake. "Call me Dezzy. Everyone else does."

"Good to meet you, Dezzy," Trent said congenially before turning to look at me, lifting the box he'd been carrying under his arm. How the man still managed to look insanely hot while holding a package wrapped in bright pink paper covered in purple balloons was beyond me, but he somehow did it. "Got Renee a little something. Where should I put it?"

"We're putting all the gifts on the dining room table."

"Gotcha." He only managed to take one step toward the open slider when my girl's voice came screeching through the air.

"*Tent! Tent!*" She ran up to us as fast as her little legs could carry her. Every bit of skin not covered by her adorable little swimsuit was coated in sand, even her face and hair. "It's by birfday! I'm fwee yeaws old!"

"I know, that's why I'm here. Couldn't miss your party."

She practically vibrated with glee. "I made a *huge* sancastle, come see!"

His eyes shifted to me when I reached out to take the present. "You go. I'll put this with all the others."

Those damn dimples made a show, and I could have sworn that every woman on my back deck nearly fainted. "Thanks."

Renee's tiny fingers latched onto his massive hand, giving it a violent tug and shake. "Come on, Tent! Come on!"

He looked down at her, his face awash with gentleness as he chuckled. "All right, Little Bit. Let's go see this sandcastle."

I stood there, clutching the gift he'd bought for my baby in my arms as I watched them walk hand in hand through the backyard and out the gate. I couldn't let the sight of them together make me soft. Trent and I were just friends, that was what we agreed on. It wouldn't do any damn good to get all gooey every time he smiled at my daughter.

It wasn't lost on me that nearly every female head in the vicinity turned to gawk as he walked by, but I was too busy doing the same damn thing to really pay it any mind.

"So that's him, huh?" Sam asked, pulling me from my reverie. "The dude who's got everyone in town talking?" I swiveled my head to look up at the big bear of a man, curling my lips between my teeth to keep from laughing at the disgruntled expression on his face. He folded his big, beefy arms over his chest and glowered out toward the water. "He's not all that."

I lost my battle and a snort broke through. "*All that*? I didn't know we are living in a high school rom-com from the late nineties."

He turned that scowl on me, but it had no effect since I knew what a big teddy bear he really was.

"I'm just as hot as he is," he defended. "Maybe hotter."

Luna came up on his other side and patted him on the shoulder, offering comfort since his wife was currently bent over, laughing hysterically at her husband's dramatics. "Of course you are, studs. Here, drink this. It'll make it all better."

Sam took the wine cooler she offered without looking at it and slugged some back.

"Damn," he grunted a second later. "That's good stuff. Got any more of these?"

Luna gave me a triumphant look. "Sure do, big guy. Follow me."

As she led him to the cooler, I burst into laughter right alongside Monica.

Fifteen

SAWYER

"Oh my God," Luna groaned dramatically from where she was splayed out across the sofa, limbs akimbo, one arm and leg hanging off the edge. "I'm never having kids. Never ever ever."

The party was officially over. Renee had been bathed—twice to get rid of all that sand—and was passed out in her bed in much the same position as Luna, having experienced a major sugar crash about an hour earlier. Everyone but Trent and Luna had headed home, the former helping me to clean up the disaster left behind from the party, while the latter continued making sounds I'd expect to hear from a bag of wet cats, lamenting all the million reasons why she was never bearing children.

Trent grabbed another plastic cup from the table and tossed it into the garbage bag he was holding, looking through the sliding door toward the living room. "She okay?"

"She'll be fine," I assured him as I tore down some of the streamers and stuffed them in my bag.

Luna's head shot up over the arm of the couch, her hair a bedraggled mess hanging in her eyes. "I am *not* okay! I think I contracted some kind of virus from that walking petri dish that puked on me. You seriously need to consider moving Renee to a new daycare. I think half those kids had tuberculosis or something."

"Randy didn't spread anything to you. He only threw up because he ate too much candy."

"So his mother said," she grumbled sullenly. "We can't really know for sure until I'm knocking on death's door."

She flopped back onto the couch. "She gets like this every year," I told Trent. "She usually bounces back within a week or so."

"Not this time!" she shouted from the living room.

Trent and I fell into silent laughter as we cleaned up the backyard before moving indoors. "I get the feeling Sam didn't like me very much," he said as he carried a load of crumb-covered trays over to the sink and turned on the hot water.

"Oh, that's because he doesn't." Around the time the boy from Renee's daycare class projectile puked all over Luna, I'd succumbed to the stresses of spending the majority of the day with eleventy-billion toddlers, and dove into her wine cooler stash. She was right. Once that film built up on my tongue, blocking the taste, they weren't so bad. I wasn't drunk, hell, I wasn't even tipsy, but the combination of the alcohol and the pure, undiluted exhaustion had stripped me of my filter completely.

His head shot around, one brow arched, dimples on full display. "Don't sugarcoat it or anything."

I laughed, shaking my head as I snatched up my wine cooler and moved into the kitchen, hopping up on the counter just like I had last time, the time we'd kissed. Had to remember not to do that this time.

"Don't take it personally. It's not because of anything you did. Monica explained it to me, but I didn't actually believe it until I saw it for myself today. He's jealous. Sam's used to being the town eye-candy. You showed up, and now he's worried about being dethroned. I'm sure he'll get over it eventually." *Like when you leave,* I thought, suddenly overcome with a ridiculous wave of sadness.

One corner of his mouth hooked up in a crooked smirk. "Well it makes sense now why he challenged me to an arm wrestling competition."

I choked on the drink I'd just taken, trying to clear my lungs of piña colada wine cooler as Trent pounded on my back. "You okay?"

"Yeah, sorry," I wheezed, batting the tears from my eyes as I laughed. "I just didn't know he'd done that."

"Yeah. That, and he kept asking how much I could bench."

I looked at him curiously. "How much *can* you bench?"

He shot me a wink as he squirted soap into the hot water, creating suds before he got to washing. "Enough."

Was that . . . flirting? It couldn't have been. Trent had made it perfectly clear where we stood, so he couldn't possibly have been flirting. So why the hell did it feel that way?

Clearing my throat, I ripped my gaze away from his smoky eyes and stared across the room at nothing as I gulped back more of the wine cooler. I had a feeling I was going to really regret drinking these come morning. The unique, intoxicating smell of his cologne was starting to make my head fuzzy. I needed to put some distance between us before I let myself get the wrong idea again. I wasn't sure what it was about this man that muddled my brain so badly, but I couldn't seem to find my footing.

Hopping off the counter, I moved around the bar and resumed my cleanup duties, stacking empty cups and plates and tossing them in the trash. "You know, you didn't have to stay to help clean up."

"I don't mind," he said as he scrubbed at one of the platters. "This place looks like a pink glitter bomb went off inside of it. Besides, it's not like I had anything else on my schedule."

"Have you seen any of the sights since you got to town?"

He shrugged and moved on to the next dish, a casserole dish that had been full of brownies earlier that day. "Not really. I've just been hanging at the house and the beach."

"There are a lot of amazing places around here you should visit before you leave. At the very least, you need to see Whisper Falls and the hot springs before your trip ends."

"Whisper Falls?"

"Yeah. It not really a tourist destination. The locals like to keep it a secret so it's not overrun during tourist season."

He shut off the water once the last dish was done and turned to face me, propping his trim hips against the counter and drying his hands on one of my dishtowels. There wasn't anything the slightest bit sexy about it, yet he still managed to make my stomach flutter just by drying his freaking hands.

"Sawyer?"

His voice jolted me back to reality and my gaze darted up to his to find his eyes shining with mirth. "Sorry. What?"

He didn't try at all to hide his dimpled smirk. "I asked if you were going to get in trouble for letting me in on a town secret. You know, angry mobs with pitchforks and stuff."

"Nah, they'll forgive me. Just as long as you don't spill the secret to anyone else."

He made a cross over his chest and lifted his fingers in a Boy Scout salute. "You have my word. I'll never tell a soul. This is a secret I'll take to my grave."

I gave him a squinty, incredulously look. "Were you even a Boy Scout?"

The corners of his mouth creeped upward, a sinful grin slowly unwrapping in the most tempting way. "For a bit. Then they told my mom I didn't follow the rules and was a troublemaker."

My eyes went wide, my brows shooting up toward my hairline. "Oh? And what rules did you break?"

"I think the easier question is which ones didn't I break."

A light giggle pushed its way from my throat. "And the trouble making?"

He held his hands up in surrender. "I might have drawn a butt on all the patches sewn on one boy's vest. But in my defense, Bobby Osborne was a little shit. He acted like he was better than everyone else because his dad drove a BMW and he got all his clothes at the mall. And he peed his sleeping bag during a campout and blamed it on his tent buddy."

"Yep, definitely sounds like a little shit. He deserved every one of those butts."

"Sure did. And when the rest of the kids started laughing and pointing at them, he cried like a little sissy. Getting kicked out was totally worth it. If I could go back in time, I'd do it all over again."

Luna chimed in from her prone position in the living room. "If you could go back in time, I'd expect you to up your game and draw penises instead of butts."

I pointed in her direction. "I'm with her."

"Valid point." He pushed off the counter and stalked closer, his thick jean-clad thighs bulging with each step as his long legs ate up the distance. He pressed his palms into the counter, arms spread wide as he leaned in and made all those muscles pop and strain against the sleeves of his gray T-shirt.

"So, about these falls. I don't suppose you'd be willing to go check them out with me on your next day off."

A warning siren went off in my head, but it wasn't

because I sensed danger. It was because I knew I was standing at the very edge of a dangerously slippery slope with nothing to hold on to. And yet, instead of making an excuse for why I couldn't or just flat-out refusing, I found myself nodding, a smile playing at my lips to match his dimpled one. "Yeah. That sounds like fun."

He hung around a while longer, helping me finish cleaning and giving Luna a hard time for being so dramatic. Once he was gone, I found and dumped the rest of her wine coolers and moved into the living room, plopping down on the love seat and kicking my feet up on the coffee table.

"God, I don't remember the last time I was this exhausted." Luna lifted her forearm from off her eyes and gave me a wry look, a low chuckle rolling from her throat. "What? What's so funny?"

"Nothing. You just didn't seem all that tired when you and Trent were getting your flirt on."

"It wasn't like that," I insisted, although there was a part of me, the part that questioned if that had really been flirting or if it was all in my head, that was still a little excited to hear Luna say that.

I quickly gagged and hog-tied that part, stuffing her into the back of a closet where she couldn't cause any more trouble. "We agreed we'd be friends."

"Friends my ass," she scoffed. "You agreed to go with him to Whisper Falls, a place, by the way, locals *also* keep a secret because tourists back in the day were also using it as a nookie spot. It's incredibly romantic."

"It's only romantic if you're going with that in mind. Trent and I aren't. I'm just showing him a bit of what makes this town so awesome. I'm not interested in him anymore."

"Oh yeah? Is that why you looked at him all moony-faced every time you saw him playing with Renee? Granted, I'll give you that, it was hot. I mean, that big mountain of a man putting that little nugget on his shoulders would get any lady engine running."

"Look, he made it clear where things stood between us, and I respect that. Unlike you, I don't need to climb every sexy man who crosses my path like a tree."

She pointed her finger at me. "Hey, don't knock it till you try it. Climbing those trees is a great form of exercise. Better than cardio."

"You're ridiculous," I said on a laugh.

"Maybe. But the truth is, it's a wonder you didn't get knocked up with all the eye-banging you guys did today. You take him to Whisper Falls, something is definitely going to happen."

I flopped back into the cushions, pressing my shoulders deeper as I crossed my arms and began to sulk. "No it's not. I have tremendous self-control."

"If you say so," she said in a sing-song voice.

I pushed to my feet, refusing to indulge in her childishness for another second. "I do say so. Now, are you staying here tonight or not?"

"Too tired to get to my car," she muttered, closing her eyes.

"Fine. I'll get you a blanket and pillow."

I stomped to the hall closet as she began singing, "Trent and Sawyer, sitting in a tree, k-i-s-s-i-n-g . . ."

She was lucky I didn't smother her with the pillow.

Sixteen

TRENT

IN THE DAYS that had passed since Renee's birthday party,
I'd gone back on nearly everything I'd told myself I had to do.
I no longer gave a shit about keeping my distance or making
sure that the line between Sawyer and me remained clear and
visible.

I was no longer driven by that moral compass I tried so
fucking hard to follow, that sense of responsibility to those
around me, of loyalty to the people I cared most about.

It wasn't about any of that. It was about my need to be
close to her, about not trusting anyone else to keep her or
Renee as safe as I could keep them. I knew the risks of what I
was doing. But just five minutes with her made it all worth it.
I'd never felt this way before, and as fucked up as the whole
situation was, I didn't want it to end.

Truth was, I felt better when I was with her than I had in

longer than I could remember. She made me want to be a better man.

In the past week and a half since the party, I'd found myself making up any excuse just to be close to her. Even though I knew it was a flat-out lie, I kept telling myself that I was just spending time with a friend. Maybe if I said it enough, I could make it true. But considering how my dick never failed to turn into a concrete pillar any time she was around, or I smelled that sea breeze and lilac fragrance that was so distinctly her, I seriously fucking doubted that. Hell, all I *really* had to do was think about her, and I was hard enough to drive fucking nails into wood. And I thought about her all the goddamn time.

I was spending all damn day, every day, in a near-constant state of arousal. If I jerked off one more time, I was afraid I might snap my dick off.

Lifting the glass to my lips, I took a pull of the whiskey I'd poured myself earlier. I usually stuck to beer, but after another afternoon spent with Sawyer at the local coffee shop, another afternoon where I sat so close but couldn't touch her, where I could see her smile but couldn't lean in to taste it, I needed something a whole hell of a lot stronger.

Leaning forward, I placed the tumbler on the coffee table, my eyes drifting to the bowl in the center of the coffee table. I wanted Sawyer's beautiful artwork right where I could see it at all times, a place of prominence. I found myself staring at it constantly throughout the day.

I was pretty sure I'd never owned anything as nice as that

bowl. Back in Hope Valley, my place was only a few steps up from a bachelor pad. There wasn't a single thing on any of the plain beige walls. The furniture was minimalistic. Not in the artsy, stylish way, but because I hadn't had the time or the inclination to bother with furniture shopping.

There was nothing special about the tiny apartment. It hadn't been anything more than a place I went to crash after working so long on a case I could barely keep my eyes open.

The beach house was a million times better by comparison. It was fully furnished with plush, comfortable furniture and decorated to fit the esthetic of a coastal beach town without being tacky. It was pleasant and airy. But it still didn't have anything on Sawyer's home. Sure, it was a little bigger, but that didn't matter.

Sawyer's house was comfortable and homey. It felt welcoming, a place that coaxed you inside and invited you to stay. It was a place you never wanted to leave. I knew that from first-hand experience.

I would have given anything to be there now, but there was something else I needed to do first.

I felt like absolute shit for it, but I'd been avoiding Dalton for a couple weeks now. It was getting harder to lie to him about where I was and what I was doing, so I'd taken the coward's way out, and instead of answering his calls, I'd responded back through short, to-the-point texts that didn't detail much.

I couldn't keep that up any longer. The guilt at avoiding him had me twisted so fucking tight I could barely sleep at night. Not that the guilt from my lying was any better. I was a fucking mess, and if I didn't figure out how to make shit right soon, it was all going to blow up in my face.

Lincoln had stopped giving me shit about telling the truth. He'd said his peace, given his advice. Now he was stepping back and giving me the space and time to make the right choice.

If only I could find the balls to actually fucking do it.

Scrolling through my phone, I pulled up Dalton's name and hit go. He answered on the second ring. "Hey brother, how's tricks?"

"Still tricky," I answered with a chuckle. "How's everything going back there."

"Same shit, different day. You know how it is. Got stuck on another assignment with Xander and Sage."

"Ah, shit."

Sage was Xander's, wife, and she had a serious knack for pushing her man's buttons. Those two loved to fight just so they could go home—or sometimes close themselves in the fucking copy room at the office—and work their shit out in ways none of us wanted to hear.

She handled the filing and most of the admin work at Alpha Omega, but the woman could be a bit of an adrenaline junky, so when she needed a fix, Lincoln would occasionally put her on a job that needed the help of a woman. Being stuck in a van while those two fought over the wire was fun for absolutely no one but them. Each job they teamed up on usually turned into a complete shit show, with Sage going off course every damn time and Xander losing his mind like he hadn't seen it coming. The woman had a wild streak a mile long, so how he managed to be surprised every time she went off script was beyond all of us.

"How the hell did that happen?"

"She brought in a cake for West's birthday, and Linc made the announcement right in the middle of us digging in. I had a mouthful of frosting and couldn't get the words "not it" out in time."

I didn't bother holding back my laughter. "Fuck. Betrayed by your love of sweets. That sucks, man. Sorry to hear it."

"Yeah," he grunted unhappily. "I'm thinkin' of cutting that shit from my diet altogether. Can't risk being caught off guard again."

I knew him well enough to know he wasn't exaggerating. Every one of us hated working jobs with the husband-wife duo that much.

"Don't blame you on that."

"Yeah, well . . ." he trailed off for a beat. "So, how're things where you are? You still on the west coast?"

"Yeah. Still here." When Linc and I agreed to keep the knowledge of Sawyer under wraps for the time being, I'd also figured it would be best not to give any specifics of where I was. If Dalton knew I'd been in one place this whole time, he'd start asking questions I didn't feel comfortable answering, at least not until I could be certain Sawyer's life wouldn't be tossed upside down when more people who knew the truth discovered her location.

"You find anything yet?"

It was the question I knew was coming, but that didn't mean I didn't hate it all the same. "Working on it." Then, for some reason, most likely immense shame, the words, "I think, I'm closing in," came spilling out of my mouth. I just couldn't bring myself to leave him with nothing. I was a prick. A prick for keeping secrets, and a prick for giving him hope instead of the truth.

He let out a soft, barely-there curse. "That's really good to hear, man. I was starting to worry all this was for nothing. Can't tell you how glad I am you think you're on to something. It'll really help Charlotte, too."

Resting my elbows on my knees, I squeezed my eyes closed and pinched the bridge of my nose as my temples began to throb. "Yeah, well, I'm not giving up, and neither should you."

Dalton let out a sigh through the line. "Thanks, man. Appreciate you saying that."

"So, anything new with Knightly? Xander and Hunt still keeping tabs on him through his phone and computer?"

There wasn't a device anywhere that Xander Caine wasn't able to hack into, and we'd stopped asking a long time ago whether or not what he was doing was legal. Hell, we didn't give a shit if it was legal or not. We'd kept a lot of people safe because of the intel Xander was able to give us, and it wasn't like we didn't all do questionable things to arrive at the same outcome. None of us were ones to judge.

"They're still keeping a close eye, but there's nothing new there. Not sure if he's just stopped looking for his wife or if he's being more careful after how bad his guy fucked up, targeting Charlotte. But either way, he hasn't been giving us shit lately."

That unsettling, twisting pain in my gut wasn't going anywhere until Graham Knightly was taken off the board for good. I didn't believe for one second that he'd given up on Sawyer, and I knew there was no way she and Renee would ever be completely safe until he was out of the picture in a permanent way.

"All right, well, keep me posted if you hear anything different."

"You got it. Talk soon."

"Yeah, brother. Talk soon."

We ended the call, and I tossed the phone on the coffee table. Picking up my glass, I tossed back the rest of the whiskey before standing and going to pour myself another.

I was going to need it after that call.

Seventeen

SAWYER

It had been three weeks since Renee's birthday, and to my surprise, Trent was still here, showing no signs of leaving, not that I was concerned about it. It wasn't like I'd miss him when he finally left. Because I wouldn't. Not at all.

I was ashamed to admit it—and there was no way in hell I'd ever tell *her*—but Luna had been right about the falls. That spot was romantic as hell, and despite my passionate insistence that I could control myself, I hadn't actually believed it. That was why I'd been putting Trent off for the past few weeks, making excuses as to why I didn't have time to take him out there to see them. They ranged from having to work, to needing to get some pottery done, to feeling a little flu-y. I wasn't proud of it, but I had well and truly chickened out.

Regardless, we still talked regularly. I occasionally met him for coffee, and he'd come over for dinner a few times. On the days I was at Warren's, he'd swing by to pick up a few items, then stick around to chat with me and Georgia for a bit. He'd even hung with me in the workshop one day, bringing cash with him to purchase that bowl he'd asked about weeks earlier.

When August started to creep to a close, Whitecap began gearing up for the Autumn Harvest Festival that took place the first weekend in September. Everyone was jazzed, and the atmosphere was electric in the days leading up to it.

One of the silver linings was that I didn't have to lie to Trent to get out of taking him to tour the falls. Each year I set up a booth where I sold my pottery, and I always made a killing, so I'd been working day and night on new pieces.

Today was the first day of the festival, and while Sam usually helped me get all my stuff there and set up, when Trent found out I'd have a booth, he'd insisted on lending a hand.

It had been funny as hell to watch Sam scowl and grunt about not needing the extra help, but it only took me half the time to get everything loaded and unloaded, and I didn't have to do *any* of the heavy lifting, so I kept my mouth shut.

Truth was, the childish rivalry between the two of them had turned into quite the show. Loyalty had been cast aside, and everyone in town was placing bets on who'd come out the victor, and, as of right then, it was split down the middle.

Of course Monica had bet on her husband because, in her words, she'd never hear the end of it. I felt like I should cast my vote for Trent. Georgia and Dezzy were steering clear,

"Like Switzerland," Dezzy had told me, and Luna was still waiting to see who'd pull ahead before putting money down on either one of them.

"There's one more box in the back of my truck," Trent said, swiping his forearm across his brow. "I'll take the dolly and grab it. Be right back."

Sam let out a snort. "Real man doesn't need a dolly for one box," he decreed, even though he looked like he was close to passing out. They'd been doing their best to one-up each other all morning long, and it was only a matter of time before one of them gave themselves a hernia.

"The box is half your size. Even you couldn't lift it on your own," Trent challenged.

Sam's chest puffed up. "Watch me."

"You break any of that pottery, you're reimbursing me," I shouted after them as they race walked back to Trent's truck. I shook my head and let out a sigh as I watched them grow smaller and smaller. "Is it just me or is this rivalry getting totally out of hand?"

"It's just you," Monica answered without preamble. "This rivalry has Sam so keyed up"—she leaned into me and whispered the rest so Renee couldn't overhear—"we nearly broke the bed the other night. I hope it never ends."

With a burst of laughter, I got to work unfolding the tables and covering them in colorful scarves while Monica and Renee unpacked boxes.

"Looks like Trent won," Monica said as we finished up with the first table.

I looked back to see Trent pushing the last box on the collapsible dolly while Sam trailed a few feet after him, looking for all the world like someone had just told him that the puppy he'd asked Santa for had fallen out of the sleigh and plummeted to his death.

"All right, I agree that this feud between them is pretty hilarious," I conceded just before the two men entered the tent through the back.

"Thanks for your help, guys. I really appreciate it."

Trent gave me those dimples, paired with a soft look. "Happy to help, darlin'."

"Happy to get in the way is more like it," Sam grumbled.

Trent looked at Sam, the picture of calm and collected. "I think you and I are gonna be best friends. I can feel it."

Monica snorted, and I didn't bother holding back my giggle.

"Come on, Mon. I need a beer."

"It's eight in the morning!" she exclaimed as Sam clamped onto her hand and started dragging her away.

"Fine. A funnel cake, then."

She looked back over her shoulder as she jogged to keep up with her husband. "Sorry, hon! Don't mind him. He gets fussy when he's hungry."

"Not a problem. Thanks for helping."

She raised her voice higher as she got farther away. "I'll swing back by later!"

I waved her off with a smile and went back to arranging everything just right.

"Mommy, whewe's my stuffs go?" Renee asked, her chubby little hands holding a green and purple mug that she'd painted a while back. She'd insisted that some of her stuff be set up for sale this year, so I'd caved and let her choose a few items I usually would have kept for myself.

I stood in front of the table and tapped my chin like I was inspecting everything closely. "I think we should put yours front and center so it's the first thing anyone sees, huh, doodle bug?"

The joy that spread across her face when I took the coffee cup from her hands and put it in its prominent place was all it took to light up my entire world.

I hadn't expected it, but Trent stuck around, helping me and my girl unload all the boxes and set everything up so it was appealing to the eye.

"So what's the story behind the festival?" he asked as he carefully unwrapped one of my larger vases and passed it to me.

"No story, really. Whitecap folks love any excuse for a big party. We have all the usual stuff, Fourth of July, Memorial Day, that kind of thing, but we also have a festival to kick off each new season. Summer's our busiest time of year, but we still get a pretty good turnout for this one and the Winter Jubilee."

He arched a questioning brow, and I held my hands up with a laugh. "Hey, I didn't come up with the names. Take that up with town council. Anyway, this one is my favorite because it's a little more laid back; not so overrun with tourists, but we still have people from the neighboring towns come to celebrate with us."

"Do you set up a booth at every one of these things?"

I snort-laughed. "Oh God no. With the number of events we have a year, it would be a full-time job. I just don't have the time."

"You could, you know."

I looked up from my table organization. "Do what?"

"Do this full-time. Your stuff is gorgeous, Sawyer."

My cheeks started to heat as that warmth unfurled in my chest again. I ducked my head to hide the blush on my cheeks behind my hair. His compliment meant the world to me. I loved working at the general store mainly because I got to spend time with Georgia and Dezzy, but if I were to imagine my dream job, making pottery for a living, putting my art out there in the world, would be it.

Unfortunately, it was impossible to start a small business without an online presence, and I couldn't do that. When I left Graham, I left those little pieces of my former self behind. If you were to google Sawyer Darcy, you'd get a string of women, none of which was me. I wasn't on a single social media platform. I still got strange looks from people when I told them as much, but it was totally worth it if it meant staying safe.

That was why I had an arrangement with shops in town, because other than these events, I couldn't risk putting my name out there to sell my pieces. It was because of their kind hearts and generosity that I got to at least live part of my dream.

"Yeah, maybe one day," I said with a small grin.

One day.

One day the nightmare would be gone, the shadow of Graham Knightly would disappear, and Renee and I wouldn't have to hide anymore. I would never give up hoping that day would come.

Trent

Seeing Sawyer in her element all day had been a high I'd never encountered before. By the time the sun had started to set, her booth had been picked over and emptied out.

The beautiful ceramics drew the people in, but it was Sawyer's smile that lit the entire place and the excitement in her voice when she talked about each piece that closed the deal. People gravitated to her. There was something about her that people wanted to be close to.

I knew the feeling all too well. It was why I hadn't been able to stay away from her. It was why I'd camped out in that tent all day long, only leaving to take Renee to get something to eat or walk around the other booths when she started to get antsy. But even for those short spurts of time, the pull to get back to Sawyer was an intense thing I could hardly ignore.

She and her daughter weren't just under my skin; they'd burrowed themselves deep into my bones. And damn if I didn't love having them there.

"This has to be some kind of record." She beamed as she looked around the empty tent. "I can't believe I've already sold out."

"I'm not the least bit surprised. You're unbelievably talented. Everyone who came by today saw that."

She smiled up at me, those eyes the color of fall leaves shining with a warmth that set them on fire. Her gorgeous face was soft and gentle, and the impact of that look hit me center mass. I felt it through every inch of my body, trailing across my skin before settling low and making my dick hard.

Christ, I was quickly becoming obsessed with this woman.

Lincoln's warning played over and over in my head, a continuous loop that left me in a near constant state of unsettled, but I couldn't bring myself to take his advice. The thought that Sawyer might not look at me the way she was just then if she knew the truth, the idea she might take herself and her daughter away from me . . . I couldn't handle it. So I kept up the lie, all the while knowing it was only a matter of time before that first domino fell, taking the rest of them with it.

"Mommy? Can we go pway games now?" Renee asked, her voice popping the bubble of heat I hadn't realized had formed around us.

Sawyer blinked her hazy eyes, clearly just as affected by

whatever had been brewing between us as I was. She took a step back, giving her head a shake in an attempt to clear it. And fuck me if knowing she was still so affected by me wasn't a turn on. "Uh, yeah. Sure, doodle bug."

With nothing left to pack up, she grabbed her bag and we started out of the booth toward the boardwalk where all the games and rides were clustered.

And I felt ten fucking feet tall as I walked through the crowds with those two girls at my side.

Eighteen

SAWYER

MONICA, Renee, and I stood a good fifteen feet back from the ring toss booth, our arms laden down with stuffed animals of every shape and color. This was only the latest in a whole slew of competitions.

When we'd run into Monica and Sam about an hour earlier, I thought we'd get to enjoy some time with friends, see the sights, maybe grab something to eat, but the rivalry between Trent and Sam reared its ugly head once again.

So far, they'd tried to out-do each other in the bean bag toss, the high striker, throwing baseballs at weighted milk bottles, and sabotaging each other at whack-a-mole.

"Ha! Yes! Suck on that," Trent crowed when one of his rings circled the top of an empty soda bottle.

"That wasn't skill. It was luck," Sam groused.

"Call it whatever you want. I still beat you." He looked

back to the kid manning the booth. "I'll take the pink panda."

I let out a sigh. That was our third pink panda so far. He'd tried to claim a goldfish in a bag of water after his win in the potato sack race, but I told him unless he planned on giving the thing a home, he needed to pick something else.

"Mommy, I'm hungwy."

Monica joined her. "Yeah, I could eat too."

I looked down at my little girl. The purple unicorn clutched in her arms was nearly as big as she was. "All right, sweetie. I'll handle it."

"This game is rigged," Sam continued to complain. "I want a rematch."

"Dude, it's a carnival game. They're *all* rigged."

I cleared my throat and raised my voice. "You do what you have to do, but we're going to get some dinner."

The three of us turned and started toward the food tents as Trent spoke up behind us. "Bet I can eat more turkey legs than you."

"You're on."

Oh, for the love of God.

The cab of Trent's truck was silent as he pulled up to the curb in front of my house and killed the engine. Renee had been fading before we left the festival, to the point that when she lifted her arms for Trent to pick her up, he hadn't hesitated.

She'd passed out the moment she was buckled into the car seat and hadn't stirred once on the way home.

"She's really out," he said softly as he twisted in the driver seat to look back at her, a tender dimpled grin on his face.

I copied his position, letting out a laugh at the row of stuffed animals lined up beside her on the back seat. To say Trent had gone overboard would have been like calling the ocean a little wet. "It was an active day. Then she got a little bored watching you and Sam act like children," I added on a giggle.

He twisted his head, those green-brown eyes smiling at me as he said in a low voice, "I'm telling you, I'm wearing the guy down. We'll be best friends in no time."

"I'm not going to hold my breath for that," I teased.

He winked and my belly fluttered wildly. "You'll see. How about I get Little Bit and you get all her new toys? Sound like a plan?"

"Works for me." I climbed out of his truck and moved around to gather up all Renee's new babies, waiting until Trent had her out of her car seat to grab the spotted puppy she'd been using as a pillow. "You know, between these and all the presents she got on her birthday, her room is overflowing with toys. It's pretty obscene."

I made the mistake of looking back as I started up the front walk. Renee's head rested on his shoulder. One of his arms was braced beneath her, his other hand running circles on her back. I quickly spun back around before I did something incredibly stupid, like kiss him again.

Damn it. I hated when Luna was right. She'd never let me live it down.

Doing my best to shift all the stuffed toys to one arm, I shoved my key into the lock and pushed the door open, stepping to the side so Trent could get Renee in out of the chilled night air.

The days were still comfortable in early September, but the nights had grown milder, especially right here on the coast. It was my favorite time of year, where I could pull out all my soft, fuzzy cardigans and leggings without shame. With autumn kissing the air, the smells were just a bit different. It was the season that led up to all the best holidays. And the biggest reason I loved fall so much . . . pumpkin spiced everything came back.

I followed Trent as he moved through the entryway and down the hall to Renee's room. Dumping her newest toys in a pile by the closet to be organized later, I tried my best not to feel it in my belly when Trent laid Renee down on her bed like she was the most fragile piece of glass, brushing the hair back from her face and pressing a kiss to her forehead before standing tall.

"I—" I cleared the croak from my throat and started again. "I'll be right out, I'm just going to get her in her pajamas and tucked in. Make yourself comfortable. I have some beer in the fridge if you want one."

"Sounds good. Want me to grab you one? Or maybe get you something else?"

"There's an uncorked bottle of wine on the counter by the fridge if you wouldn't mind."

"Not at all," he said in that soft rumble of his that did unimaginable things to my insides. "I'll see you out there."

It wasn't until he left the room and his footsteps receded down the hall that the burning pressure in my chest alerted me to the fact that I'd been holding my breath. Letting out a whoosh of air, I moved to my little girl and got her ready for bed. She was so deep in sleep she didn't stir as I moved her around; her arms and legs were like jelly as I changed her from her clothes to her PJs and got her situated beneath the covers.

"I love you so much, baby girl," I whispered against the top of her head, inhaling deeply and filling my lungs with her sweet, powdery scent. With one last kiss to her chubby cheek, I stood, staring down at her for a few seconds before summoning up the courage to leave the sanctuary of her bedroom.

I didn't know why I was suddenly so nervous to be alone with Trent, but as I moved down the hallway, my knees shook and my heart beat so hard in my chest it was a wonder Trent couldn't hear it.

When I rounded the corner into the living room and saw him sitting on my couch, the picture of relaxation, I was slammed with the thought that he looked so perfect in my house. Like he belonged. Like I never wanted him to leave.

That was a dangerous road to go down. It was full of painful potholes and dead-ended at heartbreak. So I quickly back-pedaled out of the red zone, reminding myself that we were just friends. Even though it *felt* like so much more.

When those smoky eyes, full of affection, came to me, the blood started rushing in my ears so loud it was nearly all I could hear.

"Everything good?"

I moved to where he'd placed my wine glass on the coffee table in front of the sofa and picked it up before curling into a ball against the opposite arm, pressing myself deep to maintain a good bit of space between us. "Yep. She didn't even blink. I think she's out for the rest of the night," I answered before taking a hearty sip.

"She had a big day. You have a natural born sales woman with her. When she gets older she could dominate the world."

I smiled around the rim of my glass. "I don't really care what she ends up doing as long as she's happy. Even if it is world domination. That's all that matters to me."

"As long as she has you to lead her, she'll turn out great."

Oh man. He was too much. "Thanks," I said on a breath. "That's sweet of you to say."

"Just telling the truth." His lifted his beer to his lips and took a pull, and for a second, I was transfixed by the way his throat worked around the swallow, how the thick cords tensed and his Adam's apple bobbed. Before that moment, I didn't know it was possible for throats to be sexy, but there you had it. "I had a great time today," he said, jolting me back into the present. "Thank you for letting me tag along with you and Renee."

"We liked having you with us. It was a lot of fun." I gave him a droll look. "Even when you and Sam were acting like five-year-olds."

"Yes, well, I'll let you in on a little secret. Men never really mature past adolescence."

My head tipped back on a laugh. "Hate to break it to you, but that's probably the worst kept secret of all time. And it just reiterates how lucky I am that I had a girl."

The smile slowly drained from his expression, replaced with something soft and full of heat that made my heart beat even faster. "Not sure which one of you is luckier. Renee or you."

He couldn't keep doing this. He was making this so much harder than it needed to be. "You probably shouldn't say things like that," I said in a barely-there voice.

He canted his head to the side as he slid a little closer, closing some of the distance. There was still about a foot of space between us, but it was close enough that his scent, that pine and clean laundry, was all I could smell. God, I could have drowned in that scent. "Why not?"

"We agreed to be just friends. When you're being sweet like this, it's really hard to remember that's all we're supposed to be. It isn't fair."

Something hard flitted across his features, turning his expression to granite. He squeezed his eyes closed and turned his head away, inhaling deeply through his nose as his jaw ticked. When he finally looked back at me, I could have sworn I saw something that looked a whole hell of a lot like sadness and uncertainty swimming in his gaze.

"What if I can't do it?"

My forehead crinkled in confusion. "Can't do what?"

"What if I can't just be your friend? What if I want more?"

"What—" My tongue suddenly felt too thick, my mouth as dry as the sand outside my back gate. "What are you saying?"

He scooted toward me again, closing those last remaining inches. "I thought I could be your friend, but I can't. Trying not to touch and kiss you when you're near me is just too goddamn hard."

Trent

I'd meant every word I'd just said to her. I couldn't fight this pull to her anymore. I didn't have it in me. I was crossing a line I would never be able to come back from, and I didn't care.

What I felt for her surpassed all logic. Responsibility be damned. I'd suffer whatever consequences came. I'd deal with any fallout between Dalton and me. I'd face Lincoln's wrath. It was worth it just to fucking *finally* have her.

"Tell me this isn't what you want and I'll get up right now and walk away. You say the word and this stops, here and now. But I'm telling you, Sawyer, I want you. I want to touch you and taste you. I want to slide inside you and feel you squeeze around me. I want to see your face when I make you come. If that's not what you want, I'll respect that, but I'm done fighting what I feel for you."

Those sultry eyes of hers lit with fire and passion. Her pink tongue darted out, swiping at that full bottom lip. Then she said the words that put me out of my misery.

"Then don't fight it."

That was all I needed to hear. My hand shot out, slipping beneath the thick, silky fall of her hair to grasp the back of her neck, pulling her into me and slamming my lips against hers. And just like that, I was done for.

Nineteen

SAWYER

Every inhibition I had, every doubt or fear, fell from my mind the instant his tongue parted my lips and dove inside my mouth.

The slightly bitter taste of hops from the beer he'd been drinking invaded my taste buds, making me feel nice and floaty.

His grip on my neck tightened as I met his tongue stroke for stroke, the pads of his fingers pressing into my flesh and giving me a taste of the brute force he was capable of.

But it didn't scare me. Not one damn bit.

I craved more.

I didn't want to be treated like fine china. I wanted to be taken. We could do sweet and gentle another time, but what I wanted right then was his desire for me to overcome him so profoundly that we crashed together, creating a brutal storm.

It had been so long since I'd been with a man, and even

then, my experiences with Graham over that last year had been anything but enjoyable. He'd either take what he wanted whether I was a willing participant or not, or he'd come before I was anywhere near a release of my own.

All those years of pent-up sexual frustration came to a head right there on the couch in the middle of my living room with Trent.

I wanted passion. I wanted more of that feeling he stirred inside of me. I wanted to know what it felt like to be claimed and craved and adored.

I got all of that just from kissing him, so I couldn't wait to experience what it would be like to have him moving inside of me.

"Trent," I breathed into his mouth, my heart hammering so hard that I was sure he could feel it.

"Right here, baby," he grunted, trailing biting, stinging kisses along the column of my neck.

"I want you."

"Tell me what you need," he rasped, dragging his teeth across my collarbone and sending shivers throughout my entire body. "Say it and I'll give it to you, I swear."

"I want you inside me." The brazenness of that confession made my cheeks heat, but I was too far gone to be embarrassed. I wanted what I wanted, and I didn't give a damn about anything else in that moment. "I want you to fuck me."

A primal growl ripped from his throat at my confession, setting off a million tiny fires in my blood. Grabbing me by the waist, he lifted me up like I weighed nothing at all to straddle his lap before shifting us both and placing me on my back. He laid himself over me, the weight of his massive body pressing me deeper into the cushions and surrounding me. I'd never felt so secure in my whole life.

His head came out of my neck, his eyes black with lust and need. "You wet for me, Sawyer?"

For some reason, hearing him call me that gave me momentary pause. I loved the life that Sawyer had built, and I wouldn't trade it for anything, but in that moment, with him, I wanted to be *me*. I would have given anything to be Trent and Cheyanne just then.

Shaking off the melancholy of that thought, I lifted my head and nipped at his bottom lip before breathing, "Yes."

He dropped his forehead to mine on a groan that made it sound like he was in pain and shifted his hips, pressing the steel of his erection against my most sensitive place. My head fell back on a moan as he rocked again, rubbing against my aching clit. "Trent, please." I was quickly losing my mind and loving every minute of it.

He feasted on my neck, introducing me to pleasure points I hadn't known existed as he braced himself on his forearm between me and the back of the couch. With his other hand, he touched the pulse throbbing like a drum in my throat and began dragging the pads of his fingers down, trailing between my collarbones then my breasts. "Your heart's beating like crazy," he husked out.

"That's because you're *driving* me crazy," I declared

indignantly, shooting him an impatient glare, "Touch me, Trent. Stop playing games."

I was on fire, burning alive from the inside out. And what did that jerk do? He laughed.

"But the games make it so much more fun." He kept up his torturously slow pace, sliding past my belly button before popping the button on my jeans and lowering the zipper, dipping past the waistband.

I sucked in a shaky breath when his fingertips breached my panties, excitement and adrenaline coursing through my veins at the speed of a race car circling the track.

"Jesus," he gritted when his palm cupped the very center of me, his middle finger swirling through the evidence of my arousal. "You weren't kidding, were you, baby? You're fucking soaked for me."

"Oh God," I whimpered, arching my neck and back and digging my head deeper into the cushions, desperately trying to get closer. The tip of his middle finger barely pressed inside me, and I could already feel my walls trying to clamp down around the excruciating emptiness.

"You want to come, Sawyer?"

"Yes," I nearly cried. "So bad. I'm losing my mind."

The bastard finally put me out of my misery then, shoving two fingers as deep as they could go while pressing on my clit with his thumb. I let out a sharp cry at the delicious invasion. My knees fell farther apart, one foot falling off the couch and bracing on the floor for leverage as my hands came up to his shoulders, my nails scraping across those hard, unyielding muscles beneath his shirt.

"That's it, baby," he coaxed as he finger-fucked me, my hips snapping in time with each plunge. "Ride my hand. Let me see how beautiful you look when you completely let go.

He did something just then, twisting his fingers and stirring them in a come-hither motion that brushed up against a place inside of me that no man had ever found before. That was all it took to set me off. Fireworks exploded behind my eyelids as I held on to Trent with every bit of strength I had, riding the waves of the best orgasm I'd had in *years*.

I was still coming down when Trent pulled his hand back and knifed off the couch. Before I had a chance to worry or asked what he was doing, he bent and hefted me up, throwing me over his shoulder in a fireman's hold.

"What are you doing?" I asked as he stalked from the living room to my bedroom. "We're supposed to be having sex!"

"Not fucking you the first time on your couch," he grunted. "I'm taking you to bed so I have room to play."

A smile stretched across my lips, the tingling in my core building up all over again.

A second later, he was kicking my bedroom door closed. A surprised laugh rushed from my throat when he tossed me onto the mattress so hard I bounced twice, but that humor melted away when his fingers wrapped around the waistband of my jeans. He ripped them and my panties down so fast a breeze skated across my fevered skin.

In no time at all, he had me completely naked and was staring down at me like I was a priceless work of art. "Fuck me. You're so goddamn beautiful." It was said with a reverence I'd never heard from a man before, and moved me so much the backs of my eyes began to sting.

Before the threat of tears could get any worse, Trent reached behind his neck and ripped his shirt over his head. "Holy God," I breathed, taking in all that tanned, rippled flesh. It was the first time I'd gotten a glimpse at the man's bare chest, and it was so much better than anything I could have ever possibly imagined.

"Keep looking at me like that, beautiful," he rasped aggressively. "That look on your face makes me so fucking hard."

He shed his pants and boxer briefs on that declaration, revealing the long, hard, thick truth of that statement. And *oh my God*, I wasn't sure he could fit!

"Don't worry," he said with a grin, having seen the fear on my face. I was sure I looked like a deer caught in the headlights, but in that moment, there was the very *real* concern of being impaled to death. Funny thing was, I couldn't help but think that that was the *perfect* way to go.

"I'll take care of you, Sawyer. I promise you're going to love every minute of what I'm about to do to you."

His left hand reached down to squeeze his length, stroking upward to the very tip where he twisted his wrist before traveling back down. His balls hung heavy between his thighs. He looked like a living canvas. A perfect work of art of the male form, standing naked in my bedroom.

In his other hand, he revealed a condom I hadn't seen him pull out. Bringing the foil packet to his mouth, he ripped it open with his teeth and made quick work of sheathing himself.

"On your knees, baby. Facing the headboard." His tone was gentle and thick like the purest honey, but there was no denying it was a command he expected me to obey. And I did. Happily.

Flipping over, I faced the headboard and lifted up on my knees, placing my palm in the pillows stacked at the top of the bed. A shiver trickled up my spine when the mattress depressed with his weight, and a second later his lips brushed across the left globe of my ass.

"Sexiest ass I've ever seen," he rumbled against my skin, placing a kiss on the small of my back next. "Sexiest back." Another kiss, this one just a bit higher up.

He continued to talk as he kissed his way up my spine. "Best fucking legs in the world." He complimented my arms, my hair, my breast. Hell, he even complimented my shoulders as he kissed each one, curving himself over my back and rubbing his length between my slick folds.

I'd never felt so beautiful in all my life. It was a miracle I'd been able to hold myself up, because I felt like I was melting. I was the ice and he was the flame being held up to me.

He finally reached my head, snaking his arm around and taking my chin in his big hand, forcing me to look back at him. "And those eyes," he murmured. "Fuck me, I could get lost in those eyes forever."

Oh God. I felt like I was going to cry again. My chest shuddered as I pulled in a breath and whispered, "Trent."

"You ready for me, baby?"

I'd never been more ready for anything in all my life. "Yes. Now."

Still curled around me, he tipped his hips back until the head of him notched into place, then he drove in, both of us crying out at the shock of coming together completely.

"Fucking *Christ*," he hissed through clenched teeth. "Knew you'd fit me beautifully."

His size was overwhelming, almost painful, but still the most intense pleasure I'd ever experienced. The way he filled me completely, stretching me nearly to my breaking point, brought something to life inside of me I'd never known was there. I felt wild, nearly feral.

"You okay?" he panted over my shoulder, and I could feel the strain in his entire body as he struggled to keep himself in check, holding back. I didn't want him to do that. I wanted him to *let go* and join me in the beautiful, wicked, destructive tempest we were creating together.

"I'm perfect," I said on a purr. "But I won't stay that way if you don't start moving."

He didn't make me say it twice. Grabbing hold of my wrists, Trent brought them to the headboard and wrapped my fingers around the top of it, threading his through mine to keep them in place.

"Hold on, baby."

That was all the warning I got before he pulled out to the very tip and slammed back in. Over and over, fucking me the way I'd wanted, the way I'd craved and begged for. His cock pummeled me, a driving force between my thighs, and It. Was. *Perfect*. In no time at all, that desire he'd been building inside me reached its peak. That pressure coiled so tight I thought it might destroy me once it finally snapped.

The headboard banged against the wall, a muffled thud that echoed each driving thrust and animalistic grunt that fell past his lips. I was so wet I could feel it dripping down the inside of my thighs.

My walls began to quiver, my moans turning into higher-pitched whimpers as I grew closer and closer.

"I feel it, Sawyer. You're like a goddamn glove. Let go and give it to me."

I did as he ordered, shattering into oblivion, coming so hard I saw stars and the edges of my vision began to blur.

I was dangerously close to blacking out, but I couldn't allow that to happen. I wanted to experience ever single second of this. My world exploded in technicolor as one release fed into another. Each time I crested one wave, another would sweep over me, pulling me beneath the surface until my lungs were screaming for oxygen.

"Fuck yes. Fuck, baby. That's it. I'm coming," Trent grunted before burying himself deep and coming on a groan he muffled in the back of my hair.

Twenty

SAWYER

THE SECONDS TICKED into minutes as we gently drifted back down to Earth. The air in my bedroom was humid, thick with the smell of sex and sweat.

"Goddamn," Trent groaned as he pried my fingers off the headboard and shifted us onto the bed. I sucked in a surprised gasp at the sensation when he slipped out of me, the feeling a bit raw, like a million exposed nerves.

It was *incredible*.

"My God," he panted as he rolled to his back, pulling me with him so I was nestled against his side, and flinging his forearm over his eyes. "That was . . . Shit, Sawyer. I don't have words. We need to rest up and replenish our fluids because we have to do that about a million more times tonight."

I let out a little giggle and snuggled deeper into him. "I

don't think I have a million more times in me." I was *sore*. In the very best way, but still sore. It had been *a long time*.

He tilted his chin down, looking at me with concern deep in his smoky eyes. "I didn't hurt you, did I?"

Stacking my hands on his chest, I rested my chin on top of them so I could look into those eyes I wanted to swim in. "Not at all. I feel great. Better than I have in a really long time."

"Glad to hear it," he said on a chuckle, his body shaking mine with humor.

My smile took over my whole face, splitting my cheeks. "That said, I think you might have broken me. I need some time to heal."

His expression grew serious as he reached up to brush the hair back from my forehead. "Let me stay with you tonight," he said in a soft gentle voice.

I curled my lips between my teeth and bit down. I didn't want anything more than to fall asleep in this man's arms and wake up beside him, to have his smell imprint on my sheets so it would still be there once he was gone. But I had to think about Renee.

Seeing the struggle written on my face his expression grew tender as he squeezed me tighter. "I can wake up before Little Bit, if that's what you're worried about. She doesn't have to know I was here. I'm just not ready to leave you."

God, this man already had the power to break my heart, and there was still so much of him I didn't know. And he didn't know me. Not the *real* me. Not at all.

Then there was the fact that he was leaving soon. He wasn't forever, couldn't be. His place was somewhere else. And I'd let him pull me under his spell. No, that wasn't right. That made it sound like it was his fault when it really wasn't. We were equals in this. I'd done it to myself. Unlike what I told Luna, apparently I had no self-control whatsoever.

A fact that was confirmed when my whole body melted deeper into his and I smiled with a contentment I'd never felt before. "I'd like that."

He let out a sigh like my answer had just lifted a weight that had been resting on his chest. Pulling me up higher, he pressed his lips to mine in a quick but hard kiss before releasing me.

"Let me go deal with the condom real quick and we can get some shut eye."

I rolled off him and watched as he climbed from my bed and moved across the room without an ounce of shame. Not that he had reason to feel any. The man's body could have been cut from marble, and the appendage between his thighs would make angels weep and fall to earth.

His voice held a hint of laughter as he said, "I can feel you staring at my ass."

"Of course I am. It's a great ass."

The bathroom door shut on his deep, raspy laugh, and I quickly climbed from the bed, moving to the dresser. I grabbed a pair of underwear—they weren't the sexiest, but they also weren't my period panties or laundry-day undies—and a simple cotton spaghetti strap nightgown.

He came back out of the bathroom just as I slipped the nightgown over my hips, and when he took me in, a grin tugged at his lips, poking those dimples deep.

"Christ. Just when I think you can't get any cuter, you go and prove me wrong."

I looked down at myself, brushing at my nightgown and my face flushed red. There was nothing special about it. It was plain blue with not a hint of lace or anything. The fact he thought it made me look cute made me feel like a million bucks.

He moved to his discarded clothes, snatching his boxer briefs up and pulling them back on. "You ready for bed?"

A yawn ripped from my throat before I could get a word out, answering for me. My whole body felt thoroughly used and blissfully exhausted. "Definitely." I moved to the bed, feeling a twinge between my thighs that made me smile as I pulled the covers back and climbed in. Trent moved around to the other side, turning out the light and climbing in.

It had been years since I'd shared a bed with a man, and I'd been so disgusted with Graham for so much of our marriage that I went out of my way, curling into a tight ball at the very edge of the bed, to stay as far away from him as possible. That had been fine with him. But before getting situated, Trent rolled to face me, hooking me around the middle with his strong arm and pulling me to the middle of the mattress so he could wrap himself around me, his big spoon to my little.

With that done, he rested his head on the pillow, and I

lay there, surrounded by his strength and the scent of pine and clean laundry, listening as his breaths evened out.

"Trent?" I whispered into the darkness a few minutes later.

"Yeah, sweetheart?"

"How old are you?" Now that we'd had sex, the fact that I didn't know the smallest things, such as his age, was starting to needle at my brain.

"Be thirty-five in December."

"Oh. Okay."

We lapsed back into silence for a few minutes before, "What's your last name?"

His chest shook against my back with silent laughter. "Montgomery."

"Trent Montgomery." I tested his full name out on my tongue and discovered I really liked it. "That's a really good name." The kind of name that belonged to the hero in Georgia's romance novels. Trent Montgomery could easily be a marauding pirate or rakish duke. "It fits you."

I heard the smile in his voice as he rumbled, "Thanks, baby."

Did Sawyer Darcy fit me? I hoped so. When I'd gone into hiding, I'd picked it for a very important reason. Sawyer had been my mother's maiden name, and Darcy came from her love of Pride and Prejudice. The memory of her always reading that book, of the several copies she kept lined on a shelf of prominence in the living room, was still strong. While he could be prickly, for sure, she loved Mr. Darcy. I wanted to be as close to her as possible; that was how Sawyer Darcy had been born.

It was on that thought that his arm around my middle clenched and his lips brushed the back of my head.

"Sleep, baby. It's late and you're beat."

How he sensed that my mind was racing was beyond me, but having him there, his strong, reassuring presence, calmed me, and in no time at all, I drifted off.

"Sawyer, baby. Wake up."

I let out a groan, swatting at that the offending finger booping the end of my nose as I squeezed my eyes closed tighter. "More sleep," I grunted, rolling away and yanking the covers over my head. "Too early."

A velvety chuckle flooded my belly with warmth, but it still wasn't enough to get me out of the nice, warm cocoon that was my bed. "Honey, time to get up. I need to go before Little Bit wakes up."

As much as I didn't want to—and I *really* freaking didn't want to—I threw the covers back and slowly peeled one eyelid up, blinking to bring the bleary Trent hovering above me into better focus. "What time is it?" I asked, sounding like I'd gargled rocks the night before.

"A little after five. I didn't know what time she usually gets up, so I didn't want to take any chances."

I let out a pathetic little sob and jutted my bottom lip out. "So early," I whined.

His dimples still affected me just as strongly as they always did, even though the sun had barely started to rise yet. *Damn him.* "I know, baby. But you need to lock up after me." His grin turned a bit wicked as he added, "And I want to make out at the door for a while before I have to go."

I suddenly felt wide awake. "I can get on board with that plan," I mumbled as I pushed up to sitting and swiped the hair back from my face.

"Thought that might get you," he said with a laugh, taking my hand to help me out of the bed. I wasn't so awake that I moved easily. I let out a groan and let myself go limp so he had to drag me to my feet. Was I proud of it? Not really. But Sleepy Sawyer was a bit of a mess.

I padded down the hall on heavy feet, hand in hand with Trent until we reached the front door. Turning to face me, he released my hand and placed his on my hip, pulling me flush against him. "Yesterday was really great," he rumbled.

"Yeah, it was," I replied dreamily.

One side of his mouth hooked up higher than the other. "Last night was even better."

I giggled uncontrollably. "Yeah, it *really* was." I gave my eyebrows a lewd waggle.

Reaching up, he cupped the side of my neck in his palm and traced my jawline with the pad of his thumb. "Can I see you again today?"

It was still the weekend, so I wasn't on at the general store until Monday. Georgia and Dezzy were really good at giving me the weekends off when the daycare was closed so I didn't have to scramble to find someone to babysit Renee. On the off chance there was an emergency and they needed me, either one of them would watch her for me, or they'd let me bring her in, something Renee loved because she got to play cashier.

I didn't have anything planned other than spending time with Renee and maybe spending a little time in my workshop if she was in the mood to paint.

"You can see me any day," I said teasingly. "It's a really small town, and you're staying just down the road."

He smirked, lowering one of his hands so he could give my ass cheek a pinch. "Smartass. You know what I mean."

"Yeah. I just like messing with you," I said on a shrug. "But to answer your question, yes. You can see me again. It's just me and Renee today, but I'm sure she wouldn't mind you joining us. Maybe we can head back to the Harvest Fest, this time without a ridiculous show of manliness between you and Sam. I can show you around some of the best booths."

"You wouldn't mind me crashing your time with your girl?"

I lifted up on my tiptoes, pressing my lips against his. "Not at all," I breathed.

After that, he gave me that make-out he'd promised before we finally forced ourselves to break apart so he could head back to his place. It was damn good, and by the time he left, I felt like a teenager sneaking her boyfriend out of the house.

I didn't know how long this thing between us was going to last, and I didn't know what the future held. I was almost certain I was going to suffer a pretty nasty heartbreak by the end of it, but I made the decision the night before to take Luna's advice and start living a little for myself. I was going to have fun. Consequences be damned.

Twenty-One

SAWYER

It was the Tuesday after my epic weekend with Trent, and while I was riding high, I was completely exhausted.

Renee had been a bundle of energy during the days, even more than usual thanks to Trent being around most of the time. Then at night he'd kept me up to all hours, doing things to my body I hadn't known were possible.

I'd had a smile on my face all morning long that I couldn't wipe away. It even stayed in place when I'd accidentally dozed off at the register during my shift. Georgia had sent me to lunch early, a knowing smile on her face, with orders to make sure to caffeinated myself before I came back.

I texted Luna to see if she wanted to meet me at Drip before I had to head back to work, and by the time I gave my order to Monica—a pumpkin spice latte with an extra shot of espresso since they were back in season—she was sashaying through the door, pulling her over-sized sunglasses off her face and tucking them up into her hair.

She met me at the register and gave me an appraising stare. "You look tired."

"Thanks." I deadpanned. "It's always nice to hear that I look like shit."

"I didn't say you looked like shit." She narrowed her eyes, her examination more scrutinizing this time. "You actually look really great. Like all glowy and stuff but tired—" She cut herself off on a gasp that would have put every soap opera diva to shame. "Oh my God, you had sex!" she whisper-yelled.

Like she had sonar hearing, Monica popped up right then with my drink. "What's this now?"

Luna jabbed her finger in my face. "*This* little hussy had a dirty sex romp this weekend!"

"Okay. First off, lower your voice because not everyone in here needs to know my business."

Monica let out a yelp. "Holy shit. She's not denying it!"

I chose to ignore that and kept going. "Second, I'm not a hussy, and it wasn't a dirty little sex romp. That makes it sound like we spent the entire weekend in bed. We didn't." A sly smile tugged at the corners of my mouth. "Just the nights."

My friends let out whoops of laughter that drew the attention of the rest of the patrons in the coffee shop.

"Nothing to see here," Monica said loudly. "Go back to your business or no more coffee for you." All the eyes in Drip shot away from us, the threat of not having coffee too great for anyone to attempt to call her bluff. As soon as the coast was clear, my friends turned their attention back to me. "All right, spill. We want to know *everything*."

In hushed voices, I filled them in on everything that had happened, starting with how everything had escalated the first night of the Harvest Fest. I told them about how he'd spent every night since then in my bed, sleeping tangled together until the early hours of the morning when he had to leave so Renee didn't catch him and get any ideas. I told them how he made me feel, the things he said that made me swoon, and how we couldn't seem to get enough of each other.

By the time I finished, they both looked like they'd just watched the part from *The Notebook* when Noah professed his love to Allie after so many years of being torn apart from her.

"So what does this mean for you guys?" Monica asked with stars in her eyes.

"I don't know. I mean, he's just visiting, so it's not like this is going the distance, right? He's a tourist." I looked to Luna and explained, "I'm taking your advice and having fun."

For some reason, that made her expression fall into sadness. "Normally I'd be the first to congratulate you on your sexual awakening, but are you sure you aren't maybe a little too invested in this for it to just be fun? I'm worried you're going to end up hurt."

The smile I gave her reflected some of her sadness back to

her. "I love you for being worried, but it's too late to protect myself from that." I shrugged, giving her the truth. "I'm in this now. Even if I were to end things with him tomorrow, it wouldn't matter. I feel something for him; that isn't going to change. Will it suck when he finally leaves? Absolutely. But I'm tough." Tougher than these ladies knew. "I'll get over it. I'm tired of living in this bubble. I really like Trent. I like spending time with him. But mostly, I like who I am when I'm around him. I don't want to give that feeling up just yet."

"Amen to that," Monica said, her voice thick with emotion and her eyes glistening. "You deserve to feel as special as you are, honey."

I reached across the counter and placed my hand on hers, giving it a squeeze before looking back to my best friend in the whole world.

Luna squared her shoulders and lifted her chin, standing up straight, like liquid steel had been poured down her spine. "I don't know a person walking this planet who deserves happiness more than you, so if that's what he's giving you, I'm fucking thrilled, babe. *Thrilled.* And whatever happens down the road happens. We'll be here to help you deal, whatever that may be."

"Hell yeah we will," Monica stated in agreement.

There wasn't a day that passed that I didn't thank whatever higher power was responsible for leading me to this town and these incredible people.

Thanks to the two coffees I'd downed on my lunch break, I'd managed to stay awake once I returned to work.

I was in the middle of ringing up Mr. Armstrong's weekly purchase of canned corned beef hash and microwavable dinners—the man was a lifelong bachelor—when my cellphone started ringing from my back pocket.

"Let me just put that on silent, real quick."

He gave me a kind look. "Do what you need to do. Don't you worry about me."

I pulled the phone out of my pocket, frowning when I saw the name flashing across the screen. "I'm so sorry, Mr. Armstrong. It's my daughter's daycare. Do you mind—?"

He waved off my apology. "Got nowhere else to be. Go ahead and take it, sweetheart."

Shooting the sweet old man a grateful smile, I stepped back from the register and swiped my finger across the screen before bringing my phone to my ear. "Hello?"

"Hi, Sawyer. It's Misty," the director of the daycare greeted.

"Hey. What's going on? Is Renee all right?"

"She's okay, but it seems that she may have come down with a little bug. She was fine when you dropped her off, but she started complaining that her stomach hurt shortly before lunch, and she just threw up a few minutes ago. We checked her temp, and there's no fever, but a few of the other kids have been out recently with a stomach virus. Silver lining is that it's one of those fast-moving bugs. They've been bouncing back within a day or two, but it looks like she may have caught it.

"Oh no. Okay. I'll be there as soon as I can."

"No rush, honey. She's in with another teacher right now, having a rest. We'll see you when you get here."

"Thanks, Misty."

Georgia appeared by my side before I'd even ended the call. "What's wrong?"

"Looks like Renee's come down with a bug that's making its way through the daycare."

"Poor baby." She scooted in, easing me out of the way of the register with her hip. "You go take care of that little girl. I'll finish ringing up Mr. Armstrong."

"Thank you, hon." Leaning in, I placed a kiss to Georgia's temple and unpinned my name tag from my shirt, dropping it in the little bin under the counter before grabbing my purse.

"No need to thank me. Family comes before everything. Get that precious baby better, and don't hesitate to call if you need anything."

I blew her a kiss before shoving out the door and heading for my car, thankful I'd decided to drive this morning because the forecast was calling for rain later in the day.

In no time at all, I had my girl back home and was settling her in the living room so I could be close by. "How you feeling, doodle bug?" I asked as I sat on the edge of the cushions and brushed the hair back from her face. I'd made her a little bed with a pillow and blanket on the love seat, and put the wastebasket nearby in case of more accidents. As soon as I got her comfortable, I turned on the television to one of her favorite movies.

"Yucky," she answered, her little face, normally all smiles and brightness, pale and drawn into a pout. Renee didn't get sick often, but when she did, she was usually down for the count. I hated seeing her like this.

"I know, baby. I'm sorry, but I'm going to make you all better, okay?" Seeing my baby, normally so full of life and energy, curled up in a ball because she didn't feel well never failed to leave me with this yawning sense of helplessness. All I could do was make her comfortable and wait it out, hoping it didn't take long for her to rebound.

"Will you stay wiff me, Momma?" she asked, her little voice belying just how bad she felt.

"Of course I will." I brushed me fingers through her soft hair and smiled down at her. "I'm not going anywhere."

Shifting on the love seat, I snuggled into the cushions with her and hit play on the remote. Fifteen minutes into the cartoon, so brightly colored I felt like I was on an acid trip, the doorbell rang.

"Be right back," I murmured as I placed a kiss on her forehead and stood up to answer the door. When I pulled it open and saw Trent standing on the front porch, I was hit with that sense of butterflies in my belly, their wings flapping so hard and fast it was a wonder my feet didn't lift off the floor. "Hey. What are you doing here?"

"Stopped by the store to see you, and Georgia told me

Renee was sick. I wanted to check on her, and bring her some stuff that might make her feel better." He lifted a bag with the Warren's logo on it.

I didn't even try to hide my surprise. "Wow. How did you know what to get?"

"Oh, I had no clue what I was doing," he admitted with a chuckle. "Georgia pointed me in the right direction."

God, this man. When he left it was going to hurt so much worse than I'd imagined.

"I-I can't believe you did that," I said quietly, my throat suddenly feeling a little thick.

"Of course I did. If Little Bit is sick, I want to do every-thing I can to make her feel better."

I wasn't going to cry. I *really* wasn't. *Damn it*! There was a *huge* possibility I was going to cry. "For the love of God, man, you have *got* to stop being so freaking sweet!"

His dimpled smirk was just too damn much. "You kind of want to jump me right now, don't you?"

I laughed and shook my head. "Maybe. But if I did, you'd be at risk of getting sick. These bugs are pretty contagious, and I'd hate for you to catch it from being around either one of us."

"I don't care about that. If I get sick, I get sick. If you're cool with it, I'd like to stay and help you take care of her."

How in the world was I supposed to say no to something that thoughtful and kindhearted? It was impossible.

I stepped aside so he could come in. "All right, but I'm

warning you now, things inside could get pretty messy. Hope you have a strong stomach."

He stepped into the house, but didn't move past me. Instead, he bent and pressed his lips to mine in a quick, but no less potent, kiss. "Don't worry about me, baby. I can handle anything."

Twenty-Two

SAWYER

The roar of the water falling over the blunt edge of the small cliff into the crystal-clear pool below blocked out the sound of wind rustling the leaves of the trees and birds calling out from above.

It had been a week since Renee's stomach virus, and sure enough, like I'd warned, Trent and I both caught it. The next few days had been rough, to say the least. Trent got it the worst, puking his guts up nearly constantly for almost two days, but he toughed it out with me, and all three of us were in the clear now. It took another couple days for our energy to get back to normal, but once it had, I'd decided it was time to finally take him to see Whisper Falls.

It was a bit of a hike to the remote location, but totally worth it.

"Whoa," he breathed as we stepped into the clearing,

bringing into perfect view all the beauty around us. "This place is absolutely amazing."

I smiled up at him, the sun above us shining down, making his dark, chocolate locks shine. "I thought you might like it."

Taking my hand in his, he stared at the water, the spray coming off the falls catching in the wind and traveling outward to mist our skin. "Baby, you weren't kidding. This is beautiful."

"I'm glad you like it. It's my favorite place in the whole world. The hike is a bit rough, as you know, so there aren't many people willing to make the trek. I used to come up here all the time when I needed to escape the world for a little while. I'd lie back and listen to the water and just let everything go. It's the perfect place to clear your mind."

And shortly after I'd arrived in town, after I had Renee and I was worried the choices I'd made in my life, all the regrets I had tucked away like skeletons in a dark closet, would do her more harm than good, I'd needed to clear my mind frequently.

"This place gave me a sense of peace I'd never really had before. It became kind of a sanctuary for me."

His fingers pressed beneath my chin, tilting my face around so I could see into those gorgeous smoky eyes.

"I'm really glad you had that, beautiful."

I pulled in a deep breath through my nose, filling my lungs with the crisp autumn air and the smell of pine and clean laundry. I was in so much trouble. Without meaning to, I'd gone and fallen in love with someone who was just passing through. Not only had I given my heart to this man, but I'd also allowed him into Renee's life, knowing it was just a matter of time before he disappeared.

I hadn't protected either of us the way I should have, and now it wasn't only my heart that would be broken when this ended, but my baby girl's as well.

To make matters worse, he didn't even know the real me. He didn't know anything about my life before Whitecap, about Cheyanne Knightly, and the longer I held that secret, the worse I felt. Before Trent came to town, I'd been content to live out the rest of my days as Sawyer Darcy. But for some reason, he'd changed things for me. I felt guilty for deceiving all these people who'd come to mean the world to me. They were the closest thing to family I'd had since I was seven years old, and hiding my true self from everyone who loved me was starting to tear me apart.

"What are you thinking?" he asked gently.

"Nothing important." I tried to turn back to the falls, but his grip on my chin held firm, refusing to allow me to break contact with those eyes that were the color of the densest forest.

"Baby, whatever you were just thinking, it made you sad. I can see it on your face. Talk to me. What's wrong?"

I tried to smile, but it felt as forced as I was sure it looked, brittle and stiff, seconds away from cracking. I shook my head to dislodge his hold and moved away, stepping to the edge of the pool and looking at my reflection on the surface of the water. It was big enough that the ripples created from the streaming water didn't reach the banks, making the water look as smooth as glass. "I'm just being ridiculous. Seriously, don't worry about it. I don't want anything to ruin this day."

His hands landed on my hips, turning me away from the water to see that his brows had dipped into a furrow, the skin around those smoky eyes creased deep with concern. "You aren't going to ruin anything. It's obvious there's something on your mind that took that smile away, and I can't fix it if you don't tell me what's wrong."

I wasn't sure he *could* fix it. I wasn't sure anyone could. But there was no point in trying to keep it to myself. He wouldn't stop digging until he got to the root of the problem. Letting out a sigh, I stepped closer and laid my forehead against the solid wall of his chest, hearing the steady, calming beat of his heart over the rush of the water.

"I was just thinking that you're going to leave one day, probably soon, and how badly that's going to suck." Tipping my head back, I gave him a serious look. "Newsflash: It's going to suck *really* bad. And not just for me, but Renee too."

That concern didn't fall away, if anything it became even worse, and I could have sworn I saw something else behind it, but I couldn't quite identify what it was. "Baby, that's not something you need to think about. Especially not today."

Well that certainly didn't help me feel any better.

"I know. It just kind of popped in my head. Like I said, it's ridiculous."

"Hey." God, it really did me in when he used that velvety-soft voice. It was like a soothing caress that made me want to burst into tears almost every single time I heard it. Before him, I'd never had a man speak so gently to me, like he wanted to protect me with everything he had, even his voice. "I'm not leaving any time soon, Sawyer. I swear. Not anytime soon. And you have my word, if that day ever comes, you'll know long before it happens."

Hope banged in my chest, bouncing around like a pinball. "*If*?"

His dimples pressed deep, his bright white smile and green-brown eyes all I could see. "Yeah, Sawyer, *if*."

A knot unfurled inside of me I hadn't realized was squeezing so tightly it cut my breaths short until he gave me that one word and my lungs filled completely on the next inhale.

"So, why do they call this place Whisper Falls?"

My smile was much more genuine this time as I grabbed his hand and pulled him after me. "Come on. I'll show you."

"Can you swim in here?" he asked as I led him around the pool toward the curtain of water.

"Yeah, but it's usually too cold this time of year. But the hot springs aren't far from here. I can show you those later, if you want."

He waggled his brows, his smirk playfully lecherous as he answered, "Oh, I absolutely want."

I giggled as I guided him to a small path that led behind the falling water. The grass was lush and thick, a damp, dense cushion beneath our feet. The sun blinked as we stepped behind the blanket of water into the small cavern it covered. It was already chilly back there with the seasons quickly changing, and it was only going to get colder, making it impossible to tuck into this tiny alcove without the threat of freezing to death, but it was tolerable just then.

His face lined with shadows from the pale light playing across the slick stones that formed walls around us.

"Hi," I whispered, watching his eyes widen in surprise at hearing my voice so clearly. I continued speaking in a quiet voice as I explained, "The water and the cavern create this kind of tunnel that takes noise and bounces it across the rocks, making it easy to hear a whisper."

"Hence, Whisper Falls."

"Exactly."

"I have to say, Sawyer, this is really fucking cool."

It *was* really fucking cool.

"I'm glad I got to show you this." I kept my voice quiet.

His hand came up, his long fingers tangling with my hair as he braced his palm on the back of my neck. "I'm glad I got to see it with you."

He yanked me forward, bringing me up to my tiptoes, so he could crash his lips down on mine. The kiss set my blood on fire. My whole body burned, blasting away any of the cold left in the small cave.

I could kiss him forever and never grow tired of it, not even for a second. But all it did was make me want more.

Pulling back and sucking in a much-needed breath, I tipped my head up with heavy eyelids and asked, "Feel like seeing the hot springs now?"

The craggy rumble that barreled up his throat reverberated off the stone walls. "Abso-fucking-lutely."

Twenty-Three

TRENT

IT WAS hard to believe that the woman standing before me, shedding her clothes in the middle of the woods without a single inhibition, was the same one I'd met a month and a half ago. The woman who blushed furiously every time I looked in her direction, and stuttered violently, unable to form a complete sentence without littering it with "ums" and "uhs" whenever I smiled at her.

I'd made the mistake of thinking that Sawyer Darcy was a shy, quiet woman. But she wasn't, not really. She was fiercely protective of her daughter and had loyalty that ran to her very core for those she loved. She was funny and cute, sweet but also tough when the situation warranted. There were so many layers to her, I didn't know if I'd ever reach the center, and that was fine by me. I wanted to peel each and every one back, studying everything I could and getting to know all sides of her.

She had more in common with her sister than I originally thought.

And as I sat in the hot springs, tucked deep in the trees, miles from town and the people who lived there, my throat grew dry, my heart pounding harder and harder with each article of clothing she peeled away.

Her body was made to be worshipped. All that silky soft skin was enough to drive me out of my goddamn mind. Her curves made my mouth water. Everything about her was pure perfection, from her tiny pink toes to all that long hair that was always wild, smelling like lilacs and the salty ocean breeze.

Every night I'd spent with her since we stopped with the pretenses and gave in to how we felt about each other, I'd bury my face in that hair and fill my lungs with the delicious, unique scent.

She looked back at me over her shoulder, a coy smile playing on her lips as she reached behind her and unclipped her bra. My cock went rock hard, standing tall beneath the surface of the comfortably warm water.

She extended her arm, dropping her bra to the ground beside her before going back to her teasing, sliding her thumbs along the waistband of her leggings, but not pulling them down.

My dick throbbed painfully, desperate to be sheathed inside her silky wet heat.

A growl rumbled up my throat from deep within my chest, and my fingers clenched into fists around the water, eager to grab onto her hips and keep her in place as I sank deep inside her.

"You've got three seconds to get naked and get that sweet ass in here."

She lifted both her brows, her back still to me as she cast a challenging look over her shoulder. "Or what?"

"Or you'll be walking back to the car in just your shirt, 'cause I'll have ripped everything else to shreds."

Christ, I felt like I was going insane with my need for her. I'd dug myself into a hole I was afraid I'd never be able to get out of by not taking Lincoln's advice and coming clean. I'd let my fear of losing her push logic to the back burner, and I'd let this go on for way too long. I had to figure out a way to fix it, because I couldn't lose her. I'd gone and fallen for her, and she didn't know it yet, but I had no intention of leaving Whitecap, not if it meant leaving her and Renee behind.

They were mine, and I was theirs. There was no point in denying that any longer.

Her giggle was music to my ears, and when she finally stripped out of the rest of her clothes, my body sank back into the water in relief, the tension of her being too far away for me to reach out and touch her finally melting from my muscles as she sank into the pool of water with me.

"Come here," I grunted on a breath, extending my arm and snagging her around the waist as soon as she was within reach. The feel of her bare skin brushing against mine as I pulled her against me, bringing her so close she had to straddle my lap, was pure, unadulterated heaven. Locking my arms around her, I brought my mouth to hers and feasted.

The smell of lilacs and the ocean breeze filled my nostrils. The sweet taste that was all Sawyer coated my tongue. Her needy little moans were all I heard. She overwhelmed every one of my senses. In that moment, as we kissed, our naked bodies rocking together, she was my entire world. And I didn't mind that one goddamn bit.

"Trent," she sighed into my mouth, her hands sliding up my shoulders and the sides of my neck so her fingers could tangle in my hair.

"Fuck, baby." I groaned, lifting my hips so my cock could rub against her. "I need you so bad I can't see straight."

She pinched my bottom lip between her teeth and pulled back just a bit, giving it a tiny nip before letting it go. "Then do something about it."

I kept her glued to me, taking the kiss even deeper as I reached behind me with one arm, blindly feeling around for my discarded jeans. I managed to get them and my wallet, pulling out the condom I'd stashed inside.

"Lift up," I ordered gently once I had the wrapper open.

Sawyer planted her knees on the ledge that had formed the perfect bench beneath the water, and rose above me, giving me just enough room to tip my hips and slide the condom into place.

Her breath left her in a sharp gasp when I grabbed hold of her ass and jerked her onto me in one brutal thrust. "Oh

God, Trent," she moaned, her head falling backward. "You feel so good. Always so good."

Fuck me, there was no better feeling on the planet than having her snug pussy wrapped around me. She lifted up and slid back down slowly, circling her hips on each downward stroke, ripping deep, primal grunts from my chest as she began to pick up the speed.

"That's it, baby. Ride me. Get yourself off on my cock."

"God, I'm so full," she whimpered. Those autumn-leaves eyes of hers were glassy with lust, the lids lowered to half-mast as the pulse in her neck thrummed wildly. Her hands braced on my shoulders, her nails digging half-moons into my skin as those delicate little muscles deep inside her began to tremble.

With one hand squeezing her ass cheek, guiding her to move faster, harder, I cupped one of her incredible tits with the other, bending forward to suck the turgid peak into my mouth.

Her writhing became wild with that new sensation, and I pulled deeply, sucking and nipping on her nipple until the rosy point was a nice deep red. I switched to the other, giving it the same attention as my hand on her round globe slipped and the tip of my middle finger brushed along the crease of her ass, sliding across that tiny pucker.

Her pussy clamped down and she let out a cry, her eyes going wide at the feel of me touching her somewhere so private, almost forbidden.

"You like that, Sawyer?"

"I-I don't know. I think so," she answered hesitantly, so I did it again to test the waters, applying a little more pressure.

"Know what I think?" I rasped as she started to slam herself down on me, working my cock like it was the reason she was put on this earth.

"W-what do you think?"

I pressed down one last time. "I think, one day, you're going to beg me to take this ass, and I'll make it so good for you, you'll see fucking stars."

"Jesus, Trent," she groaned, her tits bouncing as she fucked me with everything she had.

"But not now. Right now I want this pussy to clamp down around me and milk out every drop of cum I have. I want you to scream my name when I'm buried as deep inside you as I can get. You want that, Sawyer? You want to come for me?"

"Yes," she panted, her eyes wild. She was completely lost to me, just like I was to her. "Please."

Bending forward, I wrapped my lips around one of those pretty pink nipples and sucked hard before biting down. At the same time, I pressed on that little pucker and snapped my hips up. Her muscles clamped down so tight it was a wonder I could move inside her as she came on my dick, doing just as I wanted and screaming with her release.

With my arms locking around her waist, I held her in place and started driving upward, over and over, bottoming out with every thrust. She hadn't finished coming down before she started all over again.

Her back arched, her hair spilling into the water as she bucked into each of my thrusts. The tingles at the base of my spine spread like fire through my body, and my balls exploded, cum shooting from my cock so hard it was almost painful. "Jesus, you're the best thing that's ever happened to me," I groaned and panted once I was able to pull air back into my lungs.

"Fuck, I love—" I caught myself before I could finish that declaration. Even though it was the truest thing I'd ever felt, it was probably too soon to be trading *I love yous*. There were still too many secrets between us. I wanted those three words to be pure and untainted. "I love the way you feel."

She fell forward, face-planting against my chest, her back rising and falling with each labored breath like she'd just run a marathon at a dead sprint.

"Feelings mutual," she wheezed. Then she lifted up to grace me with the most beautiful smile. "I think the hot springs just became my new favorite place."

I let out a deep laugh and hugged her close. I loved that she thought that, but my favorite place would always be wherever she was.

Twenty-Four

SAWYER

WHEN WE LEFT the hot springs and hiked back to my car, there were still a few hours before I had to pick Renee up from daycare, so we'd headed back to my place.

The whole car ride home, I'd felt like I was floating. Since leaving the falls, I'd been smiling so hard my cheeks were starting to throb. I couldn't remember if I'd ever felt this happy. The best day of my life was the day Renee came into this world, but with all that joy and heart-swelling love came a near-overwhelming sense of fear that I wouldn't be able to keep her safe.

The only stain on my happiness right now was the fact that I hadn't told Trent the truth about who I really was and what my life had been before I came here.

"Get it together, Sawyer," I chastised on a whisper as I moved to the fridge and pulled it open so I could get started on a late lunch while Trent was in the shower. I'd pulled out everything for sandwiches and was in the process of spreading mayo on a piece of bread when Trent's phone started vibrating and dancing across the bar.

I glanced that way and the butter knife in my hand slipped out, clattering to the floor as a frigid chill washed over me, raising the little hairs on my arms. On wooden legs, I moved around the bar, never once ripping my eyes from the screen of Trent's phone as my heart slammed into my ribs so hard each beat felt like it was leaving a bruise behind.

The name that flashed had been the first thing to give me pause. But it was just a name. There were probably hundreds of thousands of Charlottes in the world, if not millions. No, that wasn't the name that made my blood crystalize and scrape across my veins. It was the picture that accompanied it.

It was a face I could have described with perfect clarity, a face almost more familiar to me than my own.

It was my face, but . . . not.

My body moved of its own accord, my arm stretching out and my fingers wrapping around the thin block of metal and glass.

My thumb swiped across the screen without any input at all from my brain. I was moving on autopilot as my hand lifted the phone to my ear, the shaking so uncontrollable I almost dropped it.

"Hey, Trent. Look, I'm really sorry. I know Dalton said you'd call when you had any information on Cheyanne, but you know how I am. I got antsy. Is there any news on my sister? Anything at all? Even just the littlest thing would make me feel so much better."

The blood was rushing in my ears so fast it sounded like thunder. My vision started to blur around the edges, and all of a sudden I couldn't get enough air. My head felt like it had detached and was floating above me.

"Trent? You there?" the disembodied voice of my sister asked. My sister! My twin.

"Charlotte," I breathed, that one word so soft I wasn't even really sure I'd said out loud it or just thought it.

There was a brief pause as my heart cracked and splintered into a million pieces. "Who is this?"

"Charlotte," I whispered again. It was the only word bouncing around in my brain, the only thing I could think.

I thought I heard a soft sob from across the line. "Cheyanne?"

At the sound of my old name, my *real* name, said in such a familiar voice, a sense of panic so strong it almost took me to the ground took over. Before I knew what I was doing, I'd ripped the phone from my ear and ended the call.

"Oh my God," I panted, my vision blurring as tears welled up in my eyes. The trembling had moved from my hand, spreading throughout my entire body, shaking me so hard I felt it jarring my bones. I let out a choked sob. "Oh my God."

"Sawyer?" At Trent's voice, I whipped around so fast my hair lashed at my face, making my skin sting. "Baby? What's wrong?"

He took a step toward me and I jerked, jumping back like he'd just slapped me. His forehead was chiseled with deep grooves of worry. "Sawyer, sweetheart. Talk to me. What's going on?"

"Who are you?" I asked on a whisper before something inside of me snapped, "Who *the fuck* are you?"

"What are you talking about?" He advanced again, and this time I held up the hand that was still clutching his phone to stop him. I hadn't even realized it was ringing until that very moment. "Is that my phone?" he asked, panic injecting into his eyes.

The ringing stopped and started again almost immediately. "You had a call." Accusation dripped from my words like venom as I threw the phone at him.

He caught it easily. Looking down at the screen, his face bleached of all color, turning a sickly shade of white. I could only assume it was the same person.

"Sawyer, honey—"

"Don't call me that!" I shouted. "You already know my real name, don't you? You've known this whole time. I mean, you've been looking for me, right?" I shoved my finger at the still-ringing phone he was clutching in a white-knuckle grip. "How long?"

"Sawyer—"

"How *long* have you been looking for me?" I repeated, my voice growing shrill.

He inhaled through his nose as the phone started up

again. This time, he shut off the ringer and shoved it into his back pocket. "Six months."

"Six months," I choked out, part sob, part laugh. "So all this time . . . Everything you've done, everything you've said, it's all been a lie." I reached up and raked my fingers through my hair as a deluge of tears streamed down my face. "Oh my God. I let you near Renee. I let you be a part of my baby's life, and you've been lying the *whole time!*"

He rushed me then, taking my face in his hands. "It wasn't a lie," he demanded, pulling me close and pressing his forehead into mine. "None of it was a lie, baby. Everything you felt, I felt too. Everything I said, it was all real. I tried not to want you. I tried to keep my distance. That was why I took off after that first kiss. But I couldn't stay away. I just couldn't."

His fingers pressed harder against my cheeks. "What I felt for you . . . I've never felt anything like it in my whole life. I had to be near you, and the more I got to know you, the more real it's gotten. I fell for you. I want to be with you. You and Renee. You two mean everything to me."

"Stop it," I whispered brokenly.

"I fell in love with you."

"Stop it," I repeated more firmly. I felt like I was breaking apart. I knew that it would hurt when this ended, but I never imagined it would be this bad. It was agony.

"Cheyanne. Sawyer. It doesn't matter what you call yourself. You're still the same person here." He pressed a palm against my chest right above my heart. "That's who I fell in love with."

I couldn't take it any longer. It was too much. "*Stop it! Just stop!*" Ripping away from him, I stumbled back and circled the bar, putting space and a physical obstacle between us. "Stop saying that. You don't know what the fuck that word means. You're a liar." My voice broke on a sob. "All this time," I cried, clutching at my chest. "All this time, you've known my sister. You've been a part of her life. And you've kept her from me!"

"You have to understand—"

"You heard the bedtime story!" I threw back in accusation. "You knew what that story was really about, didn't you?" He didn't bother with words, instead, he just nodded, his expression ravaged. "You knew who Renee was named after, and you *kept her* from me. My *twin*. Who does that? What kind of person could be that cruel?"

His voice sounded like he'd gargled with glass when he spoke next. "I wasn't trying to hurt you. I was trying to protect you. I saw this life you'd built for yourself and Renee, and I wanted to protect it. I was going to tell you, I swear to God. I was trying to find the right time. I thought that maybe if I could get you to trust me, it wouldn't be such a major blow. You wouldn't get scared and feel like you had to run again. But—" He stopped, giving his head a vicious shake.

"But what?" I choked out. "You decided fucking me was more fun that telling me the truth?"

The muscles in his jaw ticked, the cords in his neck tensing. "I didn't want to lose you."

The laugh that tore from my throat was bitter and acrid. "Well you really fucked that one up, didn't you?"

His breathing had grown erratic. "Please," he said so quietly I could barely hear him. "Please don't say that."

Unable to look at him for another second, I spun around and batted at the moisture on my cheeks before spying the time on the front of the microwave.

Without sparing him a glance, I turn on my heel and started out of the kitchen, snatching up my keys and purse off the bar on the way past.

"Where are you going?"

"I have to get Renee from daycare. I want you the fuck out of my house before I get back."

"Sawyer, please—"

"I'm Cheyanne, remember?" I spat back at him.

"There's so much we need to talk about—"

"I've spent as much time in your presence as I can stomach for today. When I'm able to look at you again, the only thing we have left to discuss is my sister. Other than finding out about Charlotte, I don't want to hear a word that comes out of your mouth."

With that, I slammed out of my house, not giving a damn that I was leaving it open and unprotected while I was gone. I had a handful of minutes to get myself together. There was no way in hell I was letting my daughter see me break down. I'd already fucked up by letting Trent into her life. There wasn't room for another mistake.

Trent

I stayed at Sawyer's until I heard her car pull up outside, I didn't want to leave without making sure she and Renee got home safe, so I'd waited, ignoring the incessant buzzing of my cellphone in my pocket the whole time.

Once I heard the car door close, I went out through the sliding door, slugging across the beach to my place.

I let myself into the empty place, noticing for the first time it was quiet as a tomb. Not like Sawyer's house. Her's was full of noise and life and laughter.

Moving to my fridge, I yanked out a beer and popped the cap, standing in the open door as I drained the entirety of the bottle in a few gulps. It didn't do shit to calm the storm raging inside of me.

With a second beer in hand, I slammed the door and moved to the island, finally pulling my phone out as I braced my forearms on the cool granite counter. I didn't bother scrolling through all the missed calls and messages. I figured I already knew the gist of them. Instead, I went right to Dalton's name and hit call.

"What the fuck is going on?" he barked through the line

the instant the call connected. "Charlotte's over here losing her goddamn mind. I can't understand half of what she's saying, she's crying so fuckin' hard, and you wouldn't answer your goddamn phone!"

I really was a piece of shit. "I know. I'm sorry," I told him, my throat feeling like I'd swallowed gravel. "I had something here I needed to deal with before I could call you back."

"Start talking, Trent, or I swear to Christ—"

I said the three words Dalton and Charlotte had been waiting for months to hear. "I found her."

"When?" he asked in a hard tone that indicated he'd already pieced that together from Charlotte's freak out. "And why the fuck is this the first time we're hearing about it."

Squeezing my eyes closed, I pinched the bridge of my nose and admitted, "About a month and a half ago."

"*What the fuck*?" he boomed so loud it was a wonder my eardrum didn't start to bleed.

"Look, brother, I'm sorry. I know that it probably seems all kinds of fucked up to you, but I had my reasons."

"You had your reasons?" he thundered. "You had *reasons*? Are you fucking kidding me? Do you know what my woman's been going through? She's been torturing herself day after day, you son of a bitch! All she's wanted was to find her sister, and you've known where she's been for a goddamn month and a half! You've been in Oregon this whole time, just sitting on that information!"

"I did what I felt was right. This was my assignment and I made the call. I know you're pissed, but let me explain—"

"Oh, you're gonna explain all right," he clipped. "But you'll be doing it face to face. Charlotte and I will be on the first available flight to Oregon, and you, for your own wellbeing, you better have the best reason anyone has ever had in the history of time, or so help me God, I'm going to beat you into the motherfucking ground!"

On that threat, he hung up.

"Shit," I hissed as I tossed the phone down. I lifted the second beer to my lips and drained that one too before going for a third.

If I was going to have to live through my world falling apart, I was at least going to be shitfaced for it.

Twenty-Five

CHEYANNE

I'D BEEN an anxious bundle of frayed nerves since picking Renee up from daycare earlier that day. I hadn't been able to sit for more than a handful of seconds, and it was only by sheer strength of will that I was able to hide my turmoil from my daughter.

My mind had been racing with everything I'd found out. I kept hearing my sister's voice over and over inside my head. I kept replaying that one instant when the world beneath my feet had crumbled away, taking my heart with it.

By the time Renee was bathed and tucked into bed, I was barely holding it together. So I did the only thing I could think to do to give me any kind of peace. I called Luna. That had been nearly two hours ago. On my request, she gathered Monica and Georgia and brought them to my house. I needed to be surrounded by my girls. I needed to give them the truth.

And that was exactly what I did.

I told them everything. About Charlotte and how we'd been ripped apart at such a young age. About growing up and never experiencing the feeling of being loved or wanted. Of being so desperate for love by the time I met Graham that I'd allowed myself to be fooled by a monster. I went into detail about how horrible those years with him had been. Then I explained about finding out I was pregnant with Renee and knowing I couldn't allow my baby to grow up in that world. I told them all about creating Sawyer Darcy and the abject fear I felt like a weighted blanket pulling me down the whole time I was on the run. Until I came here. Until I met these people and finally, *finally* felt safe for the first time in my life. Then I told them about what had happened with Trent, how he'd been lying since the very beginning.

By the time I was done, my mouth was dry and my throat throbbed from all the words that had been torn from it. I'd never been so physically exhausted from an onslaught of emotions and adrenaline before.

I stopped in my pacing and grabbed the glass of wine that had gone untouched during my story and gulped half of it back, needing to relieve my parched throat as well as feel the buzz of the alcohol. I hadn't been able to sit the whole time I spoke, pacing back and forth across the living room as they stared up at me, worried I'd worn a path in the floor.

I waited for one of them to break the silence that had filled the room, making the air thick and swampy with tension as the seconds ticked by. Finally, Monica spoke. Sort of. "I don't—that's just—I can't believe—" She shook her head in bewilderment, her mouth gaping open. "I don't know what to say."

I decided I'd give her a little more time to wrap her head around the bombshell I'd just dropped on her. I shifted my focus to Georgia, who'd been sitting quietly beside Monica on the couch this whole time. Her eyes were swimming with tears that hadn't fallen free, rimmed red with the same heartbreak I'd been feeling for the past several hours.

"Georgia?" I started warily, moving to sit myself on the edge of the coffee table in front of her. I was worried about her reaction the most. I loved them all equally, but Georgia and Desmond were surrogate parents to me. I was terrified that I'd lose her now that she knew I'd been lying this entire time. "Please say something. I understand if you're mad, but I swear, I wasn't trying to deceive you. Lying to you guys this whole time has been one of the hardest things I've ever done. It killed me that I couldn't tell you the truth. Please believe that."

She blinked, two tears making tracks down her face. "Oh, sweet child," she said on a shuddered exhale, "I'm not mad. How could I be? I'm just so devastated that you had to live through that kind of hell. My heart is broken."

I hated that she was in pain, even if it was for me. But I couldn't deny the relief I felt at knowing she didn't hate me was so overwhelming I thought I might crumple to the floor.

"I hate that you've had to live with this secret for so long," Monica said, finally managing to put her words together. "And I fucking *hate* you've spent all these years looking over your shoulder, scared that monster was going to find you. Is he still looking for you?"

I gave her a shrug, my smile tremulous. "Probably. He'd never willingly let me go. I was his property as far as he was concerned, and the fact that he wasn't in control of me leaving is probably eating away at him. I followed the news for a while after I first left, watching to see what they were saying about it. About a year after I disappeared, the stories in the media started to change. The police held a press conference that they'd received intel that led them to believe I was dead, so they were calling off the search."

Monica's brow furrowed. "What does that mean? Did he stop looking for you?"

I shook my head, feeling like a two-ton weight was sitting on my chest. "Not a chance. I know him. He controls the police. That was him controlling the narrative. There was no evidence I'd died. That was all Graham." And I could only imagine his reasons for making up such a story. "They made it sound like I'd been mentally unfit before my disappearance. That and my supposed death was his way of covering his bases for if or when he ever found me." Because I knew, without a doubt, that if he did, that was it for me.

"We won't let anything happen to you," Georgia spat violently. "Not ever. If Dezzy and I have to camp out on your front porch with shotguns we will. No one is taking you."

God, I loved her. I loved *all* of them, this weird, quirky family I'd built for myself in this incredible town.

Luna spoke up for the first time then. "None of us will let anything happen to you," she stated in a voice so hard, so fiercely protective, that it sent a shiver down my spine.

Twisting to face her, I reached out and took her hands in mine, giving them a squeeze. "I want you guys to know that I'm so grateful I found this place and all of you. I honestly don't know what would have happened to Renee and me if I'd never come to Whitecap."

"You'd have been fine," Georgia decreed. "Not a doubt in my mind about that. You're a fighter, sweetheart. Tough as nails. You'd never let anything happen to that precious girl."

God, I hoped that was true.

Luna spoke again. "So much about you makes sense now. I always thought you were one of those weirdo technophobes, and that was why you didn't have social media."

"And the fact you never sold your pottery online," Monica added. "I always thought you could make a living off your stuff if you'd create an online store or something. Now I get why you have the shops around town sell it on your behalf."

"I always wanted to do that," I admitted wistfully. "My dream was to sell my ceramics. Years back, I had someone in Ohio approach me about doing a showing with a collection of my vases and larger pieces. I was so excited. When Graham found out, he went into my studio and smashed every single one of them."

"That son of a bitch," Monica growled. "When I tell Sam, he's going to rip that asshole's head off."

I hesitated in what I had to say next. "You can tell Sam and Dezzy, but no one else can know who I really am. At least not right now."

"Your secret is safe with us," Georgia insisted. "All of us. We'd never do anything to put you in danger."

"I know," I whispered, feeling my eyes mist up.

"So what does all of this mean for you and Trent?" Luna asked. It was a question I'd been dreading.

"We're done," I answered, my voice cracking on those two words, the jagged edges of them slicing up my throat as I forced them out. "He's the only link I have to my sister, so I'll have to talk to him again, but we're over. I made that perfectly clear."

Something happened just then that shocked me to my core. Luna sniffled, dropping her head as tears spilled from her eyes, dropping down onto the rug at her feet. "I'm so sorry," she croaked painfully. "It's all my fault. You never would have gotten hurt if I hadn't pushed you to take a chance on him. You said you weren't interested, but I just didn't listen."

I shot off the coffee table and moved to the love seat where she was currently curled over on herself. "Oh, honey," I murmured, wrapping my arms around her. "None of this is your fault."

She looked up at me, her big eyes glassy and wet. "Of course it is. I never listen. It's what I do. I push and push people to do what I think it right for them, never stopping to consider the consequences."

"Lu, I took a chance on Trent because he made me feel something I'd never felt before, not even when Graham had me convinced he was my knight in shining armor. You aren't to blame for any of it, so don't carry that weight."

She sniffled again, wiping under her eyes while she nodded, but I knew she was only agreeing for my benefit. She didn't mean it. She wasn't finished blaming herself for my pain.

"Sawyer—I mean Cheyanne—" Monica gave her head a shake, like she was trying to clear the befuddlement. "What should we call you now?"

"Whatever you want when we're alone," I answered.

"All right." She paused, and I could tell she hadn't landed on one name or another when she started again, omitting the name completely. ""Look, I know what Trent did was a million kinds of wrong, and if you wanted to go over there right this second and set his car on fire or break his kneecaps, I'd lead the charge. Lord knows he deserves it. But . . ." She stopped, worrying her bottom lip between her teeth. I knew then she was gearing up to say something I didn't want to hear.

"But what?"

"What if he really does love you?" she finally asked, her question like a hammer to my heart. She raced on before I could open my mouth. "Yes, he lied to you, and yes, that was bad, *really* bad. But I saw how he looked at you. You can't fake a look like that. What if he really was trying to protect you by not telling you the truth in the beginning?"

"She has a point," Georgia chimed in, shocking me with her agreement. "He said it himself, he was worried about blowing up your life. If he'd told you who he was at the very beginning, can you honestly say you wouldn't have taken off?" I couldn't say that. "You probably wouldn't have believed he was here on your sister's behalf."

Monica lifted her hand in the air. "By the way, I still can't believe you're a twin. That's crazy. I've never known a twin before."

Georgia carried on like she hadn't heard her. "You'd been hiding for so long, that the moment you realized that someone, no matter who they were, had not only been looking for you, but had managed to track you down, you would have run for the hills."

It really sucked that, in the midst of my crisis, Monica and Georgia were being so level-headed and rational. I needed them to get on my level.

It wasn't lost on me that Luna hadn't thrown in her two cents in regards to Trent, but I'd let her be for now.

"It doesn't matter. It's done. We're over."

Georgia nodded resolutely. "If that's what you want, you have my support. I just want you to know that you'll still have it, even if you change your mind."

"Ditto," Monica agreed.

There was no point telling them my mind was made up, so I didn't bother. After the day I'd had, it didn't take long for the adrenaline to leech out of me, leaving me with this weary, bone-deep exhaustion that made it hard to stand.

I walked them to the door a short while later, receiving the tightest hugs from Monica and Georgia before they headed to their cars. Luna lingered in the entryway, waiting until we were alone before speaking.

"You know I'm with them, right? Whatever you want, you have my support. I love you and I just want you to be happy."

"I know." I felt some of the pressure that had been weighing me down lighten. "And I love you too, very much, Luna."

"Cheyanne," she said on a sigh. "It'll take some getting used to, but I like it. It suits you somehow."

With one last hug, Luna turned on her heel and headed down the walkway, waving over her shoulder on her way to her car.

I waited in the opened doorway just long enough for her to start the engine and put the car into gear. Then I shut the door and locked up. I killed all the lights before heading down the hall to my bedroom. I froze at the sight of my rumpled bed and the smell of clean laundry and pine trees.

The bedroom had Trent's stamp all over it. No way I was sleeping in there tonight. Instead of moving to the living room, I went to Renee, shifting her sleeping form aside so I could crawl into her bed with her and cuddle her against me. Then I slept like the dead.

Luna

Sawyer—no, I needed to remember that wasn't her name anymore. Cheyanne hadn't blamed me for being hurt. Not that I was surprised. The woman had the biggest heart of anyone I'd ever met, possibly to a fault. But that didn't mean the fault didn't lie with me.

Well, me and that stupid prick, Trent, that was.

Casting one last look at her house in time to see each light inside extinguish, I shifted into drive with the intention of heading home. But before I even took my foot off the brake, my mind changed, and instead of turning my car toward my house, I went straight to a house I'd only visited once in recent weeks.

I wasn't surprised to see that the lights of Trent's rental were burning bright. After what he'd done to my best friend today, he was probably inside, drowning his sorrows at losing the best woman on the face of the earth. As he rightly should.

After what Cheyanne had told us tonight, I wanted to hate him, I *really* did. But for some unfathomable reason, I just couldn't. And it was driving me crazy.

As much as I loathed admitting it, I was with Georgia and Monica. The dude had fucked up *big time*, but I didn't think he did it to be cruel. I honestly believed down to my soul that he loved her.

But he still had to pay. At least a little bit.

I didn't bother shutting off the engine as I climbed out

and stomped up to his front door, pounding my knuckles against the wood over and over, in rapid succession, until it finally opened a minute later.

The instant his stupid, chiseled face came into view, I balled up my fist, cocked my arm back, and let it fly, punching him right in the face so hard his head snapped backward.

"That's for hurting Sawyer—Cheyanne—whatever—you dick."

"Fuck me," he grunted, pinching the bridge of his nose and tipping his head back. "Christ, that hurt. Am I bleeding?"

"No," I snapped unhappily. "Which is very disappointing. Now my hand hurts and you're fine."

He scrunched his face a few times and pulled air in through his nostrils. "Yeah, well, if it makes you feel better, I guarantee I'll have a hell of a bruise tomorrow."

It did, actually, but I wasn't going to tell him that.

"You deserve it," I muttered, crossing my arms over my chest.

"I know," he replied on a sigh, sagging against the doorframe in defeat. "How is she?"

"How do you think she is, you dumb son of a bitch?" I threw my arms wide before slamming my hands down on my hips. "She's a fucking mess, thanks to you." Then I got down to the real reason I was here. "I can't believe I'm going to say this, because I should hate your guts and wish some sort of penile infection that will never go away on you, but you better find a way to fix this shit." I jabbed my finger in his face, taking joy in the fact that his nose was swelling up before my very eyes. "For some reason, that woman loves you, and even though she says she doesn't want anything to do with you now, something tells me that's not going to last. So you better pull out all the stops to make this right, or so help me God, I'm going to haunt your dreams for the rest of your life. You get me?"

He stared at me earnestly before nodding his head one time. "I get you."

"Good. Now go put ice on your face and come up with a game plan."

On that, I whipped around and stormed back to my running car.

Twenty-Six

CHEYANNE

I DROPPED Renee off at daycare early the next morning, but the second I stepped into Warren's General Store, Desmond and Georgia were there, gentle hands spinning me around and pushing me back out with orders to take a few personal days for myself. Normally a job like this didn't really come with sick time, but the Warrens were all about taking care of their people. And that was what they were trying to do with me when they refused to let me work my shift.

With nothing else to do, and the house too damn quiet for my sanity, I changed into my ratty clothes and headed to my workshop, hoping it would help to empty my mind, at least for a little while.

Unfortunately, that wasn't the case. The clay didn't seem to want to cooperate this morning. Every time I formed it into some semblance of a shape, it would cave in on me, over and over again until I got so frustrated I smashed the wet clay in my hands, squeezing it through my fingers before punching the ball.

Once I got all that aggression out and lowered my head, trying to pull in a calm, centering breath, I was able to feel that his presence had snuck up on me at some point.

"You feel better?" he asked in that velvet voice, clearly having witnessed my scene.

"Not particularly." Turning off the wheel, I grabbed a towel and wiped at my hands. "I have questions," I stated in a monotone voice as I swiveled on my stool to face him.

"Figured you would. That's why I'm here."

He shifted, moving so that the sun no longer backlit him and I was able to see his face clearly. His left eye was ringed in an angry blackish-purple color. "What the hell happened to your face?"

He pointed at his black eye. "Courtesy of your best friend. Was that one of your questions?" he attempted to tease, but I didn't take the bait.

"It isn't, but I can't say it's not a silver lining."

Crossing his arms over his chest, he propped his shoulder on the frame of the opened garage door and asked, "What do you want to know?"

"How do you know Charlotte?" I asked. That was the one question that had been churning in my brain since the day before. "And how did you know I was in hiding? Last I checked, the news was reporting I was dead. Why would you bother looking for me?"

He let out a sigh, and I got the impression he was gearing up for a long explanation. "After I retired from the military, I came back to the states and took a job with a security and private investigation firm in Virginia called Alpha Omega. There was a situation in our town a while back involving a known meth dealer. Charlotte was caught in the middle of it." I sucked in a gasp, a million icy pinpricks jabbing into my skin. "Your sister didn't have it easy, growing up, but she was never a bad person. *Ever*," he stressed. "She was stuck between a rock and a hard place.

"When the dealer was sent down, a few of the dirty cops who'd been on his payroll decided they wanted to pick up his work. They'd gotten used of the cash they were getting from the operation and one in particular decided to pick up the reins for himself and take out everyone else involved so he didn't have to split the take. Including an officer who had been investigating him.

"Charlotte started informing for two detectives on the force, and they pulled in my buddy Dalton, a few of the other guys I work with, and me, to keep your sister protected. During that whole thing, Charlotte and Dalton ended up falling for each other. They're together now. Engaged, actually. Set to get married early next year.

"Before we were able to pull Charlotte clear of the shit storm that had been brewing, she and another woman were caught in the crossfire. The cop was killed, but not before he hurt Charlotte. It was a big story that ended up getting national attention, and we can only assume that Knightly, or someone who works very closely with him, caught wind of it. They saw Charlotte on the news, saw the uncanny resemblance between the two of you, and started digging. One of Knightly's guys showed up several months back, broke into her place and worked her over, trying to get information out of her on your location."

Goosebumps erupted across my skin, making the tiny hairs stand on end as ice trickled down my spine. "Is-is she okay?"

"Yeah. She's good, baby," he answered gently. "A hard life made her tough. Sucks she had to go through that, but it meant she was strong enough to pull herself out of the muck and demand a better life for herself. But when she was attacked, Dalton lost his fucking mind. We started doing some digging of our own and asked the exact same question you just asked. Why would a husband send his lackey to scare a woman into giving information she doesn't have on a sister who was supposed to be dead?

"Charlotte was scared you were in trouble, and because she's one of ours, we decided we needed to find you, one: so we could protect you, and two: so we could give Charlotte back the sister she'd missed with every breath in her body."

The chill had worked its way through my body and down to my bones. As I sat on that stool in a room that had only ever given me peace and comfort, I started to shake uncontrollably.

Seeing that I was dangerously close to a nervous breakdown, Trent moved in, crouching down in front of me and taking my hands in his big, warm palms. "He doesn't know where you are. I swear to you. My boss employs some of the most talented men in the country, including hackers and guys like me and Dalton. We're two of the best trackers you'll ever meet, and it still took me six fucking months to find you. You hid yourself well, sweetheart. Covered your tracks. You and Renee are safe. You have my word."

That was a relief to hear, but that wasn't the only reason why I felt myself coming apart at the seams. "She—" I had to swallow down the wad of cotton in my throat. "She got hurt because of me," I said so quietly it was a wonder the sound didn't get swallowed up by the roaring surf outside my workshop.

"No, Cheyanne. She got hurt because of that piece of shit, Knightly. Don't take responsibility for the fucked-up shit he did. It's not on you, and Charlotte knows that."

I squeezed my eyes closed and pulled in a calming breath, filling my lungs with the salty sea air. "Is she—she's good now? Happy?"

His smile was so soft and tender, his dimples making an appearance for the first time in almost two days. "She is. Only thing that's put a damper on that is how bad she's been missing you. She's been refusing to set a date for the wedding for a long time now because she wanted to find you first so you could be a part of that."

Tears sprang to life, burning the backs of my eyes. "I've missed her too. More than anyone could possibly know."

His hands squeezed mine. "I know, honey. Knew it when

your daughter told me who she was named after, and again when I heard you telling her that story about the princesses who lived in the clouds. You've always kept her with you in the only ways you knew how to."

My throat bobbed on a thick swallow. "You said she's had a hard life. What did you mean by that?"

His chest rose on a deep inhale, his breath gently skating across my face when he finally blew it out. "That's not my story to tell. It's hers." My brow furrowed, but before I could question him, he continued. "She and her man will be here tomorrow morning. After last night, they booked the first flight they could get seats on. She couldn't wait, but if you aren't ready, you just say the word, baby, and I'll hold them off until you're okay to see her face-to-face."

My head had been swimming with everything he'd just told me, making it impossible to really focus on anything else. But at that statement, I came back to reality, pulling my hands from his grip and standing up so I could put some much-needed distance between us. "That's really not your place, Trent. I'm not your responsibility, and it's not your job to protect me."

He stood to his full height, his sheer size eclipsing everything and making the workshop seem much smaller than it really was. "That's where you're wrong, Cheyanne. I fucked up, I know that. I betrayed your trust, but there isn't a goddamn thing I won't do to earn it back. That includes protecting you from everything and everyone that could cause you the slightest discomfort, even if that person is your own flesh and blood. You're mine. You're mine and I'm yours."

I didn't have the energy to argue with him about this, not after everything he'd just piled on me. Reaching up, I massaged my throbbing temples, feeling the beginnings of a headache forming there.

"I don't want you to protect me from her," I finally said two minutes later—I knew the time because I'd counted out the seconds while willing my heart to stop racing. "I want to see her. Tomorrow, when she gets here, I want to see her, but right now, I need some space. I need you to leave, Trent."

"Baby—"

"Please," I pleaded desperately. "I just want to be alone right now."

For a moment I worried that he was going to argue, but thankfully, he relented a beat later, his shoulders falling on a sigh. "All right, I'll go. For now."

"Thank you. But—" The words fell past my lips before I could stop it. "You'll be here tomorrow? When Charlotte and her fiancé come? You'll be here?" I didn't want to need him for that, but I couldn't help it. I was excited about the idea of *finally* seeing my sister, my twin, the other half of me that I'd felt was missing nearly my whole life, but I was also scared, and for some reason, knowing Trent would be there helped temper that fear.

I remained frozen in place as he closed the distance

between us and reached up to cup my jaw. "If you want me here, I'll be here. I promise."

My breath left me on a wheeze at the intensity in his smoky eyes. I almost thought he was going to kiss me, but instead, he turned and, in two long strides, exited my workshop and disappeared.

Trent

I was on my back deck with my forearms braced on the wooden railing. I'd lost track of how long I'd been standing there, staring out at the turbulent water, but it was long enough that the sun had set, turning the swirling blue and white to an inky black that better matched my mood.

I'd been lost in thought for hours, only being pulled from my melancholy when the doorbell rang. Pushing myself up, I brought the beer bottle that had been dangling from my fingers to my lips and took a hearty pull, only realizing then that I'd apparently been out of it for so long that it had gone warm.

I choked on the sip, sputtering it up as the doorbell went off again. Placing the wasted beer on the railing, I moved through the back door and toward the front of the house as I coughed and wiped at my mouth with the back of my hand.

For the second time in two days, I opened my front door and was greeted by a fist plowing into my face. Only this one was a much bigger fist and hurt a fuck of a lot more than the first.

"Jesus," I grunted, my eyes tearing up and my vision blurring. "Good to see you too, Dalton." I should have expected it, but I was clearly off my game, because I didn't even have a chance to duck when he punched me again. Leaned out the door, I turned to the side and spit the blood that had pooled in my mouth into the front flowerbed. "Feel better?"

"A little," Dalton answered.

"Hit him again, cowboy," Charlotte said, her head popping out from behind his mountain frame and glaring at me like she wanted to set my skin on fire with her eyes just so she could watch me burn.

Dalton turned his attention to his woman, his granite expression going soft as he looked down at her. "His nose is already swelling up, Thumbelina. I think he got the message."

"Loud and clear, brother." Christ, my face fucking hurt. "I thought you guys weren't supposed to be here till tomorrow."

"We were able to get standby on an earlier flight."

"Great. Well, you want to come in?" I asked, stepping to the side.

They shoved through, both of them shouldering me back farther as they barreled in, luggage and all.

"You guys want a beer?" I asked, moving to the fridge and pulling it open, grabbing three beers before either of them had a chance to answer.

They followed me into the kitchen, propping themselves across from me on the barstools on the opposite side of the island.

"Nice place you got here," Dalton said dryly as he lifted the bottle his lips and drank. "No wonder you've been here a month and a half."

I took a swig of my own and sighed. "I'm sorry." It was all I could think to say. "I know I fucked up. I'm not going to make any excuses for what I did."

"Fine." Charlotte gripped her bottle in both hands and leaned into her forearms that were resting on the granite. "No excuses, but how about an explanation?" she demanded.

It was the very least I could give them. I told them about the call I'd had with Lincoln shortly after I got to town and realized, not only had I found her, but that I'd discovered she had a kid as well.

The only time Charlotte spoke through all of that was to murmur, "I have a niece," in a voice full of wonder.

I tried my best to explain how I wanted to do everything in my power to make sure I didn't blow up the life she'd built for herself and scare her into running again.

"I get all of that," Charlotte said in a much softer tone once I'd finished. "But a month and a half? It couldn't have taken that long to get to know her well enough to give her the truth. Why did it take so long?"

I swallowed down the lump in my throat, unable to speak past it. Throughout my whole explanation, Dalton had stayed eerily silent, scrutinizing me in a way that made me feel like I was under a microscope, his expression knowing. When he finally chimed in, I understood why.

"Because he fell in love with her." Her head whipped around to her man as I chugged back half my beer. "He fell in love with her and didn't know how to tell her without fucking it all up."

Charlotte's eyes, so much like her sisters, yet still different, flew to me and grew wide. "Is that true?"

"Yep," I admitted as I scraped at the label off the bottle with my thumbnail. "But it doesn't matter now. Like I said, I fucked up. She knows the truth now and doesn't want anything to do with me."

But then I thought of her question earlier that day before I left her in her workshop. She'd wanted me there tomorrow and was worried I wouldn't be. What did that mean for us? Could I eventually earn her trust back? I had to, I thought. There was no other option because there was no life without her and Renee.

Draining the last of my beer, I shifted the topic off me to what they were both here for. "I'll make introductions tomorrow." I looked to Charlotte as I said the next part. "She already knows you're coming, and she wants to see you."

Charlotte's chest shook on an uneven breath. "Is she—Is she good? Happy I mean?"

I couldn't help but smile. "She asked me the exact same thing about you this morning, almost word for word."

Her hazel eyes grew glassy as she smiled, letting out a watery laugh. "Of course she did. She's my twin." Her voice held a note of fondness that made me feel a little better.

I nodded in agreement. "And to answer your question, yeah. She's really happy. She's made a wonderful life here for her and her daughter after the nightmare she escaped from with Knightly. They have a lot of love in this town."

"That's good," Charlotte whispered, her focus drifting off, staring at nothing in particular. "That's really good."

"Is it cool with you if we crash here for the night?" Dalton asked. "We came here straight from the airport, didn't have time to book a room anywhere."

"Don't bother with that. Stay here as long as you want. This house is plenty big enough. You can take the room off the hall near the entryway. Second door on the left."

He gave me a short nod before rising to his feet. "Come on, baby," Dalton said gently, wrapping a big arm around his woman and helping her off the stool she'd been perched on. "Let's get some sleep, yeah? Tomorrow's a big day."

"I don't know if I'll be able to sleep. I'm so anxious I feel like I'm coming out of my skin."

I saw the smirk he gave her and caught his mumbled, "Think I can come up with some ways to wear you out," just before they disappeared out of the kitchen.

I followed suit not long after, crawling between my cold

sheets and staring up at the ceiling fan casting shadows on the walls with each slow rotation.

Tomorrow was in fact a big day. And there wasn't a chance in hell I was going to get even a minute of sleep tonight.

Twenty-Seven

CHEYANNE

I CHEWED on my lip and wrung my hands as my gazed darted all around. "Do you think I have time to pull the vacuum out and give the rug a once-over?"

Luna lifted the coffee mug to her lips and drank from her perch on the barstool. "Will you try to relax? There's no reason for you to vacuum anything. The house is so spotless you could eat off of any surface in here."

Maybe she was right, but I couldn't help it. "I'm just really nervous," I admitted as I moved to the back of the couch and began fluffing the throw pillows. Renee sat at the coffee table, coloring in one of her million books, completely oblivious to her mom's freak-out. At least she was still dressed, which I had to consider a win. "It's been almost twenty years. What if she doesn't like me?"

"Impossible. You're the most likable person on the West

Coast, if not the whole country. It's actually kind of freaky how likable you are."

I let out a snort, a shaky smile tugging at my lips. "Thanks. And thank you for being here today. I know this might be kind of awkward for you."

"Nothing to thank me for, babe. You need a support system at your back the first time you meet your sister in two decades, I'm your girl. I'm your ride or die chick. Your sister from another mister. And another mother, but that doesn't rhyme as well. I'm your—"

"I get it," I cut in with a giggle. My laughter was interrupted by a steady knock on the door. And just like that, my heart nearly exploded from my chest.

"Mommy, someone's at da doow," Renee informed me, not even bothering to lift her head from her coloring.

My eyes bugged out as I whipped around to Luna in a panic, whisper-yelling, "Oh my God! They're here!"

She hopped off the stool and came to me, clapping her hands on my shoulders like one of those coaches you'd see in the movies just as they were about to give their player an inspirational speech.

"Woman, get your s-h-i-t together. Pull up your big girl panties and go open the door."

Luna definitely needed to work on her inspirational speeches. She kind of sucked at them.

"All right." I pulled in a huge breath. Then another. "I'm going to open the door."

"Good."

"I'm going right now."

"Then go!"

I took a stumbled step from her little shove before righting myself and walking the rest of the way to the door on my own.

With a trembling hand, I grabbed hold of the knob and twisted. Trent was the first thing I saw when I pulled the door open, standing front and center.

I didn't want to be relieved at the sight of him, but damn it, I was. "H-hey," I stuttered nervously.

He gave me a tender smile, dimples in full effect. I noticed then that he had one more black eye than he'd had the day before, but my head was too overwhelmed with other things to question it. "Hey. You good?"

"Mm-hmm," I mumbled. "Come on in."

I stepped aside so he could step in, finally revealing the two people who had been standing behind him the whole time. My eyes immediately went to the woman standing beside a big bear of a man. My heart that had been banging against my ribs just moments ago suddenly quit beating all together.

"Oh my God," she gasped, her hands coming up to cover her mouth as tears sprang to her eyes. "It's really you."

I grinned, this one real but wobbly as my vision grew wet and blurry. "Hi, Charlotte."

"I can't believe you're here," she cried out, then a second later she went from being a good five feet away to pulling me into her and squeezing me tight.

Something happened the moment her arms closed around me. That empty space inside of me, the one that appeared the moment she'd been ripped away, disappeared in an instant.

I returned her embrace, closing my eyes and letting the feeling of rightness, of being absolutely complete, wash over me. I felt light as a feather just then, and I knew it was a feeling that would stay with me forever.

"I've been waiting for this day almost my whole life," she rasped.

"I never thought it would happen," I returned on a croak. "It feels like a puzzle piece has finally fallen into place."

She let out a watery laugh and pulled back, but didn't release me completely, keeping hold of my arms. "I know what you mean. The moment I saw you there was this . . ."

"Fullness," I answered for her, remembering just then how, back when we were children, we had this uncanny ability to finish each other's thoughts.

"Exactly." She beamed at me, placing her hand on her chest, right over her heart. "Right here."

I nodded, feeling like my cheeks were about to split in half with the power of my grin. "Yeah."

We sniffled and batted at our eyes, the actions so similar. It was unbelievable how that twin connection reestablished almost instantly, even after all these years. We'd been apart so much longer than we'd ever been together, but it was as if no time had passed at all.

Taking me by the hand, she turned to face the man who'd

been waiting so patiently on the front porch. "Cheyanne, this is my fiancé, Dalton. Dalton, I want you to meet my sister, Cheyanne."

The man smiled genuinely, his white teeth glinting from beneath his dark beard. "Really nice to meet you."

I took the hand he offered me, reading nothing but happiness for his soon-to-be wife in his kind gaze. For such a huge dude, he had a softness to him that made me think that Charlotte had lucked out with this guy. "It's nice to meet you too."

Trent spoke just then. "So you guys want to move this inside?"

"Yes," I answered, brightening at the thought. "There's someone I want you to meet. Come on in."

Still hand in hand with Charlotte, I led her inside, through the entry, and into the living room. Once there, I let her go in order to round the coffee table and take my baby girl's hand. "Meet Renee."

At her name, Charlotte's eyes rounded, coming to me in question. I didn't need words to know what she was asking. I nodded, that smile still firmly in place as I confirmed my daughter was named after her.

Shaking herself out of her stupor, Charlotte moved closer to Renee and lowered down onto her knees, her eyes full of awe as she stared at my girl. "Hi, Renee. It's so great to meet you."

"Hi!" she chirped. "I'm fwee yeaws old!" She curled her

chubby little fingers, trying her hardest to keep three of them up, but still having a little trouble.

"Wow. Three? That's so big."

"I know!" Renee yelped excitedly. "Whas youw name?"

"I'm Charlotte."

Renee's eyes nearly bugged out of her skull. "Like the pwincess in da clouds! Mommy says dats who I'm named aftew."

"A princess?"

"Yeah! Mommy says da stowy at night about da pwincess twins in da clouds who get stoled by da bad dwagon. Awe you da pwincess? You look jus like Mommy."

My sister looked up at me, silently willing me to help her out with the answer. "Yeah, honey. This is the princess from the story. She's your aunt Charlotte. My twin sister." Renee looked at her like she'd just met the most famous person in existence.

Charlotte sniffled back another round of tears, her voice hoarse and shaky as she said, "I'm so happy to meet you, Renee. You're such a beautiful girl."

Renee launched herself at Charlotte, wrapping her tiny arms around her aunt's neck. "Nice ta meet you too," she exclaimed before pulling back. "Dat's my Tent, and dat's my Lu-Lu," she told Charlotte, pointing out Trent and Luna. "Did you meet dem?"

I filled in introductions for her, holding my hand out toward Luna. "Charlotte, Dalton, this is my best friend, Luna."

"Hey." Luna waved at the room. "Nice to meet you guys. I'm the one who gave that dude his first black eye."

I curled my lips between my teeth to stifle a laugh just as Charlotte snorted. Dalton chuckled, before saying, "Good to meet you too. I'm the dude who gave him the second. And the busted lip."

She gave him an appraising look before nodding in approval. "You'll do just fine."

"All right," Trent grumbled. "While it's great you guys are finding common ground to bond over, what do you say we take Little Bit out to play on the beach and give the two princesses some time to bond?" He looked to Renee. "How's that sound, honey?"

Renee sucked all the air in the room into her lungs on a gasp that had Luna, Trent, and me all warning, "Cover your ears!"

Charlotte and Dalton obeyed just as Renee's excited shriek filled the whole house. "*Yeah! Yeah! Yeah*! Let's go! Come on, Tent!"

"Holy sh—" Dalton caught himself before he finished his curse.

"We spell them out in this house," Luna advised.

"Holy s-h-i-t," he started over. "Am I deaf?"

Charlotte burst into laughter, cackling so hard she fell onto her butt. "That's incredible! I can't believe she does that too."

"Too?" Trent asked, quirking a single brow. *Jerk.*

"Yeah. I used to do that when I got excited." She turned

to me. "Remember? Mom and Dad used to tease me that I'd shatter all the windows."

The memory slammed into me like a wrecking ball. "Oh my God. That's right. You did!"

"Beach! Beach! Beach!" Renee shouted, not caring that something epic had just happened.

In no time at all, Trent had Renee on his shoulders, and he and Dalton were heading across the deck toward the gate. Luna hung back for a second, looking at me to ask, "You good?"

"I am. Thank you so much, hon."

She smiled, reaching out to give my arm a squeeze. "Any and every time, babe. I'm going to head out, but it was really nice meeting you, Charlotte, and I'm sure I'll see you around."

"It was nice to meet you too," my sister told her.

Luna pulled me into a tight embrace before taking off, and for the first time in almost twenty years, I was left alone with my twin sister.

"She's incredible, Chey," Charlotte said softly.

With the guys and Renee down at the beach, I made some coffee for my sister and me—I didn't think I'd ever get tired of thinking that—and we moved out to the back deck. We were both curled up on the love seat, facing the ocean.

I felt my face get soft as I watched Charlotte's fiancé and

my baby girl burying Trent in the sand. The sight of that shouldn't have warmed me up, but it was as though I had no control over my own body. He was just so good with her. He was fully clothed, covered in sand that was probably freezing, and seemed completely content. "Yeah, she's kind of amazing, isn't she?"

"She absolutely is." Her hand covered mine, her fingers squeezing. "Thank you so much for naming her after me."

"I always had you with me, even after all the years apart, I did what I could to have you with me." We lapsed into silence when a thought came to mind, pounding against my skull incessantly. "Charlotte," I started quietly. "Trent told me what Graham had his man do to you. I'm so sorry you had to go through that."

"Stop," she ordered, turning to face me. "That wasn't your fault."

"But if I'd never married him—"

She interrupted me with fierce determination. "I wouldn't change what happened, not for anything. If that had never happened, I wouldn't be here with you right now. I can't be upset about something that led us back together."

When she put it like that, I really couldn't say I'd change anything either, even those years of misery I'd spent with Graham. In the end, having Renee and now being here with Charlotte made every bad day and night worth it.

"This is so beautiful," she murmured a few minutes later. "Being right here on the water like this, I can see why you stayed."

"It really is, but it's not just the beauty of the place that drew me in. It was the people. I never belonged anywhere until I came here. Mom's cousin didn't want me any more than she wanted you. Graham never really loved me, he just liked that I didn't have anyone I could lean on; that made it easier for him to control and isolate me. But I came here, and I was family. It was nice not to feel alone after so long."

She leaned into me. "I know the feeling. I have a friend back home in Hope Valley. His name is Micah, and he showed me what it was like to have people in my corner."

"Then you met Dalton," I said softly.

"Then I met Dalton," she agreed. "And he saved me. He gave me a family and showed me what it was like to feel treasured."

I looped my arm through hers. "I'm glad you have that."

"And I'm glad you have this."

I let out a sigh. "If only we weren't an entire country apart, huh?"

She gave me a little jostle, grinning like crazy. "But at least we know where the other is now. There will be phone calls and FaceTime. And I foresee a lot of plane rides in our future."

"This is true," I said on a giggle, feeling like I was floating on a cloud. "We finally found each other."

"And nothing and no one is ever going to separate us again."

I really loved the sound of that.

Twenty-Eight

CHEYANNE

THE DAY before had been so full of emotion that Charlotte and I hadn't really had the chance to go too in-depth about each other's lives. We were more focused on just being together for the first time in two decades.

Today was all about showing my twin the life I'd built in this gorgeous town by the ocean.

"Oh man," Charlotte said in a whisper as she stepped into my workshop. "Look at all this stuff!" Her big eyes came back around to me. "You made all of this?"

"Yep," I answered proudly. Surprisingly, all the nerves I usually felt whenever people saw my work firsthand were completely absent just then. The twenty-year gap between us hadn't made us strangers. Oddly enough, it felt like we were picking up right where we left off. Sure, there was so much we didn't know about each other, but there was plenty of time for that now that we'd finally found each other.

"This right here is my passion."

"I can see why. You're brilliant, Chey." Hearing my sister say that filled me with so much joy, I worried that it was going to burst from the top of my head and spill over. "Man, I wish I had even an ounce of your talent. I'm so jealous right now."

I knew my smile probably looked ridiculously goofy, but I didn't care. In that moment, memories of the past came flooding back. The space between when we were born might have only been minutes, but Charlotte had always taken her role as the oldest very seriously. She was my big sister, my protector. And as the "little" sister, her approval had always made me feel ten feet tall.

"Yeah, well, I could never in a million years dance like you do. I look like a fish flopping around on dry land."

I learned that Charlotte was a performer at a burlesque club in Virginia called Whiskey Dolls. After a quick Google search, I'd discovered that the club was insanely popular, and people came from all over to check out the shows the Whiskey Dolls put on. I'd even found some videos online, and I totally understood why the club had the level of prestige it did. From the snippets I'd seen, the girls were unbelievable.

Charlotte and her friends were professionals at commanding that stage. All I had to watch was some grainy cellphone video, but I was still enraptured.

"Trent has a piece of yours over at his place. I saw it yesterday. It really is stunning."

"He showed you?" I asked before I could stop myself. When I'd climbed into bed the night before, I'd berated myself for how hard I'd leaned on Trent. For how much I'd needed him on such an important day. He'd lied and deceived me since day one, and I didn't want to feel safe in his presence, but I did. Damn him, I still did.

She gave me a curious look, and I suspected that Trent had filled her and Dalton in on every detail of what had transpired between us. "He keeps it out on the coffee table," she informed me. "I saw it last night and asked him about it. He told us how talented you are."

"He said that?" I was caught off guard, and I didn't have time to hide my reaction before she saw it.

"Do you . . . want to talk about it? I mean, him in particular? I know we've just reconnected, and we've never really done the whole talking-about-boys thing, but if you want—"

I cut her off. "It's okay. There's nothing to talk about."

It took no effort at all to read her expression clear as day. She knew I was full of shit. Fortunately, Renee took that moment to interrupt us.

Skipping up from her little station at the back of my workshop, she thrust her arms toward Charlotte, a painted mug that hadn't had a chance to dry yet clasped between her chubby, now-colorful hands. "I made dis fow you, Aunt Pwincess."

Ever since I told her that Charlotte was the princess in the bedtime story I'd been telling her for the longest time, she'd taken to calling her Aunt Princess, something my sister absolutely adored. Dalton was still a little on the fence about his new name. Renee had a bit of trouble pronouncing 'Dalton,' so she'd taken to calling him Uncle Dolly for short. Something that gave the rest of us endless amusement.

"Oh wow." She went down to her knees in front of Renee, reaching out to take the coffee cup, not caring in the slightest she was getting paint all over her hands. "This is mine? I can keep it?"

"Yeah! It's a pwesent. You like it?"

"This is the most beautiful thing I've ever been given, honey," Charlotte exclaimed, the honesty of that statement radiating from her skin like a warm, soft halo of light. The gift my baby girl had made for her really and truly was the best gift she'd ever received. Her voice was hoarse with emotion as she insisted, "I love it so much."

"Yay! I'll make you a fousand mowe!"

"I'd really love that. How about a million? I could put them *all* over my house."

Renee sucked in a gasp, her eyes going big. "Dat's a *lot*."

She looked at Renee seriously. "I know. Think you're up for it?"

"Yeah!"

"Come on. I'll get this fired for you so it sets, and in the meantime, there's something I want to show you." I set the mug in a safe place and led the two of them into the house.

In the living room, I sat down on the couch and patted the cushion beside me as Renee moved to the toy bin that sat beneath the living room window and started dumping everything out, having lost interest in what the grownups were doing almost immediately. Charlotte sat down beside me, taking the box I passed her and placing it in her lap.

"What is this?" she asked, looking at me quizzically.

After everyone left last night, before going to sleep, I'd dug through my closet, getting down that box that had been everywhere with me, in every place I'd lived for years.

I was giddy with anticipation. "Open it and find out."

She flipped the lid back and stared down at the contents in silence for a few beats, blinking slowly before realization dawned. "No way!" She snatched up a stack of photos and began rifling through them. "Where did you get these?"

"They were packed up with all our stuff when we went to live with Mom's cousin. When I left there, that box was one of the very few things I took with me. I didn't need much as long as I had that. I've had it with me ever since."

"Oh my God!" Her lips split into a smile a mile wide, her face positively glowing as she flipped through the pictures at a rapid pace. Once she made it through the end of the pile, she started all over again, going much slower the second time.

"I can't believe you have these," she said quietly, her words full of awe and wonder. "I've wished for so long that I had pictures. It's weird, but I still remember what Mom and Dad look like, you know? Those memories should have faded by now, but they're still in my head, clear as day. Only, I wasn't sure if what I was remembering was right."

She lifted one of the photos close to her face. It was of our parents on their wedding day, Mom beautiful in the most stunning lacy white dress, and Dad looking so handsome in his classic tux. "Now I know what I've been remembering this whole time was real," she said in a quiet, barely-there voice.

"They were the most beautiful couple."

She looked to me, still grinning so wide I wondered if her cheeks hurt. "They really were. You have Dad's eyes."

"Yeah. And you and Renee have Mom's. And look at this." I rifled through the box until I found a picture of Charlotte and me when we were about Renee's age. I pointed to little toddler Charlotte in the photograph. "Looks familiar, right?"

She glanced at the picture, then over to where Renee was playing by the window. "Holy crap," she whispered. "She looks—"

"Just like you," I finished. "I know. It's like I've had a mini-you with me all this time."

"Shrieks and all," she giggled, and I joined in.

"Exactly." She shuffled through a few more, and we reminisced about the ones we remembered. "Tomorrow we can go into town and get copies made of all of these for you to keep. Then maybe I can show you around."

"I'd really love that," she enthused. "And I have something to show you too."

Placing the box of photos back on the table, she shot up and rushed over to her purse sitting on the bar. She grabbed it by the strap and returned to the couch. When she pulled the necklace from the inside zipper pocket, all the air whooshed from my lungs.

"Mom's locket."

She handed it to me, and I used my thumbnail to flip it open, seeing our photos on each side. Charlotte on the left, me on the right. It looked like they were school photos from way back in the day, complete with goofy smiles that were missing front teeth.

Leaning sideways, she bumped her shoulder into mine playfully. "I've had you with me all this time, too."

There was something soothing in that, in knowing that, even after all these years, we'd still been together in one way or another. There hadn't been a chance I'd ever forget her, but I would have been lying if I said I didn't worry that she'd moved on without me, that I was barely a memory for her. Knowing that wasn't the case filled me with a sense of relief.

We were two halves of one whole. Two sides of the same coin. And we'd done our best to stay as whole as possible in the only ways we could all this time, never giving up hope that we'd one day find each other.

All that waiting and hoping and wishing . . . it had finally paid off.

Twenty-Nine

CHEYANNE

"Okay, yes. This is an excellent cup of coffee," Charlotte admitted, taking another sip from the drink Monica had just made her.

I lifted my brows, only slightly bitter that I couldn't arch just one. "Better than the stuff from your place back home?" I challenged teasingly.

She rolled her eyes good-naturedly. She and Dalton had been in town for a few days now, and with Renee at daycare for the first time since they arrived, and the guys off doing their own thing, talking shop or something—I'd asked Charlotte to explain what they did for a firm like theirs, but her explanation had been both confusing and slightly terrifying—I finally had the chance to show my sister around. After getting copies of all our childhood photos made, our next stop was coffee so we could finally put to rest the debate on whose was best, the coffee from

Drip or the stuff from her favorite place back in Hope Valley, a place called Muffin Top. I relented that the name was cool as hell, but I was still convinced Drip's coffee was better.

"I think it's about tied."

I gave her a narrow-eyed look. "Then I guess I'm just going to have to visit you in Virginia and judge for myself."

Her whole face warmed, her smile infectious. "Yeah, I guess you will have to do that, huh?"

"You two," Monica said, pulling our focus to her. "Watching how you are with each other, it's just so damn adorable."

We hung around the coffee shop for a bit longer, chatting with Monica and taking the time to make introductions to the people who filtered in and out before heading off to our next stop. I was taking her to Warren's General Store so she could see where I worked and meet two of the most important people in my life, Georgia and Desmond.

We walked at a sedate, leisurely pace down the sidewalk so Charlotte could take it all in. The cute buildings, like something out of a postcard, the sound of the surf crashing against the shore not far away. I felt a sense of pride in showing her my town and letting her see the tight-knit bond everyone here had as we strolled along, waving at the people we passed by.

"So," she started as we passed the ice cream shop that would stay open year-round, even in the dead of winter. Ice cream was ice cream. Even freezing temps wouldn't keep people from the sweet, sugary goodness. "I've waited to bring it up, but I feel like it's time."

My neck twisted in her direction, my brows puckering in a frown of confusion. "What are you talking about?"

She gave me a knowing look. It was remarkable how we were able to read each other after such a short time. "You and Trent."

I jerked back around, facing forward as I lifted my paper cup and took a sip of coffee. "There's nothing to talk about."

"Yeah. I said that too. When I was falling in love with Dalton but was scared out of my mind over what I was feeling because of the ugliness in my past."

I didn't have a response to that. It hit way too close to home. She was right, but instead of acknowledging that, I made an excuse. "It's not just about that. It's the fact that he kept this huge secret. He knew who I was the whole time, and he used that to manipulate me into falling for him."

"Did he though?"

"I—" Now that she'd asked, I was having trouble answering. Because what if he hadn't? What if everything that had happened between us was real?

"Look, I'm not going to tell you whether you should forgive him or not, but I will tell you this: I know Trent. He's one of my closest friends. He's had my back and Dalton's on countless occasions. When he cares about someone, there isn't anything he wouldn't do to keep them safe. You have every right to be mad, no doubt about it. Hell, I was furious. Why do you think Dalton gave him that second black eye for me?" I couldn't hold back the laugh that bubbled up my throat. "But there's one question you need to ask yourself. Is your life better now that he's in it than it was before you met him? When you figure out the answer to that, you'll know what you need to do."

"It doesn't matter anyway," I said weakly, not quite able to give up the fight. "He'll go back to Hope Valley eventually. This is my home, Char. How is a relationship supposed to work when there's a freaking continent between us?"

For some reason, she smiled at that. "I know all the dudes that Trent and Dalt work with, and they all have one thing in common."

"Yeah? What's that?"

Her eyes grew intense when she looked over at me. "When they fall in love with a woman, they're capable of moving mountains. And that man loves you with everything he has."

We lapsed into silence the rest of the way to the general store, my mind swirling in a million different directions as I pushed through the door to the sound of that familiar tinkling bell.

Georgia's head came up from her romance novel, her smile taking over her face. "Well, there she is," she said brightly as she rounded the counter and started for me. "Dezzy!" she shouted loudly. "Get in here! Chey—" She caught herself, casting a quick glance at the few customers browsing the aisles. "Sawyer's here, and she's brought her sister!"

Word spread like wildfire that I had a twin sister who was in town, and everyone was more than eager to meet her, but the secret of who I really was had stayed between me and those people I was closest to. True to their word, they hadn't said a thing.

Dezzy came around the corner from the stockroom, his expression just as excited as his wife's. "Hey! You're here!"

My mood instantly brightened, thoughts of Trent pushed to the back burner, at least temporarily. "Guys, I want you to meet my sister, Charlotte. Charlotte, this is Georgia and Dezzy Warren, my bosses and two of the best people you'll ever have the privilege of meeting. They've helped me through some tough times."

"It was nothing. We're blessed to have this one here in our lives," Desmond stated with genuine warmth laced through the words.

"It's so nice to meet you," Charlotte said with a genuine smile as the three of them exchanged handshakes. "Thank you so much for taking care of her all these years. I can't tell you how much that means to me."

"Pleasure's all ours, believe me," Georgia informed her.

After introductions were made, the Warrens started to fill Charlotte in on every embarrassing story they had about me from the past three and a half years, like real parents would any time their child brought a friend home from school. They were in the middle of cutting up about that one time I'd accidentally stocked three whole cases of soda in the freezer instead of the refrigerator, and how they were certain it was Armageddon as all the cans started to explode, when we heard the sound of sirens whipping by the store.

It was a foreign sound here in Whitecap. There was little to no crime, so the only time we heard police cruisers or ambulances was when someone had gotten hurt.

Georgia stared through the glass, worry marring her face. "Hope old Emmet Clifton didn't try trimming his own trees again. Last time he did that, he fell off the ladder and nearly sliced himself up with his chainsaw. Got lucky he didn't really hurt himself."

Just then, another cruiser whipped by, lights and sirens blaring, followed quickly by a third. Through the glass, we could see that people were coming out of the neighboring shops and businesses, starting to line the streets.

"Whatever happened, looks like it's big," Dezzy said, heading for the door just as an ambulance raced by. We all followed after him, picking up the pace.

"What's going on?" he asked the first person he came across on the sidewalk.

"Apparently there was a shooting," Karen Norton stated, lifting a shaky hand to her mouth as all the blood in my body turned to ice, Whitecap didn't have shootings. We were a small, quiet town. Stuff like that didn't happen here.

"Where?" I asked as the panic started to set in.

She looked at me with wide eyes full of fear, and said three words that ground my world to a halt. "At the daycare."

I couldn't tell you how I got to the daycare or how much time it had taken. One second I'd been standing on the sidewalk outside the general store, and the next I was running across the street toward the daycare's parking lot at a dead sprint.

"Ma'am, I'm sorry, I can't let you in there," one of the uniformed officers said as he blocked my path.

"Please," I begged as I tried my best to look past him. "My daughter's in there. You have to let me through."

"I'm sorry." He held his arms out, thwarting my attempt to dart past him. "This is an active crime scene. You can't go in."

"Sawyer!" I heard yelled just as Trent and Dalton came running up to me. Charlotte must have called while we were on our way there, and I was beyond grateful to see Trent just then, knowing that whatever was happening in that moment, he'd do everything in his power to shield Renee and me from it. "What's going on?" he panted as he reached my side. The expression on his face was one I'd never seen before. It was the look of abject terror.

"Wait," the officer in front of me stopped trying to push me back. "Are you Sawyer Darcy?"

"Yes. I'm Sawyer Darcy. Please, you have to let me through to get to my little girl."

He looked back over his shoulder, shouting, "Sheriff, I have the mother here!"

Oh God. That couldn't be good.

The man I recognized as Sheriff Michaels lifted his head, his eyes coming right to me. "Let her through."

I didn't even wait for the man to get out of my way before I was barreling past him with Trent right beside me. "Sheriff, what's going on?" Trent asked. I was glad he was still with it enough to ask, because I was having trouble forming words.

"Sir, are you with Ms. Darcy?"

"Yes, he is," I bit out. "He's with me. Now please, tell us what's going on. Where's my daughter."

"Ms. Darcy, I'm sorry to have to tell you this, but your daughter was taken."

Just like that, everything went black.

Thirty

TRENT

I WAS RUNNING on nothing but adrenaline and rage by the time I got to Cheyanne's house. Renee had officially been missing for an hour and a half, and each minute that passed felt like a knife being plunged into my chest over and over again.

Cheyanne had collapsed the moment the sheriff told her what had happened. I'd had Dalton take her back home with Charlotte and the Warrens so I could stay back and get the full story from the sheriff.

A man had come in, posing as a parent who was trying to find a daycare for his son. Of course, all the information he'd given had been fake, but the staff there couldn't have known that, at least not right then. One of the workers had taken him on a tour, and when they got to the classroom Renee was in, he'd pulled a gun. The worker who'd been showing him around tried to intervene when he snatched Little Bit and was shot. According to the sheriff, it hadn't been fatal, but the woman was currently in surgery.

Cheyanne's house had been a whirlwind of activity for the past forty-five minutes. Georgia had shown up with Dezzy, followed closely by Luna, Sam, and Monica. They were all doing what they could to keep Cheyanne from losing it completely while I did everything in my power to locate her little girl.

The deputies had been there as well, doing what they were trained to do: asking Cheyanne one question after another. None of which would get Renee back to us any faster.

Did she have any enemies that she could think of?

Yes.

Was there anything in her past that might indicate who had taken her daughter?

Yes.

Did she have any idea who was behind the kidnapping?

Hell fucking yes.

I knew they were only doing their jobs, they couldn't just take us at our word when we told them who was responsible and why. They needed evidence. They had to work the case their way.

Fortunately, I had the skills to work it my way at the same time. And my way was a fuck of a lot faster, no evidence required.

"Where are we with the security footage?" I barked as I paced the area between Cheyenne's kitchen and living room.

"Linc put Xander on it," Dalton answered from his place at the bar, hunched over his laptop. "He caught something on one of the cameras from a business right across the street from the daycare center. He's sending it through now."

In that very moment, I was grateful that Xander Caine was our resident techie at Alpha Omega. There wasn't a computer or camera in existence he couldn't hack.

I moved in behind him, leaning forward to get a better view of the video that had just started playing. My heart wedged itself in my throat as I watched the scene play out. It showed a man running from the building with Renee tucked in one arm and a gun in the other hand. The image was grainy, and there was only a flash of his face before he climbed into the backseat of a dark-colored sedan that had been idling in the parking lot. The car peeled out before the guy's door was even fully shut.

"Two people," I grunted, fire coursing through my veins. I didn't recognize either of them, but that wasn't going to stop me from make them pay in the most painful ways for daring to touch my girl.

"The gunman and a driver," Dalton confirmed. "From the looks of it, neither was Knightly."

I stood tall, raking my hands through my hair in agitation. I felt like I was coming out of my skin. With each second that passed, anxiety and fear clawed my insides to shreds. "Of course not. That motherfucker never gets his hands dirty. We got facial recognition on that son of a bitch yet?"

"Nothing that'll tie back to Knightly. Just like that prick back in Hope Valley that came after Charlotte, there's nothing that links either of these guys to him. He's good at keeping his nose clean."

"It doesn't matter." At the new voice in the room, Dalton and I spun around. Cheyanne was standing at the mouth of the hall with Charlotte beside her, and the whole family she'd created for herself and Renee here in Whitecap at her back. My woman was looking at me with sheer determination setting those fall-leaf eyes on fire. She might have broken down for a bit, but she was strong as hell, and I could see it written all over her hard face now, she was ready to fight.

"What do you mean, baby?"

"We don't need to know who those guys are to Graham, because he reached out."

She held out her arm, her cellphone resting in her palm.

I moved to her and took it, looking down at the text chain she had open on the screen.

There was a message from an unknown number that read '*You didn't really think you could hide from me, did you?*' accompanied by a video. I clicked play and felt all the blood drain from my face while acid churned in my gut.

"What is this?" Dalton asked, watching the short clip over my shoulder.

"It's from the Harvest Festival," Cheyanne answered. "That's how he found me. Someone must have been live streaming on their phone."

The person holding the phone was panning around, showing all the different booths that lined the street. The video paused on Cheyanne's booth. She was standing right there behind her table, a smile full of happiness and light on her face as she held Renee in her arms.

Through the haze of red coating my vision, I was able to read the message that had come in right after the video.

Trade. Her for you.

My eyes shot to Cheyanne's, and the determination staring back at me coated my throat in fire.

"No fucking way."

Cheyanne

I felt my spine go hard, like it had just been coated in steel. My bones and muscles rigid, I squared my shoulders and lifted my chin. "I'm doing it, Trent."

"Not a goddamn chance," he barked as all the color bleached from his face. "No, Cheyanne. I'm not letting you do that."

"It's not your call!" I cried out, snatching my phone back. "He has my baby! *My* daughter. If you think I'm just going to sit here and do nothing, you're out of your fucking mind and you clearly don't know me at all."

"There has to be another way," he mumbled to himself,

pacing the floor like a caged lion. I'd never seen him like this before. There was something feral in his eyes, something positively wild and filled with terror. He was a man on the edge, terrified of losing something he had come to love.

"Just give Dalton and me some time. We can come up with a plan."

"There's no way for any plan to work that doesn't involve me. That's my little girl." My voice broke and I had to swallow down the tears that wanted to break free. I didn't have time to fall apart. I didn't have time to curl up in a ball and cry, no matter how badly I wanted to. Not when that monster had my child.

"I've sworn to protect her since the moment I found out she was growing inside me. That's why I took her from him in the first goddamn place! I'm going to get her back. There is no plan without me, so I suggest you figure out a way to keep me safe so I can get my baby and bring her home."

His gaze darted frantically around the room looking for someone who would agree with him. "You guys can't be okay with this," he said, his voice pleading. "This is insane."

"It's not insanity," Georgia stated firmly. "It's a mother willing to risk everything for her child. There's nothing stronger on the face of the earth than that."

Clearly he wasn't going to be getting any help from her, so he tried a new tactic. "Charlotte, you know she can't do this. We'll get Renee. Dalton and me, you know we will. You have to make her see reason."

"She's my twin," my sister said in a way I knew meant

she'd be backing whatever play I made. "We're one and the same, Trent. If you weren't able to stop me from getting in the middle of a bunch of dirty cops, what makes you think you have any chance of stopping her when it's her own child's safety on the line?"

Trent rocked back on his heels, so off balance it looked like he could have been knocked over with a feather.

Closing the distance between us, I stepped up to him and lifted my hands, the scruff coating his jawline abrading my palms as I cupped his cheeks. "Trent, I trust you," I whispered, the sincerity of that statement dripping from my words, because it was the God's honest truth. There had been no one in my life for the past twenty years that I trusted the way I trusted Trent. "I know you would never let anything happen to me or Renee. You'd protect us with your life. I believe that down in my soul. And I know you'll protect me. So help me, please. Come up with a plan that will keep me safe and get my daughter back. If there's anyone who can do it, it's you."

He stared down at me, love so strong it overrode everything else shining in his eyes. My heart beat wildly in my chest as I waited with bated breath for him to say something, *anything*. And when he finally did, I felt a glimmer of hope for the first time since Renee was taken.

"All right. But if we're doing this, you have to do *exactly* what I tell you."

 Thirty-One

TRENT

I COULDN'T FUCKING BELIEVE I'd agreed to this. My heart was lodged in my throat, taking up so much space it was nearly impossible to breathe.

Dalton clapped me on the shoulder. "She's got this, brother. Don't worry. She's a Belmont, just like her sister. No stronger women in the world."

It wasn't that I didn't agree with what he was saying. I knew he was right. But that didn't mean I wouldn't burn the fucking world to the ground if something happened to Cheyanne or Renee. There were no lengths I wouldn't go to in order to make those who harmed them pay in the most brutally painful ways.

After I let her talk me into this insanity, we'd sat down to form a plan. She texted back, agreeing to the exchange, and within five minutes that son of a bitch had responded with the location and orders not to tell the cops or he'd kill Renee.

The one thing we had going for us in all of this was the fact that the man's ego was so big he hadn't bothered to do his due diligence. He didn't know anything about Dalton or myself, and we planned to take full advantage of that.

I'd left her place only long enough to run back to my rental to grab my gear. When I returned to her house and started pulling everything out, she's looked at me with wide, shock-filled eyes.

"I can't believe you have all this," she'd said on a breath. "I mean, who has thermal vision and recording and listening devices? This isn't normal everyday stuff you'd find around your house."

I wasn't feeling it, but in an attempt to put her at ease, I'd given her a wink, a sly smile pulling up my lips and pressing my dimples deep. "I was a Boy Scout, remember? We're always prepared."

"You were kicked out!" she exclaimed nervously.

"Yeah, but not before they taught me that."

Once we'd gotten the location, with Xander's remote help, we'd been able to pull up the blueprints of the building, as well as a satellite view of the area.

It looked to be some sort of abandoned industrial warehouse in a remote location in the middle of nowhere, twenty miles outside of town.

Cheyanne, Dalton, Charlotte—because she refused to stay behind, goddamn Belmont women—and myself had arrived an hour before the scheduled meet time, taking two cars and parking a mile up the road to stay out of sight.

Dalton and I went ahead to scope the place out and decided on the perfect vantage point for him to set up. He'd been an expert marksman back when he was a Ranger, so he'd provide eyes on the outside as well as cover if it came to it, and I'd take my place near the rear entrance we'd spotted.

According to Xander, who'd hacked into God knew what, there'd been four heat signatures in the building. One was substantially smaller than all the rest and had to be Renee. She was located in a room at the very back of the building, only a few yards from the rear exit.

"She's five minutes out," Dalton said, pulling me back to the rescue. "Get into position."

"I'm going with you," Charlotte stated, pushing up determinedly from her crouch.

"Not a fucking chance—" I started, but I should have known it was pointless to argue.

"That's my sister, down there. I only *just* got her back, and I promised her there wasn't anything or anyone who'd keep us apart ever again. I intend to keep that promise."

I turned to look back at Dalton, who was staring at his woman with fierce pride. With one quick nod, he reached around and pulled out the handgun that had been tucked into the waistband of his jeans at the small of his back and passed it to her.

After Charlotte had been shot and nearly killed, she'd developed a fear of guns. Dalton had worked with her for a while to teach her there was nothing to be scared of if you respected the weapon in your hand and were properly trained to use it. Now the little firecracker was a crack shot.

"You remember everything I've taught you?" he asked as she took it from him and checked the safety before tucking it into her own pants.

"Every lesson," she confirmed with a resolute nod.

"All right then. Let's get this done."

Cheyanne

Nerves were making me shake so hard my bones were rattling as I drove my car along the abandoned gravel lane toward the building.

I couldn't remember a time in my life when I'd been so scared, but I couldn't let it control me. This plan would work. I just knew it. Trent had come up with it, and if there was anyone who could get Renee and me out of here safely, it was him.

Blowing out a tremulous sigh, I spoke into the empty car.

"Can you guys hear me?" I asked.

A second later, Trent's disembodied voice filled my ear from the microscopic earpiece he'd given me back at my house. "Loud and clear, baby. Got visual from the button cam as well. I'm right here with you. Just remember the plan. Keep him talking so I can get in and grab Renee."

"Got it." That wouldn't be hard. If there was one thing I knew for certain about Graham, it was that the man loved the sound of his own voice. He was a narcissist through and through. That, combined with the fact he was a total sociopath, made for an extremely dangerous person. He really was the perfect politician.

"Once I get her clear, I'm coming for you. You have my word. If things go sideways, Dalton's got your back."

"Roger that," Dalton confirmed in my earpiece. "Got eyes on you right now, sweetheart. You're all good."

I was putting my complete faith in one man I hardly knew and another who had been lying to me the entire time we'd known each other. And for some weird reason I couldn't even begin to comprehend, I felt like that was the smartest decision I could ever make.

Trent's voice returned. "Cheyanne," he said in that strong, husky tone that sent shivers down my spine. "This ends today, baby. From here on out, Graham Knightly will be nothing more than a memory. You hear me?"

"I hear you," I whispered as I pulled to a stop outside the building.

"Good. I love you, sweetheart." I swallowed past the lump that had filled my throat, desperate to return those words, but unable to speak. "See you on the other side."

I shut off the engine and climbed out, my knees knocking violently as the door to the warehouse creaked open, revealing the man who had haunted my every living moment all these years.

The slick, oily smile that made my skin crawl stretched across his face. "Ah, if it isn't my lovely wife. Please, come in. I've been eagerly awaiting our reunion."

He stepped aside and extended his arm like he was welcoming me to a dinner party and not a rusted-out, abandoned building crawling with tetanus and God only knew what kind of rodents. The dilapidated relic of a warehouse was the stuff of nightmares. Fitting, considering who was currently setting up shop inside.

"Where is she?" I demanded, coming to a stop in the middle of the cavernous space. The main area was one long, open room with a few doors equally spaced along the left side of the building that led to what I assumed had been offices back in the day. There were only two exits, both in plain view. The one I'd come through, and the other at the very back of the building just ahead of me.

The ceiling was two stories high, the first twelve feet from the ground up was solid, the whole right side of the warehouse covered in rusted steel siding that was riddled with holes, while the upper level of the building was wrapped on all sides by dingy windows, most of which had been busted out from time, weather, and if I had to guess, kids with nothing better to do.

There were lewd drawings and graffiti made with spray paint covering the walls. I wasn't sure what this warehouse had been used for back in the day, but now it screamed *setting for a gruesome horror movie*. I hated the fact that my daughter had been in here for more than three hours now, and I was desperate to get us both out.

"Don't worry, she's safe," Graham said, circling around to come stand in front of me, his back to the rear exit. His hired guns came to stand behind him, a few feet back, one to his right and the other to his left. The three of them formed a perfect triangle, and I couldn't help but wonder if they'd rehearsed it. It was like something out of a cheesy, poorly scripted action movie.

The goon on his left was short and compact, his frame covered in ridiculous muscles so big they swallowed up his neck. He was the one who'd taken Renee. The one on his right was the complete juxtaposition. Tall and lanky, his dark hair slicked back with so much product it shimmered under the muted sunlight that filtered through the dirty windows. Clearly, these men had seen one too many mafia flicks.

I narrowed my eyes, every ounce of hate I felt for this man seeping from my pores. "You'll have to excuse me if I'm not willing to take you at your word. I want to see her."

He laughed, that smarmy, kissing-babies, shaking-hands, politician laugh that I'd always hated. "I'm not so sure you're in the position to be making demands, seeing as you really were stupid enough to come here with no backup." He let out a sigh, like he was dealing with an insufferable child. "But I suppose it doesn't really matter. I'm a generous enough man to allow you one last look before you take your last breath."

He waved his hand lazily at the goon on his left, a silent order to let me see my daughter.

I locked my knees to stay on my feet as my heart pounded in my ears. I'd always known this was Graham's end game. He wasn't just going to take me back, force me into pretending I was the long-missing wife he'd pined for all this time, finally come home at last. Oh no, he planned to dispose of the problem.

No Neck yanked open the last door on the left, and the sound of my daughter's screams filled the whole warehouse as he disappeared inside. A moment later, he stepped back out, holding her like a sack of potatoes as she screamed and cried uncontrollably.

"You're scaring her!" I shouted, taking a step forward, ready to lunge.

"Ah, ah, ah," Graham tsked as String Bean pulled a gun from inside his jacket and leveled it at my head. "None of that now, or this meeting will be over far too soon."

Renee's head came around, her eyes big, stark with fear. "Mommy!" she screamed, holding her arms out to me, begging me to get to her, to take her out of here. "Mommy!"

"It's okay, doodle bug," I called out, my voice thick with tears. My legs wanted to run. My heart hammered helplessly with the need to get to her. "It's all right. Mommy's here, baby. It's all going to be okay."

At the second flick of Graham's wrist, No Neck disappeared back behind the opened door. I wasn't sure how I managed to stay upright as he shut Renee back in that dark room all by herself, the thick metal of the door muting her cries, but I told myself that it was almost over, just a while longer, and this nightmare would finally end.

"We have confirmation," Dalton said into my ear, having seen everything I just saw from the camera feeding live to wherever he was. "She's in the back room. Move now."

"There," Graham started as No Neck resumed his place behind and to his left. "You've seen her. Feel better?"

"Not particularly," I answered through gritted teeth. It took an act of strength I didn't know I was capable of to keep my eyes pinned to my husband and not allow them to dart to the back door, but I couldn't risk drawing his focus that way. "I'm still stuck here in your presence."

His top lip curled up in disgust. "You always did have a mouth on you," he spat disapprovingly. "I was always surprised that none of my . . . *lessons* managed to bleed that out of you."

He'd always referred to his beatings as lessons, as though that somehow made them more acceptable. Looking at the man just then, I wondered how I'd ever been blind enough to think he was anything but a disgusting, slithering snake.

"That makes two of us, because I was always surprised by how easily you were able to con all those idiots in the state capital for all those years."

Before I had time to register it was coming, Graham's arm whipped around, his knuckles slamming into my cheek and setting fire to my skin.

I righted my head just in time to catch a glimpse of Trent

slowly creeping in through the back door from the corner of my eye. He'd just witnessed the smallest taste of the brutality Graham was capable of, and I was worried it would cause him to react. That couldn't happen. He had to stay focused on Renee.

I let out a low, brittle laugh as I turned my head and spat the blood that had filled my mouth onto the dirt-covered floor. "You still hit like a bitch," I taunted, anything to keep his focus on me.

He pulled a handkerchief from the pocket of his slacks, wiping my blood off his knuckles. I noticed with disgust that he still wore his wedding ring. Always playing the part.

I'd pawned mine, along with all the other expensive jewelry I'd accumulated during out marriage, at the first shop I came across once I got out of Ohio. The cash I got from all of it had made a hefty down payment on my beach cottage. Bet he would have loved that.

"You always were a piece of trash," he hissed. "I honestly don't know why I wasted my time on you."

Motion from the back of the room caught my eye, but I refused to look that way as the door to the office Renee was in inched open and Trent slipped through.

"You know, I've always wondered the same thing. You could have just let me go. Why bother spending all this money and energy trying to track me down?"

In the blink of an eye, he was in my face, his own ruddy with rage as he thundered, "Because you don't get to win! You belong to me, you're my property! Do you understand?

Mine to do what I want with. To use and defile in any way I choose!"

His rampage was cut off by my daughter's high-pitched cry. "*Mommy!*"

I looked toward the back of the warehouse just in time to see that Trent had my little girl in his arms and was only feet from the back door.

Panic latched at my chest as everything began to move in slow motion. "Trent, *run!*" I screamed. Then all hell broke loose.

Before String Bean had the chance to lift his hand that still held the gun in their direction, glass shattered from above us and a bullet slammed into the side of his head, taking him to the ground. Kill shot.

"What the fuck are you waiting for!" Graham shouted at No Neck. "Get them!"

No Neck turned and lumbered off just as my husband reached around and pulled a gun out of his waistband, prepared to shoot in Trent and Renee's direction.

"*No!*" I shouted, launching myself at him. We landed on the floor in a heap of tangled, clawing limbs, and I knew this was it.

My last chance.

As long as Trent and Renee got out, nothing else mattered.

Thirty-Two

TRENT

I BURST through the back door, my eyes going right to Charlotte who was still standing where I'd left her.

"Take her," I barked, shoving Renee into her arms. "Run and don't stop until you get to Dalton." There was no time. I had to get back in there. I had to get to her. My heart was beating so fast I felt winded, but I forced myself to push past it.

She looked at me in sheer panic. "Trent—"

"Now!" I bellowed, and like a shot, Charlotte took off at a dead sprint, clutching her niece in her arms.

I yanked the rear door to the warehouse open just as the fucker, who had kidnapped Renee and shot a gun in a building full of children, reached it. The hand holding the gun came up, but before he could take aim, I was there, grabbing his wrist and twisting it around, out of the line of fire. He let out a shout of pain as I pulled his arm back at an unnatural angle and used my elbow to snap his forearm like a twig.

Unfortunately, the son of a bitch didn't go down.

He whipped around, breaking from my hold, and his other arm swung wide. I barely had enough time to jump back to avoid the blade clutched in his fist.

This guy's muscles were all for show. He didn't have a goddamn clue what he was doing, but he was standing in the way of me getting to my woman, having to grapple with him was wasting precious seconds.

I could hear Dalton's voice in my ear just then, barking as I dodged another swipe of that knife. "Trent, get the fuck in there, I don't have a clear shot on Knightly."

That was gasoline thrown on the fire that had been raging inside me this whole time. With a feral yell, I grabbed the asshole's wrist and bent the knife back toward him, then I pushed with all my weight, shoving the blade into the center of his chest, right into his fucking heart.

Cheyanne

"You goddamn fucking *cunt!*" Graham shouted at the top of his lungs, grabbing me by the ankle as I crawled across the floor, trying to get to the gun. He yanked, pulling my leg out from under me, but as I hit the ground, I kicked back with my other foot, connecting with his face.

The roar he let out sent terror racing down my spine, but I couldn't quit. I couldn't stop fighting. He crawled over the top of me and I squirmed closer to the gun, reaching out, but it was still too far away. My fingers dug frantically in the dirty ground as I bucked and kicked, trying to get out from under him.

"You're dead, bitch!" he snarled in my ear as he flipped me onto my back. Spittle flew from his mouth as he hissed, "Fucking dead!"

His hands closed around my neck and began to squeeze. "You belong to me," he seethed in my face. "*I* say what happens to you!"

Like fucking hell. I was *not* going to die by this man's hands!

"I never belonged to you," I wheezed. I reached up and dug my nails into his forehead so deep blood welled up instantly and ripped downward, carving deep, gnarly slices into his face. He screamed out and released my throat. I sucked in a huge lungful of air as he reached for the gun, and a second later, a shot went off.

Time seemed to pause as the bang ricocheted through the air. I stopped breathing as Graham's eyes came to me, wide with surprise. His mouth gaped open, but no sound came out. It felt like we stayed like that for an eternity. Then, just like that, someone pushed play, and things started moving again.

Graham went down, but before he could collapse on top of me, I shoved with all my might, rolling him onto the filthy ground beside me.

I lifted up, crab-walking away from his prone body, and whipped my gaze up to Trent, standing three yards away, his arms raised, his eyes and still trained on the now-lifeless body of Graham Knightly.

"Trent," I breathed, rising to my feet on wobbly legs. Those beautiful smoky eyes finally came to me. His chest shuddered on an exhale, and something told me he'd been holding his breath that whole time. The relief that filtered across his gorgeous features ripped at my heart. A sob tore from my throat, my hands slapping over my mouth as he shoved the gun in the holster at his waist and rushed me, taking my face in his hands.

"Baby, are you okay?"

I cried uncontrollably, nodding my head as my vision went blurry. "Renee?" I sobbed, the fear for my daughter still holding me in a death grip.

"Charlotte got her out," he assured me, then to drive that point home, Dalton spoke in both our ears. "We have her. We're in the truck on the way to you."

My whole body collapsed, my face planting in Trent's chest as I inhaled the scent of clean laundry and pine. "I knew you'd save us," I breathed, speaking those words I felt down to my very soul.

Cupping my cheeks again, he lifted my face to his so he

could riddle it with kisses. "You're safe now," he said, his words a promise. "You and Renee are safe, I swear."

"Because of you," I whispered, clutching his shirt in a tight fist. "You made us that way, because you love us."

He brought his forehead down on mine. "I do, baby. With all my heart."

"That's really good," I told him on a sniffle, "because we love you too."

His arms came around me, squeezing me tight to him, and in his embrace, I'd never felt safer. "Let's get to our girl, yeah?"

That was the best offer I'd ever been given.

Trent

The past two days had to have been the longest days in the history of time. Graham Knightly was dead. The threat constantly lurking around the corner, the nightmare that had plagued every one of Cheyanne's days, was gone for good.

I'd driven my girls straight to the hospital from the scene so they could be looked over. Cheyanne had assured me she was fine, but I wasn't willing to take any chances with either of them.

While we were there, deputies had shown up to question us. We'd done our best to remain patient, but after the events of the last several hours, we were holding on to calm by the tips of our fingers.

Fortunately, the cam footage we had of the whole thing made their case pretty cut and dry. An abusive, psychotic husband had tracked down his wife and daughter, hiring criminals to kidnap his own flesh and blood and kill his wife. That was all the sheriff's department needed to know to close their case, something they did quickly in order to allow Cheyanne and Renee to put this all behind them.

Thanks to my brothers at Alpha Omega, that footage was leaked to every media outlet in the country. The truth about Graham Knightly was out there now, and the world knew once and for all the kind of man he really had been. To put it plainly, he wasn't going to be missed.

I hadn't been able to pry myself away from either of them for more than a second in the past two days, terrified that if I looked away, they'd somehow disappear.

I kept seeing the fear on Little Bit's face. I kept seeing that piece of shit on top of Cheyanne. It had fucked with my head in a really big way.

I stood on Cheyenne's back deck, staring out at the turbulent water crashing against the shore as the sun set, thinking that was exactly how I felt inside.

Charlotte and Dalton were back at my rental, but I was still here, unable and unwilling to leave.

I was pulled from my melancholy by Cheyenne's soft, musical voice.

"What are you out here thinking about so hard?"

I turned around just as she reached me, and to my pleasant surprise, she didn't stop until her arms were wrapped around my waist and her lush body was snuggled into mine.

For the past couple days, our sole focus had been on Renee, on guiding her through the trauma of what had happened and reassuring her she was safe. There had been no more admissions of love or talks about what all of it meant for our future. But that was okay. I was willing to wait as long as it took.

I returned her embrace instantly. "Nothing much," I lied. "I was just watching the water, thinking about how beautiful it is here."

"Liar," she mumbled into my chest before tipping her head back to look up at me. "I know you're out here worrying, but I'll let it slide for now and say, I'm glad you think it's so beautiful here. Maybe . . ." She trailed off and pulled her bottom lip between her teeth. "Maybe the beauty of this place will be enough to get you to stay."

My muscles locked tight, my arms clenched around her. "What are you saying?"

She closed her eyes and pulled in a fortifying breath. When her lids flitted open again, those eyes were alight with a passionate fire. "I'm saying, Charlotte and Dalton are going back to Hope Valley in two weeks, and . . . I don't want you to go with them. I want you to stay here. I want you to build on to this life with me and Renee. I want you to make Whitecap your home, because I'm so in love with you, Trent.

My life is better for having you in it, better than it ever was before I met you. If that's not what you want, I totally understand. I just—"

I silenced her with a hard, searing kiss. "I had no intention of ever leaving," I rasped, feeling something inside of me click into place, making me whole. "I decided at the falls there was no way I could ever leave you. Wherever you and Renee are, that's my home. Besides, I've become pretty fond of a certain hot spring, and I'd hate not to be able to visit it regularly."

Her smile was so beautiful it lit up my whole world. "I'm glad to hear that," she said, her voice thick with emotion. "Because you're my protector. And I'm never letting you go."

I didn't have a single problem with that.

Epilogue

TRENT

THREE WEEKS later

Sam grunted as he lifted the box out of the back of the moving truck, a sweat beading across his forehead.

I'd told Cheyanne that I was never going to leave her, but that hadn't been completely right. When Dalton and Charlotte returned to Hope Valley a week ago, I had, in fact gone with them, but only for as long as it took to pack my stuff and drive it back across the country to my girls. To my forever.

Now I was back where I belonged, at the beautiful beach cottage full of so much love and life.

"Jesus," Sam grumbled. "What the hell all did you put in here?"

I looked to the word I'd written across the side in big black letters. "Books. There's a dolly behind you if you finally want to admit defeat."

He and I had been going steady since I pulled the truck up in front of my and Cheyanne's home an hour ago, neither of us willing to slow down, trying to show each other up with who could carry the most boxes.

"Maybe you need a dolly. But I'm fine."

His face was so red I was actually a little concerned he was about to pull something. But even with all his grumbling and complaining, the man had shown up to help me unload without me even having to ask. His silent approval as far as I was concerned.

"I'm growing on you," I teased as I hefted a box of my own, this one much lighter than his. "Just admit it."

"Like a fungus," he groused before taking off toward the house.

Like I'd told Cheyanne, it was only a matter of time before that man and I were BFFs.

Moving down the ramp toward the walkway, I looked up and spotted Cheyanne standing in the opened doorway, her brilliant smile lighting my whole world as she waited for me to finish.

Oh yeah, I thought as I moved toward her, toward my future. *This is most definitely my favorite place.*

Cheyanne
  Three and a half months later

"So? What do you think?"

I lifted the cup to my lips, keeping my eyes pinned on my sister as I took a slow sip, just to drag things out and drive her crazy.

"It's . . ." I scrunched my lips to the side and feigned contemplation before finally admitting, "It's really good."

"See!" she crowed. "I told you. Muffin Top coffee is the best!"

Time had continued to tick by, the world had continued to spin, and after four months, I was finally in Hope Valley for my twin sister's wedding.

Having a whole country between us after just finding each other wasn't the easiest, but we talked and FaceTimed every single day. For Thanksgiving, we'd taken a trip to a place in Wyoming called Pembrooke to spend the holiday with Dalton's family. The two of them had come back to Whitecap so we could have a big family Christmas. And now, we were finally getting to see the beauty that was my sister's home.

And to finally put to rest the argument of who had the best coffee.

I held up my hand to stop her. "I didn't say it was the best. I said it was really good. Now that I've tried it for myself, I have to agree with you that it's tied with Drip. I can't, in good conscience, pick a clear winner."

She studied me for a second before nodding her head. "I can accept that. But wait until you try the cronuts. You're going to lose your mind!"

God, I was happy to have my sister back.

Two days later

Crouching down in front of my daughter, I booped her nose and tucked a strand of her hair behind her ear. She looked so adorable in her little flower girl dress. And I'd only had to stop her once from ripping it off and running through the wedding venue in her underwear. That was winning.

"All right, doodle bug. You remember what to do?"

She nodded solemnly. "Yu-huh. I frow da flowers. Walk to da front. And go to Tent."

"That's right, baby. You ready?"

"Yeah!" she screamed with enthusiasm. A second later, the wedding coordinator opened the door to let her out. Before it closed behind her, I heard my girl shout so loud it could be heard over the music, "Hi Tent! Hi Unca Dolly! Look at my pwetty dwess!"

I shook my head and laughed as I turned around to face my sister.

"She's my favorite human in the whole wide world," Charlotte giggled. "I'm so glad she called Dalton Dolly in front of the guys he works with. He's never going to live that down."

"Glad my girl could be of service." I reached out and took her hands in mine. "I'm so thankful I'm here. And we get to celebrate this big day together."

"I am too, honey," she whispered, pulling me into a hug. "I spent twenty years missing you."

"Same, but now we get to spend the next twenty making up for lost time."

We separated, and she beamed at me. "I really like the sound of that. And hopefully one day soon, we'll be able to switch roles. You'll be the bride and I'll be the matron of honor."

I didn't have to say anything. She could read my face clear as day that I loved the idea of that.

Sniffling back the happy tears, I waved at my face and declared, "All right, enough mushy stuff. Let's get you married."

After one last hug, I moved to the doors, clutching my bouquet in my hands and waiting for my cue.

As soon as the door opened, I stepped out onto the aisle, my eyes going straight to the altar at the front.

To where Trent stood. Holding my little girl in my arms.

He gave me that dimpled grin, mouthing the words, "I love you," down the aisle.

Oh yeah, I thought as I started toward them, the love I

felt for them pouring out of me. I couldn't wait for the day my sister and I got to switch roles.

The End.

***Read Charlotte and Dalton's story,
Playing for Keeps, now.***

Stay With Me
Out of the Darkness
The Second Time Around
Waiting for Forever
Love to Hate You
Playing for Keeps
When You Least Expect It
Never for Him

REDEMPTION SERIES
Bad Alibi
Crazy Beautiful
Bittersweet
Guilty Pleasure
Wallflower
Blurred Line
Slow Burn
Favorite Mistake

THE PICKING UP THE PIECES SERIES:
Picking up the Pieces
Rising from the Ashes
Pushing the Boundaries
Worth the Wait

THE COLORS NOVELS:
Scattered Colors
Shrinking Violet

Love Hate Relationship
Wildflower

THE LOCKLAINE BOYS (a LOVE HATE RELATIONSHIP spinoff):

Fire & Ice
Opposites Attract
Almost Perfect

THE PEMBROOKE SERIES (a WILDFLOWER spinoff):

Sweet Sunshine
Coming Full Circle
A Broken Soul

CIVIL CORRUPTION SERIES

Corrupt
Defile
Consume
Ravage

GIRL TALK SERIES:

Seducing Lola
Tempting Sophia
Enticing Daphne
Charming Fiona

STANDALONE TITLES:

One Knight Stand
Chance Encounters
Nightmares from Within

<u>DEADLY LOVE SERIES:</u>
Destructive
Addictive

About Jessica

Born and raised around Houston, Jessica is a self proclaimed caffeine addict, connoisseur of inexpensive wine, and the worst driver in the state of Texas. In addition to being all of these things, she's first and foremost a wife and mom.

Growing up, she shared her mom and grandmother's

love of reading. But where they leaned toward murder mysteries, Jessica was obsessed with all things romance.

When she's not nose deep in her next manuscript, you can usually find her with her kindle in hand.

Connect with Jessica now
Website: www.authorjessicaprince.com
Jessica's Princesses Reader Group
Newsletter
Instagram
Facebook
Twitter
authorjessicaprince@gmail.com

www.ingramcontent.com/pod-product-compliance
Lightning Source LLC
Chambersburg PA
CBHW032339310726
48973CB00007B/1765